THE GREAT HEATHEN ARMY

By

H A Culley

Book one of the Saga of Wessex

Published by

oHp

Orchard House Publishing

First Kindle Edition 2020

Text copyright © 2020 H A Culley

Cover Image: © Shutterstock¦ Nejron Photo

TABLE OF CONTENTS

Place Names

Note: *In my last series of novels I used the modern names for places in Anglo-Saxon England as some readers had said that my earlier novels were confusing because of the use of place names current in the time about which I was writing. However, I had even more adverse comments that modern names detract from the authentic feel of the novels, so in this series I have reverted to the use of Anglo-Saxons names.*

Acemannesceastre	Bath, Somerset
Æscesdūn	Location unknown, possibly near Uffington, Oxfordshire
Aldburgh	Aldborough, North Yorkshire
Alnwic	Alnwick, Northumberland
Basinges	Old Basing, Hampshire
Basingestoches	Basingstoke, Hampshire
Beamfleote	Benfleet, Essex
Berrocscir	Berkshire
Brydancumb	Burcombe, near Wilton, Wiltshire
Catræth	Catterick, North Yorkshire
Cantwareburh	Canterbury, Kent
Certesi	Chertsey, Surrey
Cilleham	Chilham, Kent
Coventre	Coventry, Warwickshire
Dyfneintscir	Devon
Danmǫrk	Denmark
Darenth	River Darent
Ðarcy	River Aire
Dorcesterscir	Dorset
Dùn Èideann	Edinburgh, Scotland
Ēast Seaxna Rīce	Essex
Eatun	Eton, Berkshire
Eforwic	York, North Yorkshire.
Ferendone	Great Faringdon, Berkshire
Fŏs	River Foss
Fŏsweg	The Fosse Way (Roman road)
Gæignesburh	Gainsborough, Lincolnshire
Godmundcestre	Godmanchester, Cambridgeshire
Grante	River Cam

Grantebrycge	Cambridge, Cambridgeshire
Grantesete	Grantchester, Cambridgeshire
Hægelisdun	Possibly Halesdun, Essex. Location disputed
Hamtunscīr	Hampshire
Hapesburc	Happisburgh, Norfolk
Hagustaldes	Hexham, Northumberland
Hreopandune	Repton, Derbyshire
Hrofescæster	Rochester, Kent
Hymbre	River Humber
Inglefelle	Englefield, Berkshire
Irlond	Ireland
Ligeraceaster	Leicester, Leicestershire
Lindocolina	Lincoln, Lincolnshire
Lindesege	The district of Lindsey, Lincolnshire
Linne Foirthe	Firth of Forth
Lundenwic	London
Malsenþorp	Melsonby, North Yorkshire
Meretum	Merdon Castle, Hampshire
Midweg	River Medway
Newercha	Newark-on-Trent, Nottinghamshire
Norweġ	Norway
Orkneyjar	The Orkney Islands
Oxenaforda	Oxford, Oxfordshire
Readingum	Reading, Berkshire
Salteode	Saltwood, Kent
Sarum	Salisbury, Wiltshire
Sandwic	Sandwich, Kent
Silcestre	Silchester, Hampshire
Snæland	Iceland
Snotingaham	Nottingham, Nottinghamshire
Stanes	Staines-upon-Thames, Surrey
Stanforde	Stamford, Linlconshire
Sweoland	Sweden
Sūþrīgescir	Surrey
Suindune	Swindon, Wiltshire
Suth-Seaxe	Sussex
Taceham	Thatcham, Berkshire
Tarentefort	Dartford, Kent
Tateshalla	Pontefract, West Yorkshire
Theodforda	Thetford, Norfolk
Temes	River Thames
Tes	River Tees

Tinan	River Tyne
Trisantona	River Trent
Turkilestun	Thruxton, Hampshire
Wejr	River Wear
Weolud	River Welland
Wiltun	Wilton, Wiltshire
Wiltunscir	Wiltshire
Winburne	Wimborne Minster, Dorset
Wintanceaster	Winchester, Hampshire
Uisge	River Ouse
Verulamacæstir	St. Albans, Hertfordshire

List of Principle Characters

Historical figures are in bold.

Jørren – The narrator
Jerold – Thegn of Cilleham and Jørren's uncle
Æscwin – Jørren's eldest brother
Alric – Jørren's fourteen-year-old brother
Æthelred – King of Wessex
Ceolnoth – Archbishop of Cantwareburh
Baldred – Ealdorman of Cent
Cei – A slave belonging to Jørren's family
Redwald – The son of a poor farmer who joins Jørren
Erik, Ulf and Tove – Three Danish boys captured by Jørren
Edyth – A charcoal burner
Nelda – Her daughter
Leofflæd – A merchant's daughter
Ecgberht – Leofflæd's brother
Ælle – King of Northumbria
Osbehrt – His brother, deposed by Ælle but now his ally
Jerrik and Øwli – Two Jutes enslaved by the Danes
Wigestan – A warrior in the service of Edmund of Bebbanburg
Cináed and Uurad – Two young Picts enslaved by Vikings to serve as ship's boys
Ceadda, Hroðulf, Sæwine and Wealhmær – Bernician scouts serving Edmund
Cynemær – A Bernician thegn, father of Ceadda
Ívarr the Boneless – Principal leader of the Great Heathen Army
Halfdan and **Ubba** – His half-brothers
Dudda – Reeve of Silcestre
Ælfred – Brother of King Æthelred of Wessex
Wulfthryth – The Lady of Wessex, Æthelred's wife
Æthelhelm – Their elder son
Asser – Bishop of Wintanceaster
Pæga – The Hereræswa (army commander) of Wessex
Burghred – King of Mercia
Tunbehrt – Shire reeve of Hamtunscīr
Cuthfleda - Jørren and Leofflæd's daughter
Merewald – Ealdorman of Hamtunscīr
Swiðhun and Wolnoth – Other members of Jørren's warband from Bernicia
Ealhswith – Mercian noblewoman, later Ælfred's wife and Lady of Wessex

Ulfrid – her youngest brother
Hunulf and Ædwulf – Thralls rescued from the Danes, later scouts for Jørren
Ethelwulf - Ealdorman of Berrocscir
Heahmund – Bishop of Sherborne
Æscwin – Leofflæd and Jørren's son
Ælfric - Archbishop of Cantwareburh after Ceolnoth
Eadda – Hereræswa after Pæga's death
Æthelwold – Æthelred's younger son and a contestant for Ælfred's throne
Acwel and Lyndon – Young scouts in Jørren's warband
Odda – Ealdorman of Dyfneintscir
Wulfhere – Ealdorman of Wiltunscir
Drefan – Ealdorman of Alnwic
Rigsige of Bebbanburg – Earl of Bernicia, later King of Northumbria

Glossary

ANGLO-SAXON

Ætheling – Literally 'throne-worthy. An Anglo-Saxon prince

Bondsman – a slave who was treated as the property of his master

Birlinn – A wooden ship similar to the later Scottish galleys but smaller than a Viking longship. Usually with a single mast and square rigged sail, they could also be propelled by oars with one man to each oar

Burh - fortified settlement

Byrnie - A long (usually sleeveless) tunic of chain mail

Ceorl - Freemen who worked the land or else provided a service or trade such as metal working, carpentry, weaving etc. They ranked between thegns and villeins and provided the fyrd in time of war. Also spelt churl.

Cyning – Old English for king and the term by which they were normally addressed

Cyningtaefl – Literally *king's table*. The game was not dissimilar to the later game of chess, except that the contest was between two unequal forces: a weaker force in the centre of the board surrounded and outnumbered by an attacking force stationed at the perimeter of the board

Ealdorman – The senior noble of a shire. A royal appointment, ealdormen led the men of their shire in battle, presided over law courts and levied taxation on behalf of the king

Fyrd - Anglo-Saxon militia that was mobilised from freemen to defend their shire, or to supplement the king's army. Service in the fyrd was usually of short duration and members were expected to provide their own arms and provisions

Gesith – The companions of a king, prince or noble, usually acting as his bodyguard

Hereræswa – Military commander or general. The man who commanded the army of a nation under the king

Hide – A measure of the land sufficient to support the household of one ceorl

Hundred – The unit for local government and taxation which equated to ten tithings. The freemen of each hundred were collectively responsible for various crimes committed within its borders if the offender was not produced

Seax – A bladed weapon with one sharp edge and a long tapering point. It is somewhere in size between a dagger and a sword. Mainly used for close-quarter fighting where a sword would be too long and unwieldy

Settlement – Any grouping of residential buildings, usually around the king's or lord's hall. In 8th century England the term town or village had not yet come into use

Shire – An administrative area into which an Anglo-Saxon kingdom was divided

Shire Reeve – Later corrupted to sheriff.   A royal official responsible for implementing the king's laws within his shire

Thegn – The lowest rank of noble. A man who held a certain amount of land direct from the king or from a senior nobleman, ranking between an ordinary freeman or ceorl and an ealdorman

Tithing - A group of ten ceorls who lived close together and were collectively responsible for each other's behaviour, also the land required to support them (i.e. ten hides)

Wergeld - The price set upon a person's life and paid as compensation by the killer to the family of the dead person. It freed the killer of further punishment or obligation and prevented a blood feud

Witenaġemot – The council of an Anglo-Saxon kingdom. Its composition varied, depending on the matters to be debated. Usually it consisted of the ealdormen, the king's thegns, the bishops and the abbots

Villein - A peasant who ranked above a bondsman or slave but who was legally tied to his vill and who was obliged to give one or more day's service to his lord each week in payment for his land

Vill - A thegn's holding or similar area of land in Anglo-Saxon England which would later be called a parish or a manor

VIKING

Berserker – Literally bear coat.   Feared Viking warriors who wore animal skins and

 who fought with wild and uncontrolled ferocity

Bóndi - Farmers and craftsmen who were free men and enjoyed rights such as the ownership of weapons and membership of the Thing. They could be tenants or landowners

Byrnie - a long (usually sleeveless) tunic of chain mail

Hirdman – A member of a king's or a jarl's personal bodyguard, collectively known as the hird

Hersir – A bondi who was chosen to lead a band of warriors under a king or a jarl. Typically they were wealthy landowners who could recruit enough other bóndi to serve under their command

Jarl – A Norse or Danish chieftain; in Sweden they were regional governors appointed by the king

Mjolnir – Thor's hammer, also the pendant worn around the neck by most pagan Vikings

Nailed God – Pagan name for Christ, also called the White Christ

Thing – The governing assembly made up of the free people of the community presided over by a lagman (*q.v.*). The meeting-place of a thing was called a thingstead

Thrall – A slave. A man, woman or child in bondage to his or her owner. Thralls had no rights and could be beaten or killed with impunity

LONGSHIPS

In order of size:

Knarr – Also called karve or karvi. The smallest type of longship. It had 6 to 16 benches and, like their English equivalents, they were mainly used for fishing and trading, but they were occasionally commissioned for military use. They were broader in the beam and had a deeper draught than other longships·

Snekkja – (Plural snekkjur). Typically the smallest longship used in warfare and was classified as a ship with at least 20 rowing benches. A typical snekkja might have a length of 17 m, a width of 2.5 m and a draught of only 0.5 m. Norse snekkjas, designed for deep fjords and Atlantic weather, typically had more draught than the Danish type, which were intended for shallow water

Drekar - (Dragon ship). Larger warships consisting of more than 30 rowing benches. Typically they could carry a crew of some 70–80 men and measured around 30 m in length. These ships were more properly called skeids; the term drekar referred to the carvings of menacing beasts, such as dragons and snakes, mounted on the prow of the ship during a sea battle or when raiding. Strictly speaking Drekar is the plural form, the singular being dreki or dreka, but these words don't appear to be accepted usage in English

Prologue

Autumn 865

I was one month shy of my fourteenth birthday when the Danes came.

My name is Jørren, an old Jutish name. My father was a ceorl, a freeman who tenanted a farmstead owned by the thegn, Jerold, who was my father's elder brother. Jerold's vill was called Cilleham and it lay in the Kingdom of Cent. This was something of a misnomer as the kingdom comprised the shires of Ēast Seaxna Rīce, Sūþrīgescir and Suth-Seaxa as well as Cent.

I had two brothers and two sisters. My eldest brother, Æscwin was five years older than me and we didn't have much to do with each other. In comparison I was very close to my other brother, Alric, and not just in age. He was a year older than me and we did practically everything together. In many ways I supposed that he was a kind of hero to me.

My father had told me that many of the inhabitants of Cent, including our family, were Jutes who had come over from Jutland at the same time as the Saxons had settled the rest of southern England and the Angles had conquered East Anglia, Mercia and Northumbria. However, Cent was now a vassal of the Kingdom of Wessex and the distinction between Jutes and Saxons had almost disappeared.

Cilleham was neither large nor small as far as vills go. The settlement itself boasted a mill and a church with a priest and there were a dozen hides of land. Jerold couldn't afford to pay professional warriors, but there were thirty one freemen over the age of fourteen - including my father and my two elder brothers - who were obliged to take up arms when the fyrd was called out by our ealdorman.

The reports that reached us said that a large fleet of longships carrying nearly three thousand of the heathen devils had landed at

Sandwic on the south coast. It was an enormous number if the rumours were anywhere near accurate. Sandwic belonged to the Archbishop of Cantwareburh and, without waiting for the authority of King Æthelred of Wessex, he sent messengers to the ealdormen of Suth-Seaxe, Sūþrīgescir and Ēast Seaxna Rīce to raise the fyrd and muster at Cantwareburh. It was a reasonable thing to do as the king was at his capital, Wintanceaster, a good three or four days ride away. It would have been at least a week before he got a reply.

The archbishop, Ceolnoth, was now an old man, having been in post for over thirty years and the dean of the cathedral before that. He was no warrior and so he asked Ealdorman Baldred of Cent to command the army gathering to oppose the Danes.

Of course, I was too young at the time to understand much of what was going on, but I knew that my father and brothers would be leaving to join the shire's fyrd. That left me as the man of the place, though I'm not sure my mother saw it that way. Come to that, neither of my sisters seemed to think that I was now in charge either. I could understand the attitude of the elder, Godifu, as she was betrothed to marry her cousin, Jerold's youngest son, but I had expected a little more respect from Sibbe, who was over a year younger than me.

Once they left it meant that all the work of looking after our farm fell on those of us who were left. There was no more time for hunting or learning how to fight; my days from dawn to dusk were filled with milking the cows, feeding the swine, weeding the fields and tending the sheep and the chickens. Luckily father and my brothers had taken the two horses we owned with them and so at least I didn't have to muck out the stables.

The girls seemed to think that all they had to do was to help mother inside the small hall where we lived. Thankfully we had four slaves to help me on the farm, a Welshman called Bedwyr, his wife and their two sons: Cei, who was fourteen, and his sixteen-year-old brother.

It was three weeks before any tidings reached us, and then it was scarcely good news. The Danes had defeated Ealdorman

Baldred at Salteode and scattered his army. We had no word as to the fate of my father or my two brothers. Alric was fifteen then and hadn't been training to be a spearman for long. I feared that he stood little chance in combat against a big, hairy Danish axeman. At least my eldest brother, Æscwin, was nearly fully grown at eighteen. He was a skilled archer and would doubtless be employed as such.

I was also worried about father. He owned a chain mail byrnie, a pot helmet and a good sword. His shield was made from the best lime wood that grew on our own farm and it was banded with bronze. That meant that he would have been chosen to fight in the front rank with the nobles and other professional warriors. I knew, even at my tender age, that father and his companions would have to bear the brunt of the fighting.

It wasn't until Æscwin returned home wounded that we heard what had happened. He had been grouped with all the other archers and so he'd been separated from father and Alric before the battle. He was a skilled hunter and his bow and the arrows he made himself were well suited for killing deer and other animals. However, it wasn't as powerful as a proper war bow, nor were his arrows intended for piercing chain mail.

Not all Danes could afford byrnies – the tunics made of linked iron rings – or even leather armour, and he told us that he concentrated on those Danes dressed in woollen tunics like most of our fyrd. Æscwin and his fellow bowmen managed to inflict significant casualties at first; then the Danes formed what he called a shield wall and it proved almost impossible to hit the Danes after that.

I was enthralled by my brother's account of the battle but mother and the girls were naturally much more concerned about what had happened to father and Alric. However, Æscwin knew nothing of their fate, nor that of Thegn Jerold and his two sons. Godifu was almost hysterical with worry about her betrothed and burst into tears.

To my shame, I was impatient to hear more about the fighting and regarded Godifu's anguish as an unnecessary distraction. If he was dead, he was dead and there was nothing anybody could do about it.

I was even more annoyed when mother declared that she wanted to hear no more about fighting; it was just too distressing for everyone – well, not for me it wasn't. I had to wait until later that evening when we retired to the small bedchamber I shared with Æscwin and Alric before I was able to ask him to tell me what else he knew.

'I don't really know what happened, it was all so confusing, and terrifying,' Æscwin began. 'We were in front of our own spearmen and axemen and so I had a clear view of the Danes at first. Thankfully they didn't seem to have many archers of their own but, as they came closer to us, a hail of javelins rose into the sky and came down amongst us causing a lot of deaths and injuries. I was lucky not to be hit but the men on either side of me were both killed. After that we retired – fled would be more accurate – through our own shield wall to the rear. From there we sent our arrows at high trajectory over the heads of our own men and into the rear ranks of the enemy.

'I have no idea how much damage we did, nor indeed how the battle was progressing as all I could see was the backs of the rear rank of the fyrd's spearmen. They were pushing at the backs of the men in front to hold the line steady. The next thing I knew was that men started to break away from the line and rush past us, throwing away their shields, spears, axes and anything else that would impede their flight. I knew then that the battle was lost.

'The archers fled along with the rest, but at least we kept stopping in groups to send a few arrows in the direction of our pursuers. I like to think it bought us a little breathing space and eventually we reached a large wood just before night fell. By that time I was with a dozen men I didn't know and I had no idea where the other archers from Cilleham had gone. We found a stream and drank before resting. A few had some stale bread and cheese and they shared it with the rest.

'We put more distance between us and our pursuers that night but they may well have given up the chase by then. It took me two more days to get home, begging for scraps of food from settlements and farmsteads on the way. It wasn't that the people were unwilling to give me food but there were so many of us that they couldn't feed everyone.'

'So you didn't see either father or Alric after the rout began?' I asked.

Æscwin shook his head and looked at the floor despondently before speaking.

'If they had escaped they should reach home tomorrow or the next day, if they don't we have to assume that they are either dead or prisoners of the heathens.'

'If they've been captured what will happen to them?'

My brother looked at me bleakly.

'I've heard that they either kill their captives, and none too quickly either, or they'll make them thralls.'

'Thralls?'

'Slaves, but not like our slaves who we treat well. I have heard tales that all Scandinavians treat their thralls worse than dogs.'

'Then I pray that they died in battle. That way they will have kept their honour.'

I lay down but I found it difficult to get to sleep. When I did eventually drop off I had nightmares about Danish axemen trying to chop off my head.

✝✝✝

It was three days before we had news of father and Alric. They had fought alongside the other men from Cilleham and, as they drifted back, many of them wounded, we heard what had happened from those who had fought alongside them. Father and Uncle Jerold had been together in the front rank and both had been killed during the first attack by the Danes. Some had seen both of Jerold's sons fall too. Alric was towards the rear of the fyrd because of his age. The reeve told us that my brother had survived unwounded and had fled with him and a few others when the army broke.

The reeve's group had made it safely to some woods. Foolishly they lay down there for the night instead of putting more distance between them and the pursuing Danes. The reeve had been lucky. He had gone further into the woods and was squatting down to defecate when the enemy had surrounded the rest of his companions.

He had watched, powerless to help, as a few who put up a fight were killed and the rest were carted off as prisoners. It was a full moon that night and, even under the tree canopy, he had recognised Alric as one of those being led away.

Godifu had lost her betrothed and was inconsolable, but all of us were distressed by what had happened to our family. We didn't even have their bodies to bury. It wasn't until the reeve came to see Æscwin a few days after his return that the consequences became apparent to us.

The reeve pointed out that Æscwin was Jerold's heir now and so he would become the Thegn of Cilleham once he had paid the inheritance tax to the Ealdorman of Cent. The trouble was that Baldred had also fallen at Salteode and he had no living sons. Until the king appointed a new ealdorman Æscwin's inheritance would remain in limbo.

The situation was made even more complicated by the fact that the victorious Danes were rampaging all over Cent and so it was unsafe to send a messenger to the king.

Everyone waited with trepidation to see what the invaders would do next. My brother half expected them to attack Cantwareburh, as they apparently had done fifteen years before, but we heard nothing further for a month. For some reason the Danes had decided not to complete their conquest of Cent, but to sail up to East Anglia instead.

I had been fretting over the enslavement – or worse – of Alric and grew ever more resentful when Æscwin seemed more concerned about securing his position as thegn than he did about the fate of our brother. When he let our farmstead to a tenant and we all moved into the hall at Cilleham I decided that, if he wasn't going to do anything, then I would have to.

I might have been young but I wasn't naïve. I knew that if I told my family about my intention to go looking for Alric they would have stopped me. Looking back on my decision now I think I must have been mad!

I didn't want to go alone so I involved Cei in my plans. He was a year older than me and the chance of escaping the drudgery that was his everyday life in exchange for excitement and adventure blinded him to the dangers and he had no hesitation in becoming my willing accomplice. Neither of us thought about the consequences. The punishment for a slave who ran away was death, whatever the circumstances, and I would be in serious trouble for abetting him.

I waited until everyone was asleep. Now that Æscwin was the thegn, albeit unconfirmed, he had his own chamber and so I had a small cubicle off the main hall all to myself. The servants slept in the main hall but, if any were awake, none paid me any attention as I crept out at midnight. Cei was waiting for me at the stables with two of the Thegn's riding horses already saddled. I had hidden a sack containing food for a few days, a water skin, a change of clothes and my warmest cloak under a pile of straw. Collecting that, together with my bow and a quiver of arrows, I mounted and Cei did the same.

Apart from my bow I also had a seax – a short single-edged sword – and a dagger. Cei, being a slave, wasn't allowed to handle weapons but at least he had an eating knife in his belt.

We led the horses until we were out of the settlement and then we mounted.

'Where to, master?' Cei asked, his eyes shining with excitement in the moonlight.

'North, into East Anglia. We need to find the Danes' camp.'

What on earth we were going to do once we found it, I didn't know. It wasn't something I'd thought about. It all seemed so simple as we rode away that night: find the Danes, locate Alric and rescue him. Little did I know then that it would be decades before I saw Cilleham once more.

Chapter One

Late Summer 865

We stopped for the first night at Hrofescæster, which meant the camp on the summit. It was where the Roman road known as Watling Street crossed the River Midweg. It was only a settlement but, because of the bridge, it was a staging point on the route from Lundenwic to Cantwareburh and boasted a sizeable tavern which had a similar layout to the ruins of a Roman villa I had once seen.

The taproom lay across the quadrangle from the gate. Between the two on one side lay the stables and on the other there were cubicles for those staying the night. A colonnade ran around three sides of the quadrangle, giving it a rather grand appearance.

Staying anywhere, other than in an isolated spot, was a risk but we were tired, hungry and very saddle sore. Cei's mother was something of a healer and he had the foresight to steal an earthenware jar of her soothing balm before he left. I was used to riding, but not over such a long distance, and my inner thighs were sore. Cei's must have been in an even worse state. Not only was he no more than an occasional rider, but his legs were bare and I saw that he was red raw where his legs had rubbed against the saddle. The balm helped but neither of us were that happy to remount afterwards.

I had dug up the small chest of coins which was hidden in my chamber before I left so I had money. It wasn't a fortune by any means, but it should meet our expenses if I was careful. I had distributed the silver pennies between the pouch which hung from my belt, the saddlebags containing our provisions and spare clothes, and a money belt that Cei wore around his waist under his tunic.

Of course, I had no way of being certain that the slave wouldn't desert me and steal the coins I had entrusted him with, but I was as certain as I could be that he wouldn't betray me. He and I had grown up together on my father's farmstead and we were as near to being friends as we could be, given our respective places in the social hierarchy.

After riding for thirty miles with few rests along the way we were tired and filthy. We were also hungry having eaten nothing but a chunk of stale bread and some cheese for twenty four hours. The tavern appeared to be clean and the payment asked for a cubicle for us to share, stabling for the horses, a bowl of hot pottage and fresh bread seemed reasonable, so I paid up before we went down to the nearby river to wash ourselves. We then applied more balm to relieve the soreness.

When we went into the taproom to eat I was immediately conscious that our clothes made us stand out. I wore a linen shirt beneath a fine wool tunic dyed light blue with embroidered border sewn around the neck, hem and bottom of the sleeve and red woollen trousers tied below the knee with yellow ribbons. I looked like the son of a noble whereas Cei's rough brown tunic made of coarse wool marked him out as a slave or a poor villein. Neither would normally be away from the settlement where they were born, lived and eventually died.

We sat in a corner eating an insipid pottage made of root vegetables and mopped up the last drops with coarse rye bread. We washed down with some foul muck that passed for ale in this place. The tavern might look grand, but the fare offered was anything but.

Unfortunately, we had attracted the attention of the dozen or so men in the taproom when we entered and I noticed out of the corner of my eye that two unsavoury looking characters at a table near the door continued to take a particular interest in us.

I suppose that a well-dressed boy of thirteen and another dressed like a pauper was an odd combination to be seen eating together. There wasn't much I could do about our age, but I could alter our clothing and I resolved to do so as soon as possible. In the meantime I unsheathed my seax and placed in on the table. I hoped that it would serve as a warning that we were not entirely defenceless. In retrospect I now realise that I was being naïve. The two men saw us as easy pickings and the fact that I has a seax wasn't going to deter them.

Our ground-floor cubicle had a stout door with a locking bar that was held in place by two U shaped brackets. There was a small window at the back of the room which had a shutter that could also be barred on the inside. I therefore felt reasonably safe as we lay down for the night. I took the narrow truckle bed and Cei slept on the floor by the door. It was sometime after midnight when Cei woke me with his hand over my mouth. I could just see him holding his finger to his lips in the dim light indicating I should be quiet, then he withdrew his hand.

'Someone is trying to lift the locking bar,' he whispered almost inaudibly in my ear.

I gestured to him to open the shutters over the unglazed window whilst I quietly put on my shoes. I motioned for him to climb out of the window and handed the saddlebags and our cloaks out to him, then I put on my belt and drew my seax.

I went and stood by the door and watched as someone outside tried to lift the heavy oak bar with a sword which he had pushed into the gap between the side of the door and the frame around it. He was evidently having difficulty in getting enough purchase but I'd seen enough.

I was about to join Cei outside the window but he whispered something to me that I should have realised. The gates leading into the courtyard would be locked from the inside and there were no windows in the stable block. Once we were outside the tavern there was no way that we could get our horses and we weren't going to get far on foot.

Suddenly I spotted my bow and quiver in the moonlight which I had put in a corner of the small room and then forgotten about in the excitement. I rushed over to grab it and then climbed out of the window to join Cei. I didn't have long to wait as moments later the man with the sword succeeded in lifting the bar out of its bracket and it fell to the earthen floor of the cubicle with a loud thump.

As soon as the first man rushed into the room I let fly my first arrow. The light from the moon was poor but he was a mere six feet away from me. I couldn't miss and the arrow struck him in the throat. He fell to the ground, gurgling and trying ineffectively to pull the arrow from his neck; not that that would have saved him. Instead the increased loss of blood would have hastened his end.

I nocked a second arrow to my bow string and let fly in one smooth motion that took no more than a second or so. A second man stood stock still in the doorway, paralysed by the unexpected fate of his companion. This time my arrow struck him in the centre of his chest, entering his heart and killing him instantly.

I thought that I had dealt with both of the robbers, but the roar of rage that came from the other side of the doorway told me that the pair from the taproom were not alone. That was unexpected and I hadn't drawn a third arrow from my quiver before two more men rushed into the room. I ducked down before they saw me and heard them asking one another where the devil we were. Just as they realised where we had gone I succeeded in nocking another arrow to my bow and, rising up, took quick aim and let fly a third time.

It was a hurried shot and the arrow lodged in someone's shoulder. There was no time to shoot another arrow before the fourth man reached through the window and grabbed me by the front of my tunic. He had a dagger in his other hand and I watched in horror and he thrust it towards my neck.

Inches before it struck Cei stabbed his eating knife into my assailant's hand. The man yelled in pain and dropped the dagger. A split-second later Cei slit his throat. The man fell to the hard-packed earth inside the room and Cei leapt over the sill to dispatch the thief I had wounded in the shoulder in the same way.

We stood there, Cei inside the cubicle and me outside it, feeling drained and exhausted as the adrenaline wore off. However, the disturbance had been loud enough to wake others. The partitions between the cubicles were constructed of thin planks of timber and did little to attenuate sound.

'Go and unlock the main gates,' I told Cei. 'I'll meet you there.'

I gathered everything in my arms and ran around the outside of the tavern and waited impatiently for Cei to open the gates. Moments later he did so and we ran into the stables.

We could hear the commotion as the bodies of the four men were discovered and a hue and cry was raised. I felt that we had every justification for killing those men but that would mean explaining what had happened to the local thegn and more than likely to the shire reeve as well. That would mean revealing who we were and, at the very least, we would be taken back to my brother and he would be asked to pay wergeld for the dead men. His inevitable reaction didn't bear thinking about. I would be punished severely and Cei would be executed as a runaway slave. I therefore decided to flee before we could be detained.

We saddled up and rode out of the stables. Thankfully no one had yet noticed that the compound's gates were open and we cantered through them before anyone could stop us. We rode across the timber bridge over the river at a fast canter then slowed to a trot after a short while, but we didn't stop for two hours, by which time we were at least fifteen miles away from the tavern. Our horses were blown and we were shattered; after all we had only managed to grab a few hours' sleep in the past two nights.

The moon had long since disappeared behind clouds and now a fine drizzle was falling, soaking us and the horses. We had stayed on Watling Street and shortly after we recommenced our journey we could see the lights of what looked like a large settlement ahead of us. It was hardly a good idea to arrive in the early hours of the morning so we left the old Roman road and followed a track to a farmstead. There was a barn which was unlocked and so we rubbed the horses down with straw and lay down for a couple of hours sleep.

Luckily no one came near the barn at daybreak, although we could hear sounds coming from the hut a hundred yards away. We saddled the horses and led them until we were out of sight. Then we rode a little way down the track until we found a stream. We let the horses drink and eat some grass whilst we dined on yet more stale bread and hard cheese. It was a wonder that neither of us broke a tooth.

We rode into the place we had seen the night before, which turned out to be called Tarentefort, a crossing place over a small river which ran into the Temes close by. Because it had been raided countless times by Vikings sailing up the Temes it sat behind a thorny hedge and the one set of wooden gates was guarded by two bored looking sentries. Thankfully they took little interest in us amongst the carts and other people entering the settlement, mainly on foot, but a few were mounted like us.

The good Lord must have been with us because we had arrived on the monthly market day. Not many stalls had been set up as yet so I bought two meat pies from a baker and Cei and I ate them ravenously whilst we waited. During the morning more and more stalls appeared and I was able to buy less distinctive clothing for both of us. Cei had never worn trousers or leather shoes and was dubious about putting them on, but I told him that he would soon get used to them; being barelegged and barefoot marked him out as a slave or a member of a very poor family. Such folk didn't ride expensive horses. I also bought him a warm woollen cloak with a hood. It was impregnated with lanolin so it would keep out the rain as well as being warm.

Next I bought sheepskin covers for our saddles; they would be much kinder to our skin. I also managed to find a small leather tent to sleep in as we would be avoiding taverns from now on. We stocked up on fresh provisions and then made for the gates. That was when we ran into trouble.

Few others were leaving so early in the day so we stood out. In our new clothes both Cei and I looked like the sons of poor ceorls but something must have aroused their suspicions.

'Hold on boys, who are you and where are you going?'

27

'Back to our farm,' I replied on impulse, hoping that the nervousness I felt didn't show on my face.

As soon as I had spoken I realised that it would have seemed odd for the younger one of us to have answered.

'Cat got the other boy's tongue then?'

'He's a mute,' I replied, feeling that I was digging a bigger and bigger hole.

'Oh, poor lad,' he said insincerely. 'Those are fine horses for farmer's sons to be riding.'

'Yes, my father doesn't normally allow us to ride his best horses but he let us do so today. He breeds them you see.'

'Ah! That explains it,' he said giving our animals an envious look. 'Go on, on your way then.'

I nodded my thanks and we rode out of the gates, breathing a collective sigh of relief once we were well away from him.

'I thought he was going to detain us,' Cei said with a broad grin. 'You were great. I don't know how you remained so calm.'

Then his face fell.

'I'm sorry master; I was too familiar and I misspoke.'

'No, that's fine, Cei. We're in this together and we're taking equal risks. No more master and slave. Call me Jørren from now on.'

'Yes master.'

We broke into laughter and grinned at each other.

'Yes Jørren,' he corrected himself.

†††

Just after midday we clattered across the timber bridge that spanned the Temes and entered Lundenwic. I had been to Cantwareburh a few times and I had thought that it was big. It may have been – it had nearly a thousand residents – but it was no way near the size of Lundenwic. It sat on the north bank of the River Temes to the west of the ruins of the old Roman city. The latter was mainly uninhabited because it was full of ghosts and evil spirits, or so I had heard.

Someone told me later that some ten thousand people lived in the narrow streets to the west of the old city. It certainly smelt like it. As we rode though the hovels that had sprung up outside the timber palisade that surrounded the original burh of Lundenwic our noses were assailed by a mixture of rotting garbage, faeces, urine and smoke.

Once into the narrow streets on the far side of the bridge the stench got worse. The place reeked so much that I thought I was going to vomit. Dead animals lay where they'd died and naked children played in the filth. I pressed on hoping for inspiration. I had hoped that we might get some news about the Danes there as it was the capital of Mercia and a major trading port. However, I had no idea where to go to obtain that sort of information.

I was on the point of turning around when we reached the waterfront. Here at least there was a wind blowing downriver to clear the air somewhat, although the river resembled a cesspool. It carried the detritus of the settlement eastwards with the current, but then the incoming tide brought it back again.

In my innocence I thought the best thing to do was to ask one of the port labourers if he knew where the Danes had gone. The man I asked spat at me and said that he didn't know, didn't care and then indicated that I should return whence I'd come, although he put it in much more colourful terms.

I was wary of staying at a tavern again but we could hardly sleep in our tent, so I asked the way to a monastery. This time we were given a more helpful answer and we rode out of the settlement to Saint Peter's Monastery on the banks of the river a mile upstream.

Most religious houses offered accommodation to travellers and by convention expected to receive a donation in accordance with the traveller's means. Saint Peter's was the exception. I suppose it was reasonable as, being so close to the largest settlement in Mercia and a major port, it would otherwise be swamped by visitors looking for a cheap bed. I was happy to pay as monks were notorious gossips and I anticipated obtaining some useful information as well as a bed. I was not disappointed.

Because of our age we were shown to the novices' dormitory instead of the men's guest hall. The young monk who escorted us could not have been more than eleven. He was a talkative lad and told us that he had been given to the monastery at the age of eight because his elderly father thought that, by so doing, he would increase his chances of entering heaven.

When I asked about the Danes he didn't seem to think my question was a strange one. He unthinkingly replied that a vast fleet had been seen heading north past the entrance to the Temes estuary a week previously. Various rumours abounded as to their destination. Some thought that they were headed back to their home in Danmǫrk whilst others maintained that they planned to raid the coast of East Anglia.

I hoped it was the latter as I had absolutely no chance of finding my brother in Danmǫrk; even to try would inevitably mean that Cei and I would end up as thralls like him, or more likely dead.

As he went to leave he asked us where were travelling to and I told him I was going to stay with my uncle at Wintanceaster as he was poorly and not likely to last the winter. He seemed satisfied and left.

As guests we were expected to eat with the monks in the main hall and to attend services in the small timber church. I discovered that this was one of the drawbacks of staying in a monastery as their wretched bell seemed to wake you up every time you managed to get to sleep. We staggered out of bed several times to endure yet another lengthy session of prayers and homilies in their cold and dank church.

After morning mass the sub-prior sidled up to me as we made our way to the hall to break our fast and asked about my uncle.

'Who is he? I was a monk at Wintanceaster before coming here as sub-prior,' he said with a false smile.

Evidently our friendly novice had spoken to the inquisitive monk and that placed me in a difficult position. I could hardly admit to lying but I knew no one in the main part of Wessex, let alone in its capital.

'Edgar the goldsmith,' I blurted out, that being the first name that came into my head.

'Really? I didn't know he had any siblings, let alone a nephew. I'm sorry to hear he's ill. I will pray for his swift recovery.'

I had hit upon the name of an actual person purely by chance. I breathed a sigh of relief as the man went on his way, apparently satisfied that I was who I said I was. I had to resist breaking out into a fit of the giggles, such was my relief. Later I recognised that I should have chosen someone more a little more obscure than a goldsmith. There must be thousands of people in Wintanceaster but everyone would know who the leading citizens were. I'd been a fool, but a lucky one.

We left the next morning heading along the old Roman road called Ermine Street. It was only then that I realised that I knew absolutely nothing about East Anglia or its geography. Cei was of no help, of course. We had made it so far, more by luck than by good judgement, but now I was bereft of ideas.

Chapter Two

Autumn 865

That night we camped by a stream in a wood well away from the road. We didn't bother with the tent, but in the middle of the night it began to rain and we hurriedly put it up. The next morning we discovered that there was one problem with a tent. You get soaked rolling it up again. Luckily it had stopped raining by then so we risked lighting a fire to dry out by and to make a pottage from dried meat and barley.

We returned to Ermine Street and two days later we reached Godmundcestre. We had passed several groups on the road, travelling in both directions, but thankfully no one seemed to take much interest in us. We were a long way from Cent but the theft of the horses and my brother's hoard gave me a guilty conscience and I half expected the next person we saw to accuse me of the crimes.

Killing the robbers at Hrofescæster had affected me as well. Of course, they deserved to die; if Cei and I hadn't killed them we would have ended up dead instead. Somehow that didn't help ease my conscience though. I needed to make confession to a priest but for some reason I kept putting off doing so. Perhaps I didn't altogether trust them.

Although we had avoided any settlements since we left Lundenwic, I needed to find out where the Danes were. I therefore risked entering Godmundcestre and stopped the first person I saw.

'Are there Danes anywhere near here?' I asked the man, who looked to be poor ceorl from the way that he was dressed.

He looked at the two of us suspiciously.

'Why do you want to know?'

'So that we can avoid them,' I replied. 'My servant and I are travelling to Lindocolina to live with my uncle.'

I prayed that the man wasn't from there and asked who my uncle was. Thankfully he didn't and he seemed satisfied with my answer.

'All I know is that the priest says that they landed at some place called Hapesburc and marched inland, pillaging and murdering their way across the countryside towards Theodforda.'

'Theodforda?'

'Yes, it's a large settlement of some two thousand people, or so I'm told. Mind you, there will probably be a lot less than that once the bloody heathens get there.'

'And is it near here?'

'Thank the Lord, no. It's well the other side of Grantebrycge and that's over a day's walk away.'

I thanked the man and we left the settlement. Now all I needed was someone to tell me the way to Grantebrycge.

†††

The farmstead looked peaceful enough. Sheep were grazing on pasture that sloped down to the hut where the family presumably lived. There was a barn and another, smaller hut which was probably for the slaves. Judging by the squeals coming from a fenced off compound with a small outbuilding attached to it, they had pigs and several chickens pecked around the space between the huts and the barn. On the side of the farmstead away from the pasture there was a patch of ground where crops were evidently grown and another for root vegetables.

As we watched a man appeared and went into the barn. He emerged a little while later with a pair of oxen in harness. Evidently he meant to plough the arable land now that the crops had been harvested, ready for next year's sowing.

Two boys came out of the house and made their way over to the midden heap where they proceeded to shovel manure into a cart ready for spreading so that it could be ploughed into the soil to fertilise it. It all reminded me of my old home near Cilleham, except that our farmstead had been much larger.

A third boy appeared and went into the barn before bringing out a horse to hitch to the cart. Two little girls went down to the nearby stream with wooden buckets and filled them. I began to wonder how many lived on the farmstead when a family of five came out of the slave hut and set off to weed the area growing root vegetables. It didn't seem a large enough a farm to support so many people.

We normally steered clear of places like this but I needed information; in particular I wanted to know if I was on the right road for Grantebrycge. I thought it probably was as it was evidently an old Roman road, albeit a minor one, but it was in poor repair and long stretches of it were no more than muddy tracks. Presumably the cobbles used to pave the road had been taken over the centuries and reutilised elsewhere.

I left Cei looking after the horses and walked across to the larger of the two huts. One of the boys loading muck onto the cart came across to see what I wanted. He looked to be about fifteen or sixteen and had shed his tunic to carry out the filthy task. He had a broad shoulders and powerful arms. I suspected he might be an archer by the look of him.

'What do you want, boy?' he asked me gruffly.

'A little information for which I'm willing to pay,' I replied with a smile.

His frown disappeared and he looked relieved.

'You're a Saxon,' he said in relief. 'We've heard tales that there are Danes not that far away.'

'I'm a Jute from Cent,' I replied, 'but near enough as we're now part of Wessex.'

'You're a long way from home,' he commented as he washed in the horse trough and pulled his rough woollen tunic over his head.

I saw no reason to lie to this boy and so I told him the truth.

'My brother was captured by the Danes and I'm on a quest to find him and free him.'

'What!' he exclaimed in surprise. 'Just you? What are you; thirteen or fourteen? I'm surprised you got this far.'

'You know where Cent is then?' it was my turn to be surprised.

'I was a novice with the monks of Ely for six years. My father said he couldn't afford to feed all of us and so he gave me to the monastery when I was eight.'

'So why are you back at home?'

'I ran away when I was fourteen, just before I was due to take my vows as a monk. I couldn't stand the boredom anymore. In any case I wanted to be a warrior, not a churchman.'

'So you've been training as an archer?'

'Ever since I returned,' he said, nodding. 'I was hoping that King Edmund would muster the fyrd but instead the coward has given the Danes hundreds of horses and allowed them to stay for the winter in return for keeping his throne,' he said, spitting in the dirt to express his disgust.

'What's going on? Why have you stopped working? It's difficult enough to feed you all without you shirking?' the man who was presumably the boy's father demanded angrily.

Then he spotted me.

'Who's this? What are you doing here?'

'I'm looking for a guide to lead me and my companion to Theodforda.'

'Theodforda? Why?' He looked at me suspiciously. 'That's where the Danes are rumoured to have set up camp for the winter.'

'They have my brother and I intend to rescue him.'

'Then you're a fool. There's thousands of the pagan swine by all accounts. Are you that eager to die?'

'I'm a good hunter and tracker,' I boasted. 'They won't know I'm there.'

He studied me for a long moment.

'You'll never get there on foot.'

I put my fingers in my mouth and whistled. Seconds later Cei appeared from the trees leading our two horses.

'We've been travelling for weeks,' I told him. 'I am told that Theodforda is only two days ride from Grantebrycge so I think our horses can make it, don't you?'

He glared at me and I instantly regretted my impudent remark.

'I'm sorry,' I said contritely. 'That was crass and rude.'

His face softened and he looked at his eldest son.

'Well, Redwald, you wanted adventure. If your mother was still alive she would never let you go off on such a dangerous and foolhardy undertaking, but she isn't, God rest her soul. If you want to go with these two, I won't stop you.'

My opinion of the man sank. He was evidently only too glad to get rid of his son and didn't care that he was probably sending him to his death. However, Redwald didn't hesitate.

'Wait here,' he called as he dashed off towards the hut. 'I won't be a minute.'

Half an hour later he was mounted behind Cei whilst my horse was loaded with the tent and our other possessions. I was now feeling more optimistic as we rode away from the farmstead and headed for Grantebrycge.

✝✝✝

The settlement was quite a large one and housed perhaps as many as six hundred souls. It sat astride the River Grante but we didn't cross it there. Instead Redwald guided us to a vill called Granteseta to the south west where he said there was a horse stud.

The ceorl who owned it sucked his teeth when I said that we wanted to buy a good riding horse and a packhorse.

'The king has bought most of my stock to give to the bloody Danes,' he told us. 'What I have left I need to keep as breeding stock.'

I looked at my two horses. They were both mares and were of a type called palfreys, the best class of riding horse. However, they were exhausted after coming such a long way.

'Have you seen brood mares as good as these two?' I asked.

The horse-breeders eyes lit up greedily, then he hooded them and put on a doubtful face.

'They look pretty knackered to me.'

'They are tired after a long journey, yes, but they will swiftly recover and produce many fine foals for you.'

'I thought you were after more horses, not selling the ones you have?'

'I was thinking more in the way of an exchange,' I replied.

'What, these two for two of mine?'

His eyes lit up again.

'No four of yours, and they'd better be good ones,' Redwald cut in before I could reply. 'Three rounceys and a pack pony but I'll need to see them and make sure that they're not some elderly nags on their last legs.'

'Don't worry,' he said with a grin, 'I got rid of all those to the king's men.'

We spent another hour bargaining but we ended up with three riding horses and a pony which both Redwald and I were happy with. It was getting on towards dusk and so we retraced our steps along the River Grante until we found a hollow in which to camp for the night.

The next day we left Cei at the campsite and rode into Grantebrycge. It wasn't market day but there were several weavers, an armourer and a fletcher in the settlement. I bought Redwald better clothes, including a padded gambeson and a cloak; then decided that it wouldn't be a bad idea for Cei and I to have gambesons to give us some protection in combat. Unfortunately no one had one in my size and so I eventually settled for a leather over-tunic.

I bought my new companion a seax, a dagger and a helmet at the armourer's workshop, then purchased a seax for Cei as well. By now my stock of silver pennies had diminished considerably but I made one more investment. We spent some time at the fletchers whilst Redwald tried out various bows, eventually settling on a war bow which was much more powerful than mine. I bought him a quiverful of arrows and a small barrel of spares now that we had a pack animal.

Cei was suitably grateful for the gambeson, which would keep him warm as well as protecting him to some extent. He was less sure about the seax.

'But Jørren,' he said doubtfully, 'I have no idea how to use a blade, other than my knife.'

'Then Redwald and I will teach you.'

Both of us had been taught how to defend ourselves by our fathers, but our new companion was much more skilled than I was, so he ended up teaching both of us every spare moment we had. We also put our bows to good use and supplemented our diet with ducks, plovers, grouse and geese.

We had crossed the river in Grantebrycge. Now we had the burly Redwald riding with us we attracted far less attention than we had when we were two young boys on their own. Although Cei was nearly fifteen he was small for his age and consequently looked younger. The road to Theodforda was little more than a muddy track so we made much slower progress. I estimated that we made less than fifteen miles that day and when rain threatened we hastily found a spot by a stream to camp.

Our little tent was a bit of a squeeze for two, let alone three, but in any case I had decided that one of us should stand watch at night in case we encountered parties of Danes from now on. Both Redwald and I had hunted at night and so we were used to the strange sounds of the woods in the dark; not so Cei. He woke us with false alarm twice that first night and so we took it in turns to sit up with him until dawn pointing out what each sound meant. I also told him what sounds to listen out for if there were men in the vicinity.

We didn't return to the road the next day. To do so would have risked running into a patrol, or more likely a Danish forage party, as we were now less than twenty miles from Theodforda. Redwald said that we should head north east through the trees and we did so but in a manner I would have never have thought of. Either

Redwald or I would advance a hundred yards on foot and then, all being clear, the other two would catch up leading the horses. It made for slow going and we camped early in order to hunt and train Cei in the use of his seax.

Of course, he became far from proficient in such a short time but he was a quick learner and he knew the basic defensive moves by the time we encountered our first group of Danes.

It had taken us three days to get near Theodforda, especially as we had to skirt open areas of pasture or arable land. We saw black smoke rising into the still air at one point and surmised that the heathens had sacked and burnt a settlement or a farmstead. On the fourth day we came across a small settlement I never did know the name of. What I saw from just inside the treeline shocked me.

Women and girls, some much younger than my little sister, were being repeatedly raped by groups of men whilst others plundered the huts and the Thegn's hall. I saw some coming out of the small timber church carrying a silver cross and other precious items. Then three men pushed the priest ahead of them so that he stumbled down the steps and fell into the mud. They picked him up and then proceeded to pinion his arms and feet to the door of the church with their daggers in a ghastly parody of the crucifixion.

I had my bow strung and was pulling an arrow from my quiver when Redwald stopped me.

'There are too many of them,' he hissed in my ear, 'but I have an idea. Come.'

He dragged me away fuming and thirsting for revenge but I soon realised that he was right. If we attacked the pagan bastards we might kill a few but we would die ourselves, and that wouldn't help my brother.

'I think I know in which direction Theodforda is from here. If we climb the trees we can pepper them with arrows on their return.'

'Won't they still be able to kill us?'

'Not if we're quick and climb down before they get to us. They'll search for us in the trees and that will enable us to pick more of them off as we retreat. Either they'll give up or we make a clean break after a while and return to where Cei will be waiting with the horses.'

Perhaps I should have thought about his plan a little more, but hate clouded my judgement and I nodded eagerly.

At first it worked like a dream. There were a score of Danes, some were quite elderly and a few were boys like us. That shocked me a little and I reflected on how different our cultures must be. Four were mounted and the rest, including three young boys, trudged along on foot carrying what few pitiful items they'd pillaged from the settlement.

Redwald's first arrow drove through the chainmail byrnie of the leading Viking and he toppled from his horse without a word. I released my own bowstring a split second later and hit another man in chainmail in the throat. At first the pagans didn't know where the attack had come from and cast around seeking us out at ground level. By then we had both nocked and released a second arrow. This time Redwald killed the only other man wearing a byrnie and I wounded a man in a leather jerkin in the shoulder. We had time for a third arrow, each of which killed another Dane before we climbed down and retreated just before the rest of them charged into the woods looking for us.

Redwald disappeared in one direction and I in another. It was our good fortune that the Danes had no archers with them. I could afford to come out from behind a tree and release my bow and dart back into cover without fear of being hit myself. One or two spears were thrown at me but I was too far away. When a throwing axe lodged in the tree beside me I knew that I had allowed them to get too close. I released one more arrow and then ran.

I calculated that I had killed or badly wounded six Danes. If Redwald had managed the same there could only be eight left. Surely they would give up the chase after suffering so many losses, but they didn't. I wounded another one in the thigh. It was only after I'd taken cover behind yet another tree that I realised that he could have been no older than me. I had a picture of the horrified

40

look on the boy's face etched on my retina and I wanted the killing to end.

I had to tell myself that it was them or us, then I remembered what had happened to the women and the young girls in that settlement and my resolve hardened. I jumped out from behind a tree and saw two Danes before me. Both were young, perhaps thirteen or fourteen, and both looked scared out of their wits.

'Throw down your weapons,' I yelled before realising that they didn't understand English.

I pointed the arrow at one and indicated as best I could that they should throw down their spears and daggers. One was brighter than the other and threw away his spear whilst holding his other hand up in a gesture of surrender. I changed my aim to the other and he hastily did likewise. I kept an arrow trained on them as I approached them. One obviously thought of running but the brighter one said something to him and he stayed where he was. Obviously he realised that I could aim and release an arrow before the boy was out of range.

I dropped my bow and drew my seax before they could react and held the blade against the throat of the brighter boy and indicated that the other one should use the spare bow string, which I threw at him, to tie up his companion. He did so with shaking hands. No doubt the death of so many of his fellow Danes had unnerved him. He offered no resistance whilst I unstrung my bow and tied his hands together. I then tied the other boy's hands a bit tighter. Pushing them in front of me with one of their own spears I took them to where Cei waited with the horses.

I had picked up the two daggers and the other spear and I handed one to Cei. We then sat down to wait for Redwald. When he hadn't appeared after what seemed to me to be hours, but which was probably no longer than a short while in reality, I grew concerned.

'Keep an eye on them. If they move kill one of them,' I told Cei and went in search of our guide. Redwald had proved a real godsend so far and I felt lost without him. I prayed fervently that he was alright.

I retraced my steps to the road. It was littered with the Danes we'd killed. The one I'd wounded in the thigh had bled out but another, presumably one that Redwald had injured, was screaming in agony. I drew my dagger and took a deep breath. A second later I had cut his throat and was busy vomiting all over him. I felt better after that, but I was still shaken. Killing a man in cold blood is not an easy thing to do, especially if you're only thirteen years old.

My instinct was to follow Redwald's trail immediately, but first I collected the four horses the Danes had been riding and tied them to a tree to make sure they didn't stray – or worse return to the heathen army's camp. I wanted to collect everything of value: namely hacksilver, arm rings of gold and silver, swords, daggers, spears, axes, shields, helmets and byrnies but that would have to wait. I set off on foot to follow the clear trail left by the Danes who had pursued Redwald.

It was an even easier trail to follow at first because of the dead Danes. I counted four of them before they petered out. Then I heard a faint scream. I frantically searched in my pouch for another bowstring but didn't find one. I cursed, my spares must be with my gear on my horse and that was some distance way with Cei. I drew my seax and my dagger and ran towards the sounds of someone in intense pain.

Chapter Three

October 865 to March 866

I realised that crashing through the wood, snapping twigs and rustling the fallen leaves was foolhardy and I slowed down after a couple of minutes, but I found it difficult to curb my anxiety. I was naturally light-footed and made scarcely a sound as I carefully crept forward to the lip of a hollow. Below me I saw Redwald stripped to the waist and tied to a tree whilst two men slowly and systematically flayed the skin from his torso. The blood ran down his chest in thick rivulets and I knew that he was badly injured. A third Dane – a boy like the two I'd captured - watched fascinated.

Thankfully the screaming ceased when Redwald blacked out. The Danes, robbed of their pleasure, stopped what they were doing and one of them handed his helmet to the boy and barked something at him. He scurried away into the woods.

I racked my brains trying to think of what to do. I would be committing suicide if I charged the two men. They were big brutes armed with swords and there were two battle axes leaning against a nearby tree. Then I had an idea. I circled around the hollow and set off in the direction taken by the young pagan.

I couldn't bring myself to kill him. He was bent over on the bank of the stream trying to reach the water below him. I crept up behind him and brought the pommel of my seax down on his head quite hard. He was wearing a fur cap on his head and I found it difficult to gauge how hard to hit him to ensure unconsciousness without killing him. I must have judged it well because he collapsed without a sound. I just managed to catch him before he toppled into the stream but he let go of the helmet, which fell into the water and sank. I laid him down and put my ear to his lips. Happily he was still breathing, albeit faintly.

I jumped into the stream and retrieved the helmet before filling it with water and climbing out again. I carefully put it against a tree and stripped the boy of his outer clothing. All Vikings wore trousers which were much baggier than ours and the ribbons they used to bind them up to the knee were much broader. It took me a little while to get them looking right and then I pulled on his light blue tunic, his leather body armour and his fur cap before setting off back to the camp. The clothes were a tight fit and I worried that the Danes would notice that I was bigger. Luckily the boy had long fair hair, much like mine, and I pulled it over my face to hide it as much as possible.

I had to leave my seax behind as the Danish boy only had a dagger; it would have to suffice. I kept my head down as I made my way into the small clearing where Redwald was still unconscious. Both the Danes shouted at me; presumably cursing me for being so slow. I walked up to the one who looked to be in charge and, just as he recognised that I wasn't who he thought I was, I threw the helmet and the water in his face and drew my dagger.

He was so shocked that he stood there for a moment and that gave me enough time to thrust my dagger into his throat. Without waiting to see whether the wound was fatal I darted over to the tree with the two axes leaning against it and picked one up, kicking the other away.

It was much heavier that I had expected and that nearly cost me my life. The other Dane gave a roar of rage and came at me with his sword. I swung the axe intending to cut into his side but it was too heavy and it chopped into his leg instead. He dropped to one knee, but still managed to swing his sword at me. I jumped backwards and thankfully the point just missed me. This time I lifted the axe as high as I could and brought it down onto his sword arm.

I heard the bone crack and blood spurted out of the wound. He let go of his sword with a shriek of pain and I picked it up. He was still trying to get to his feet when I put all my weight behind it and pushed the point into his eye socket. He fell to the ground and I retched for the second time that day.

I was trembling all over and wanted to collapse, but I forced myself to do what was necessary. I ran back to the stream and retrieved my seax and changed my clothes, ignoring the fact that my trousers and shoes were soaked from jumping into the stream.

I heard a groan as the boy woke up and clutched at his head. I held my seax to his throat and told him to get dressed. Of course, he didn't understand but he got the gist. Ten minutes later we were back in the clearing.

The young Dane's eyes opened wide when he saw the two dead men and he asked me something. Even though English and Danish were different languages they had the same roots as we had all originated in the same part of the world. I understood him to ask if I had killed them. I nodded and he looked awestruck. From then on he acted as if he was frightened that I would kill him too and he became amazingly compliant.

I lowered poor Redwald to the ground and took the boy with me to fetch water to wash his wounds. There was little more I could do for him then, so I left him and went and fetched the horses. I got the Dane to gather up everything of value and we put them in sacks before tying them to two of the horses. Then we went back and I wrapped Redwald in my cloak before putting him across a horse. I mounted another one and hauled the Dane up in front of me. I showed him my dagger and pressed it into his side. He nodded to show he understood and we set off to find Cei and the other two Danes.

I tied the three boys up sitting around a tree whilst Cei and I did what we could for Redwald. We bathed his wounds again and Cei spread honey on the raw flesh before putting moss on top of it and binding it in place with strips torn from a spare white linen tunic. Then we set about getting a meal organised. We had to hand feed the three prisoners; I wasn't going to risk releasing their hands. When we'd given them a drink one of them thanked us in accented English.

'You speak our tongue?' I exclaimed in surprise.

He shrugged. 'I got one of my father's Saxon thralls to teach me in case it came in useful.'

'What was the name of this thrall?' I asked casually.

'Alric, I think; something like that anyway.'

I tried not to get excited. Alric was a fairly common name.

'Do you know where you captured him?'

'Why, what's with this sudden interest in a thrall?'

I hit him in the mouth.

'Just answer my questions if you and your friends want to live.'

'In Cent,' he replied resentfully. 'He was knocked unconscious during a battle and I asked my father not to kill him. He kept him as thrall to serve me,' he replied sulkily.

In that instant I regretted hitting him. It seemed that I might owe my brother's life to this boy.

'What are your names?' I asked after a pause.

'My name is Erik. My friend is called Ulf and the runt in the fur hat is Tove.'

'Well Erik, is anyone likely to ransom for any of you?'

'I doubt it,' he said giving me a venomous look. 'You and your friend there,' he said nodding towards the unconscious Redwald, 'managed to kill all three of our fathers together with my uncle, who was our hersir.'

I gathered that hersir meant leader. He went on to say that his father, and that of the other boys, were bondi; what we would have called ceorls. Then he surprised me by giving me a sly grin.

'You will be a great warrior when you grow up. Perhaps we shouldn't have written the Saxons off as a bunch of women if they can produce a cub like you.'

I didn't follow everything he'd said, but I did pick up on the word Saxon.

'I'm a Jute not a Saxon,' I replied tersely. 'Several centuries ago the people of Cent and several other places along the south coast of England came from Jutland. It's...'

'I know where Jutland is! It's where we come from,' he cut in.

I grinned at him and said mischievously 'perhaps we are distantly related?'

'I doubt it!' he shot back, glaring at me. He paused. 'Mind you, you fight well, enough to be a Dane,' he admitted reluctantly.

I thought I detected a glimmer of admiration in his last words and I patted him on the shoulder in a friendly fashion before getting up. A glimmer of an idea had begun to form in my head.

That night Cei and I took turns to stand watch. We felt shattered the next morning and infuriatingly the Danish boys slept well all night long. I'd found some mead in a flask on one of the dead Danes and Cei and I dribbled it into Redwald's mouth from time to time to dull his pain.

The next morning we made a stretcher of sorts to carry Redwald and slung it between two of the horses. I would ride the leading one and Cei the lead horse of the other two, trying to keep the stretcher as steady as possible. The problem I was left with was the three Danes. If I let them go they would doubtless tell their countrymen what had happened and we would become fugitives. I ruled out killing them and so I was in something of a quandary. To add to my problems I quite liked Erik, who I thought was probably the same age as me.

'What will happen to you if I let you go?' I asked Erik after we'd broken our fast.

'We have no family left in England now; our mothers and sisters are back in Danmǫrk and they will have a hard time with no man to support them. No one here will want us either. We're too young to be warriors so no jarl or hersir will let us join him.' He paused and looked at the others, who both looked at the ground. 'Orphans usually end up as thralls,' he muttered gloomily.

'Then I have a proposition for you, if you can fight,' I gave Erik a steady look to let know that I was being serious. 'Can you?'

He shook his head. 'Danish boys like us are just old enough to start our training. That's why we were brought along – for the experience - but we couldn't fight anyone yet. And now there is no-one left alive to teach us.'

47

'There is.'

'Who?'

'I will. I'm teaching Cei to fight, to track and to hunt. I can teach you as well.'

'Why? Why would you teach Danes how to kill Saxons?'

'Because I'm obviously hoping you won't do that. I want you to join my warband.'

Erik translated for the benefit of the others and suddenly they brightened up, looking eager. It had been a gamble but I thought it might work. I knew enough about Danes to know that, once they had pledged their loyalty to their jarl, they were honour bound to honour it.

'Will you give me your oaths?' I asked.

'Does it mean we'd have to kill other Danes,' Erik asked doubtfully.

'Don't Danes ever kill other Danes if their jarls fall out?'

'True,' he admitted. 'Very well. I will join you and I'm sure the others will follow my lead.' He paused. 'Jarl.'

Erik grinned and I chuckled but Cei looked upset by this turn of events. I think he resented the increase in the size of our group. It was certainly true that from then on we were no longer as close as we had been.

✝✝✝

Now we had eight horses we used two to carry Redwald on a makeshift stretcher; one in front and one behind. Cei took the reins of the lead horse and I rode alongside the rear one to make sure it kept the correct pace and jolted the litter as little as possible. Erik and Ulf rode ahead of us and Tove followed on with the pack horse. There was too much booty I'd taken from the dead Danes to load on one horse so we all had to carry some of it. I had chosen a good sword for myself and hung two byrnies and several helmets in a sack from my saddle horn.

We needed to find somewhere safe where Redwald could recover. We daren't stay on the road and obviously we had to keep well clear of Theodforda. As the day wore on I despaired of finding anywhere, and then we emerged from a wood into a clearing with a charcoal burner's hut in the centre.

Smoke was coming from the mound near the hut indicating that charcoal was being produced so we knew that the hut was occupied. Leaving Cei with Redwald and the horses the three Danes and I warily approached the hut. Suddenly the door flew open and a middle-aged woman appeared holding a spear. A girl of about eleven stood behind her carrying a knife.

'Be warned, Danes. We'll sell our lives dearly.'

Then she stared at us open mouthed.

'You're just young boys!' she exclaimed.

'And we mean you no harm.' I reassured her. 'I'm no Dane and we seek your help. We have a boy with us who the Danes have half-flayed.'

'Leave your weapons there and bring him inside,' she ordered briskly.

We did as she said and half an hour later she had treated and re-bound Redwald's wounds with clean bandages. He was in considerable pain and the flask of mead was finished. However, the woman, whose name I learned was Edyth, gave him something which put him to sleep.

'We need somewhere to stay for the winter,' I said. 'If we hunt for food and do what we can to help you, will you allow us to stay?'

'I suspect that you could have easily killed us if you wanted to and taken the hut for yourselves, so yes, you can stay. To be honest my daughter and I will be glad of the company.'

The daughter's name was Nelda, a rather shy girl, not saying anything to us for the first three days we were there. However, I noticed her making calf-eyes at Tove so I encouraged him to talk to her. Once the floodgates had opened she wouldn't shut up. She got on my nerves but Tove seemed as enchanted with her as she was with him.

49

October passed into November and then the snows came. By now Redwald was healing well and he was no longer in such pain, although he would always bear the scars. He started to exercise and by the middle of December he was fully recovered. I was eager to return to Theodforda to try and find Alric but there was no chance of going anywhere. The snow covered everything in a blanket of white and, as Erik pointed out, the Danes wouldn't be leaving until the spring.

Confined to the hut, the camaraderie that had developed between us began to deteriorate. Cei had become aloof almost from the moment that the three Danes had joined us and now he devoted himself to helping Redwald recover, shunning the rest of us. Erik and Ulf started to pick on Tove, teasing him about loving Nelda and he reacted by sulking. I found myself getting irritated by their petty squabbles and I also became isolated from the rest.

However, that was the least of our problems. We had lived well at first, but then food became a concern. There were few wild animals to hunt and we also needed more fodder for the horses. Thankfully, a sudden thaw set in a week before the celebration of Christmas and we were able to ride into Godmundcestre with Edyth's charcoal cart.

Everyone's spirits picked up once we had escaped the confines of the hut and we laughed and joked amongst ourselves. Even Cei seemed more at ease with the Danes now.

When he and I had been on our own, I had dreaded being challenged due to our youth. Redwald looked like a young man and after he'd joined us I stopped worrying. Now, with the presence of three more boys in our group, we excited attention again as we entered the settlement.

Whilst Edyth and Nelda were selling the charcoal, Redwald, Cei and I left the others to look after the horses and went to the street where there were two armourers' workshops. We had various Danish byrnies, helmets and swords for sale and I was hoping to get a good price for everything bar six of the best swords.

The first armourer offered us a derisory price so we went next door. Immediately the first man rushed after us and the two armourers started bidding against each other. In the end we sold everything to the first man and then I explained to both of them what we wanted.

The swords I'd kept were too heavy and too long for any of us except for Redwald. I wanted them cut down but the armourer said it would make the swords unbalanced. He offered to make us swords to suit each of us, although it would cost more. Next we asked if he could alter the helmets to make them smaller and to look more like the pattern that Anglo-Saxons wore. Again he said that it would be easier to melt them down and make new ones.

When he said it would take a month to do the work I went next door and asked the other armourer if they could do it in two weeks if I split the work between them. That's what we agreed and the first man paid me the difference between what we had agreed and the cost of the swords and helmets. He would pay the other armourer for his help. I went away well satisfied thinking I had a goodly sum to add to my stack of coins; then Redwald whispered something in my ear that I should have thought of.

'A leader should always split the loot he gains with his men. It is the custom amongst the Danes as well as our nobles.'

I should have thought of that myself and nodded my thanks for his suggestion. It would bind the boys closer to me and raise their morale. I would still keep half though. I had half an eye on the future and my aim, apart from rescuing my brother, was to gain enough money to buy at least five hides of land somewhere. Then I could call myself a thegn. Of course, that would be several years in the future, but it gave me a goal.

Next we sought out the appropriate merchants and purchased hay and oats for the horses, flour and root vegetables for us and bows for the three Danish boys that were suited to their build. I also bought more arrows so that that they could start training as archers.

Once reunited with the others, Edyth accompanied us with the cart to collect our purchases. She insisted on sharing the cost of the food but I told her that we wouldn't accept it. She had given us shelter so that Redwald could heal and a place to see out the winter. That was enough.

In mid-March we decided that it was time to leave. We had collected our new swords and helmets and had spent three weeks practicing with them. We were hardly formidable swordsmen but at least we had mastered the basic parries, cuts and thrusts.

I had given each of the others a small purse of silver pennies. They hadn't expected it and they were suitably grateful. Cei was especially moved to have money of his own. I glanced at Redwald and nodded my head in appreciation for his suggestion.

We were all sorry to say goodbye to Edyth and Nelda, especially Tove. Nelda hugged him hard and gave him a kiss on his cheek before running back into the hut to hide her tears. We were in a sombre mood as we rode away, but soon the thought of the excitement to come lightened the atmosphere. The others didn't seem to have a care in the world, but I was apprehensive. Spiriting Alric away from the middle of the Danish camp was an almost impossible task and I had no idea how we could accomplish it.

Chapter Four

Spring / Summer 866

We attracted a few curious glances as we rode through the narrow streets of Theodforda. We had approached the place with extreme caution, Redwald and I taking turns to scout ahead of the rest, but the Danes had gone. They hadn't sacked the settlement, but they had stripped it bare of horses, provisions and any money and other valuables that they could find. A lot of girls and some older women were showing signs of pregnancy and I suspected that there would be a lot of Danish bastards born over the coming months.

We needed more food, leather tents and a second pack horse or pony but none were available. I also needed to know where the Danes had gone so we went in search of a priest. My father had always said that churchmen were a lot of old gossips and knew far more about what was happening than the rest of us.

At first the priest was wary of us, despite our youth, and I realised that the cause of his caution was the Mjölnir hanging around Ulf's neck. The others also wore one but kept them tucked inside their tunics. The Mjölnir – or Thor's hammer – was a talisman worn by many pagans and was of similar significance to them as a crucifix was to us. The priest would be all too familiar with it after a winter spent in close proximity to the Danes.

The fact that half of my little group was Christian and the other half heathen hadn't been a problem up to now. I had shown little interest in the Norse pantheon of gods and the three Danes had shown absolutely no desire to learn about Christianity. My policy, had I thought one necessary, would be that each was free to follow his own beliefs just so long as he kept it to himself. However, I didn't expect the priest to take the same view.

'Redwald, why don't you take the others off to an alehouse and have a drink whilst I talk to the priest?' I suggested.

Once they had departed I dismounted, tied my horse to the rail outside the priest's hut and produced a silver penny, saying that I would like to make a donation to the Church. He nodded, although he still looked suspiciously at me, and I followed him inside the hut. His wife and a little girl beat a hasty retreat to the corner of the only room. The mother ignored me but the girl stared at me wide eyed.

I gave him a brief outline of my adventures to date, leaving out anything to do with killing. He wouldn't have believed me if I said that I had killed three robbers and several Danes anyway; he'd think I was boasting. He seemed to accept that I was searching for my brother but he said he knew no more than the fact that a third of them had ridden off northwards whilst the others had headed eastwards on foot.

Perhaps my father had been talking about monks, rather than priests, when he said that they were the best sources of the latest information?

To me what the priest had said indicated that they were all heading towards Northumbria; those on foot returning to their ships before sailing to the north. I thanked him and left.

The others had made for the nearest tavern and were drinking ale when I joined them. We had all been brought up on weak ale, it being safer to drink than polluted water. Cei poured me a flagon from the earthenware jug in the middle of the table and I took a mouthful. It was pretty foul, and stronger than I was used to, but I was thirsty so I grimaced and took another swig.

It seemed that Redwald had had more luck than I had. Danes in their cups were a talkative lot and the tavern keeper had told him that they intended to invade Northumbria. There was some story about their king, Ælle, having thrown the father of some of the leaders into a snake pit to die. Their motive seemed to be revenge as much as anything else and their first objective was to take Eforwic, Ælle's capital.

The Danes had a four day start on us but I knew that two thousand warriors plus their camp followers and baggage train would do well to make twenty miles a day. I wished I knew what lay eighty miles from Theodforda but none of us had more than the haziest notion of how far away Northumbria was. What we did find out was the Ermine Street led there, so it looked as if we would have to retrace our steps along the way that Cei and I had taken and re-join the Roman road. I don't suppose that this was the route along which the Great Heathen Army had marched – they would have taken a more direct road but, unlike us, they presumably knew where they were going.

†††

It took us a week to reach Lindocolina. The three Danish boys could ride, but they had never ridden for any great distance and we soon ran out of Cei's mother's balm. We managed to buy more sheepskins to make their saddles more comfortable and we stopped at a monastery where the infirmarian gave us some unguent of his own devising in exchange for a donation. By the end of the week we were all used to spending several hours in the saddle at a time.

We approached Lindocolina cautiously. It was the seat of the Ealdorman of Lindesege and it looked to be quite a large settlement, but it had evidently been attacked. It sat on the top of a hill and so we could see the black smoke from miles away. I studied it carefully as we approached it but there didn't seem to be any sign of life. I hoped that the inhabitants had managed to flee in time, but I feared that we would still find many dead in the streets. Cei suggested that we by-passed it but we needed more provisions and I hoped that the Danes might have left something.

Evidently, whatever the route taken by heathen army when they left Theodforda, they had now joined Ermine Street. The huts, workshops and stores were still burning so they couldn't be that far ahead of us.

We strung our bows and nocked an arrow as we approached the outskirts on foot. Tove and Cei led the horses as they were the worst archers, although they were improving all the time. As I had anticipated, there was no sign of life, but there were a lot of dead bodies, nearly all Anglo-Saxons. The people of Lindocolina had obviously put up a fight as there were numerous blood stains everywhere. The fact that the bodies had been taken away for cremation indicated that the blood came from Danish casualties.

When we reached the far side of the settlement we hurriedly retreated back into the shadows. Below the hill, not six hundred yards away, the enemy army had built a series of pyres on which lay at least three score bodies. The enemy were gathered around the various pyres whilst some sort of ceremony took place. Then men stepped forward with torches and set the pyres alight.

It was only then that I noticed that each of the pyres had a living person tied up amongst the corpses.

'It is customary amongst the Norse to sacrifice a few thralls to serve the dead in Valhalla,' Erik whispered to me.

'The Norse?' I queried, watching horrified as the flames consumed living human beings along with the dead.

'Vikings from Norweġ, Snæland and Orkneyjar. Not every warrior down there comes from Danmǫrk. There are some from Sweoland as well.'

I wasn't really listening. I had a horrible thought that Alric might be one of those poor thralls being roasted alive. Then I told myself that I couldn't think like that. They were more likely to be people captured in Lindocolina. I turned back into the settlement saying that we needed to find food. It was an excuse; I couldn't bear to watch the cremations any more. The others seemed equally glad to tear their eyes away from the grisly sight.

We were in a sombre mood as we started to check inside the buildings that hadn't been torched. We didn't find anything, which is what we'd expected. What we hadn't noticed was how dark the sky had become, mainly because of the pall of smoke overhead. Then the wind got up, blowing the smoke away and I saw a flash of lightning illuminate the greyness. A few seconds later a crash of thunder overhead made the horses buck and rear so that Cei and Tove had trouble controlling them.

'We need to find shelter,' I yelled. 'Heavy rain is coming,' I added pointing to the east where you could see thick streaks slanting down from the clouds overhead.

Ulf spotted a small hall nearby, probably the home of a wealthy merchant or a minor noble. It had a building to the rear which proved to be stables; even better there was hay and a barrel of oats. After we had unsaddled and fed the horses Cei and Tove volunteered to stay and calm them whilst we checked the hall. By now torrential rain was falling outside and we made a hurried dash for the door into the hall.

We were so intent on not getting soaked we forgot the usual precautions and the four of us tumbled into the hall without checking it first. It was gloomy inside, so much so that at first we couldn't see anything. Then I suddenly became aware of somebody running towards me with a spear held horizontally.

Thankfully I reacted quickly and I jumped to one side, just avoiding the point. The person wielding the spear couldn't stop in time, so intent were they in thrusting their spear into me as hard as they could. I raised my fist and punched him on the point of his chin. My assailant crashed to the floor unconscious whilst I nursed my hand, convinced that I'd broken one or more bones as a result of the impact.

A sharp cry came from my right and I whirled around, my hand reaching for my sword. Erik had raised his arm to ward off a blow from an axe wielded by what looked like a girl. Thankfully it was the haft, and not the sharp blade that had connected with his forearm. Redwald leaped at whoever it was and the two of them crashed to the ground, the axe spinning free.

Our eyes were now getting accustomed to the dark interior of the hall and I could see that Erik's attacker was indeed female. By her size she appeared to be fifteen or sixteen. She fought like a she-wolf as Ulf and Redwald hauled her to her feet. I turned the spearman onto his back and saw that it was a boy a year or so older than me.

I went and found some rope in the stables, getting thoroughly drenched in the process, and we tied the vixen of a girl and her unconscious companion to two stout chairs. I examined Erik's arm, which seemed to be no more than badly bruised, and then sat down opposite our two captives and waited patiently for her to calm down and for him to wake up.

✝✝✝

We mean you no harm,' I told them when the boy eventually came to and groggily looked around him.

'You're not Danes?' the girl exclaimed in surprise.

'Some of us are,' I admitted. 'But they are my men and I come from Cent.'

When she looked blankly at me I added 'from Wessex' and she relaxed a little.

'Where are your parents?' I asked after introducing myself and the others.

'The Danes murdered them,' she said she said looking at Erik venomously. 'And my betrothed.'

'I'm sorry. We've followed the heathen army across half of England and I fear it's an all too familiar story,' I smiled at her sympathetically and she nodded. 'How did you two escape?'

'Father built a small chamber under the floor for exactly this sort of emergency. Regrettably they were out visiting the Ealdorman when the alarm was sounded. They rushed back and put us in the hole but, before they could join us, some pagans rushed into our hall and killed them both.'

'They didn't find you?'

'Obviously not,' she said with some asperity. 'We heard them searching the place and then they left. Thankfully we stayed where we were because another group came and ransacked the place again the following day.'

'You had food and water down there?'

'Untie me and I'll show you.'

'Only if you promise to behave.'

58

'You can release Ecgberht too,' she said nodding.

'The boy who tried to run me through?'

'Yes, who else?' she said scathingly. 'He's my brother.'

'And what's your name?' I asked. 'Leofflæd?' I suggested sarcastically.

It meant *beloved beauty* and was the most unsuitable name I could think of for this fiery little vixen.

'How did you know?' she asked, looking genuinely surprised.

I shook my head, amazed that I'd guessed correctly.

'Very well, cut them free,' I told the others.

The chamber under the floor was well concealed. Unlike most floors of beaten earth, this one was made of timber planks. The entrance looked like the rest of the floor and was located under a large coffer that stood open and empty. Steps led down into a small room lined in more timber.

There was a bench to sit on and even a small table, but what caught my eye was the shelves on which sat several large cheeses, haunches of smoked ham and venison, apples and earthenware jars full of lentils, flour and pulses. Several strings of onions hung down from the ceiling and there were leather flasks full of ale and mead. It was a virtual treasure trove. Coupled with the fodder in the stables, there was enough there to keep us provisioned for some time to come. The problem would be carrying it all.

'We'll let you have it if you let us come with you,' Leofflæd said, drawing me out of my daydream in which I was feasting on what lay before me.

'I was thinking of buying it from you,' I replied.

'And then what would we eat?' she scoffed. 'Besides, there is nothing here for us now. Our parents are dead and our friends will be too, or worse – they'll be slaves.'

'Can you fight?' I asked. I expected her to admit that she couldn't; I could then use that as an excuse not to take a girl along with us.

'Better than I can,' Ecgberht said, speaking for the first time.

'Can you use a bow?' I asked her, recovering from my surprise.

59

'Yes, as well as any boy, and some men come to that.'

'If you can beat me with five arrows, I'll think about it, but the others will have to agree as well.

'Where are you?' a plaintiff voice drifted down to us.

The storm had passed over and Cei and Tove had come looking for us.

'Down here,'

I climbed back out of the hiding place and told them what we'd found.

'We need to find a cart to carry it all,' I said after everyone was back in the hall, 'but first we need to agree whether Ecgberht and Leofflæd should join us.'

Opinion was divided. I think the girl frightened some and others thought that she would be more of a hindrance than a help. Her younger brother was accepted but, of course, he refused to go if his sister was left behind. Then there was the question of the supplies. Leofflæd quite reasonably said that we could only take the contents of their hiding place if they were allowed to join us. Ulf muttered in my ear that we could just kill them and take the food anyway, but I ignored him. I wasn't going to murder anyone in cold blood.

In the end we went outside and put three battered and discarded shields up on a wall as targets and Redwald paced out a hundred yards. I let Leofflæd go first and she put her first arrow near the boss in the Centre of the shield but it was three inches off target. Her brother went next and his was a good six inches too high. I took careful aim, allowing for the wind and trajectory over that distance and put mine in the centre of my target.

After shooting all five arrows I had hit the bull three times and had two near misses. Ecgberht had improved slightly, but only scored one bull. Leofflæd had surprised us all by scoring four bulls after her initial attempt. We were all impressed and even Ulf said that she was welcome to come with us. My little warband now numbered eight.

†††

I sent Cei and Erik to shadow the Danes the next day to see where they were headed. When they came back they reported that the army was headed for the south bank of the River Hymbre. I assumed, correctly as it turned out, that they were meeting their fleet there who would ferry them over to the north bank. I wondered why they would go to all that trouble but I was soon to find out.

We took the longer, but essentially much quicker road which crossed the River Đarcy at Tateshalla. Both ended up at Eforwic, which was the most logical destination for the Great Heathen Army. East Anglia had already submitted; if they took Eforwic they would control the North and from there they could sweep down into Mercia. Then only Wessex would remain to oppose them. I feared for our future. By our, I mean that of the Angles, Saxons and Jutes who had made our home on this island for the past three centuries. The name England only emerged as a term for all the Anglo-Saxon kingdoms much later in my life.

Although we were fairly certain that all the Danes travelling overland into Northumbria had headed due north to cross the River Hymbre, we weren't taking any chances. Two of us took it in turns to scout ahead of the rest of us, encumbered as we were by the cart. It took us three days to reach Tateshalla and when we did Erik and Tove, who were acting as our scouts for the day, came riding back to say that there was a great host defending the bridge over the Đarcy. They were adamant that they weren't Danes and so I was left with the conclusion that they must be the army of Northumbria. If so they were in the process of being outflanked.

We rode forward to the south bank of the river and halted a hundred yards from this side of the bridge. I dismounted and walked forward flanked by Redwald and Ecgberht.

'Leave your weapons the far side of the bridge,' a large man on a horse called across to us.

I beckoned Cei forward and we handed our swords, seaxes and daggers over to him. Then we walked forward onto the bridge.

Three men approached us from the north bank. The one in the Centre was wearing a chainmail byrnie whilst the other two wore leather armour. I took them to be members of some noble's gesith.

'Who are you boy? What are you doing here?' the leader barked at me.

'My name is Jørren and I'm the youngest brother of a thegn in Cent.'

He started in surprise.

'Cent? You're a long way from home!'

'My other brother is a captive of the pagan army and I seek to rescue him.'

All three men laughed and I flushed with annoyance. It caused me to brag, something I usually tried to avoid.

'We've killed a score of Danes. How many have you slain?' I asked belligerently.

'You lie, boy.'

'No, he doesn't.' Redwald said. 'I was being tortured by three Danes and he killed two of them and captured the third. Tove, come here,' he called.

The Dane, who was now thirteen and who had put on several inches over the winter, came forward to join us.

'These men don't believe that we killed all the Danes in your group and that Jørren rescued me singled handed.' Redwald said.

'It's true' he said in slightly accented English. 'Jørren knocked me out and captured me. Only three of us survived the attack; he, Redwald and Cei killed seventeen men.'

'And now you've joined him?'

'Yes, all three of us did. He is now our jarl, er, leader.'

The man in the centre pursed his lips.

'You had better come and tell your tale to the kings.'

Two men stood together at the far side of the bridge. The one on the left was a giant wearing a byrnie, which had been polished until it shone, over an embroidered crimson tunic, an ornate helmet inlaid with gold and a sword with a large jewel for a pommel. It marked him down as important; it also demonstrated that he was vain. The other man looked like him, but he was smaller and less flamboyantly dressed.

'I'm Ælle, King of Northumbria,' the giant said in a deep, impressive voice.

Even in Cent we'd heard that he and his brother Osberht were rivals for the throne. The last we had heard was that Ælle had deposed Osbehrt, but the latter wasn't about to give up easily and had raised an army to try and regain the crown. I was therefore surprised when the king introduced the man standing to his right as his brother. Evidently the two rivals had combined their forces in the face of the Danish threat.

'Cynige, you will wait here in vain for the heathen army. Their fleet is ferrying them across the Hymbre as we speak. They will be at Eforwic in two days or less.'

A look of panic flitted across Osbehrt's face but Ælle was made of sterner stuff.

'How do you know this?'

'We arrived at Lindocolina just after the Danes had left it. We watched them cremate their dead on the plain below and then many hundred headed off up Ermine Street whilst some two thousand set off towards the coast, presumably to re-join their fleet. The smaller party headed directly north from where the road divides; we took the left fork.'

'It's true, Cyning,' Ecgberht cut in. 'My sister and I survived the sacking of Lindocolina and joined Jørren. What he says is correct. We shadowed the Danes heading north for a time.'

The two men glanced at each other. They knew that they'd been outwitted. Most of their warriors were on foot, whereas the Danes were either mounted or they could sail up the River Uisge to Eforwic. It would take the army of Northumbria at least two days to get there. It would be a close run thing, but my money was on the Danes reaching Eforwic first.

They broke camp immediately but by the time the last group had departed there was only a few hours of daylight left. We were forgotten in the rush and I decided to camp on the south bank, away from the detritus of the abandoned camp. We were mounted and could easily catch the Northumbrians up the next day, even with our cart.

†††

We passed a few stragglers as we came to Loidis, the main settlement in Elmet, once a separate kingdom, but now part of Deira, that part of Northumbria south of the River Tes. I saw no point in joining the Northumbrian host; we weren't here to fight the Danes, just to rescue Alric. So we stayed in Loidis for a few hours.

It gave me the opportunity to buy helmets and seaxes for Ecgberht and Leofflæd. There was no time to order byrnies to fit them but we did find padded gambesons that would give their bodies some protection. I also bought a barrel of arrows tipped with iron that would penetrate chainmail at close range. My stash of silver was running low again, but I hoped we would have the opportunity to obtain more ere long.

We camped north of Loidis that night. I had asked how far Eforwic was and I was told it was a day's journey on foot. From that I calculated that the Northumbrians, encumbered as they were with a large baggage train, would arrive there the next morning. We spent the next night in a glade by a small river well away from the road some four miles short of the settlement. Tove proved to be an expert trout tickler and the fish made a nice change from our diet hitherto of smoked ham, hard cheese and pottage made from barley, lentils and turnips.

The next day we followed the Uisge to the north-west until we found a crossing place. As we crested a rise I saw Eforwic ahead of us. It was bigger than Cantwareburh or Lindocolina but not nearly as big as Lundenwic. Being an old Roman city it was surrounded by high stone walls, but over the last four centuries stone had been taken for buildings, leaving big gaps. Other sections had just collapsed leaving a pile of rubble.

Succeeding kings of Northumbria had mended the walls by inserting sections of timber palisade across the gaps, but two of these sections had recently been torn down, presumably by the Danes during their assault. Whatever garrison had been left behind - probably old men and the youngest members of the fyrd - had obviously been overcome. Now the banners of the pagan leaders flew from the walls.

We didn't have long to wait until the Northumbrians appeared and deployed ready for battle. As they did so the Danes streamed out through the gaps in the defences and formed a continuous shield wall some six ranks deep outside. I couldn't understand why they hadn't made temporary repairs to the walls so that they could defend the settlement, but the reason for that became all too obvious later.

'Where will the thralls be?' I asked Erik. 'In the settlement?'

'No,' he said shaking his head. 'Most likely they will have been left with the fleet.'

'Then we need to find the ships.'

'I have heard that the River Uisge is navigable up as far as Yorvik,' Ulf said.

'Yorvik?'

'Our name for Eforwic,' Erik explained.

'Where is the fleet likely to be?' I asked.

All three Danish boys shrugged.

'It numbers between fifty and sixty longships and so it would need a stretch of beach or river bank long enough to take it,' Tove answered.

'Although they could have moored many of the ships in the middle of the river,' Ulf said thoughtfully.

'Then we need to explore the north bank of the Uisge downstream from here,' I decided. 'Ulf, you're about my size. May I borrow your Danish clothes?'

'Does that mean I have to stay here?' he asked unhappily.

'I'm sorry, but I'm the only one who can recognise my brother.'

We made our way to a wood to the north of Eforwic, well away from the fighting, so that Erik, Tove and I could change clothes. Leaving the others to watch the battle, we set off to reconnoitre the river bank.

As we were dressed as Danes we saw no point in trying to be clandestine and we rode openly down to the banks of the River Fŏs intending to make our way down it to its confluence with the Uisge to the south of Eforwic. However, we didn't need to travel that far. There was a large lake to the east of the settlement through which the Fŏs flowed. The majority of the Danish and Norse fleet was anchored in the middle of this lake. Much of the land bordering it was marshland and I wondered how the crews reached their ships.

We rode a little further up onto a small hillock. From our vantage point I could see that the Fŏs narrowed and then broadened out again before narrowing once more before joining the Uisge. There was a bridge over this narrow section of the river which led to a second part of the settlement. This explained why the longships moored in the lake had lowered masts which lay in cradles on their decks. It had been necessary so that they could be rowed under the bridge.

This had evidently been built by the Romans as the two end spans were constructed in stone, not something that we Anglo-Saxons were very skilled at. The centre span must have collapsed a long time ago as it had been rebuilt in timber.

There was a wooden quay along the broader section of the river where ten longships were moored alongside. There were also a number of smaller rowing boats. I assumed that these were used to ferry the crews out to the ships in the lake as necessary. The general impression given was that the Danes and their Norse allies were here to stay for some time, perhaps over winter. That is, if they weren't defeated by the Northumbrians.

What I didn't see was any compound where the thralls and other captives might be being held. We weren't able to ride any further because the walls around the main part of the settlement extended into the beginnings of the marsh and it barred our way. It seemed as if the only way of making further progress was to enter the settlement and make our way back to the banks of the Fŏs inside the walls.

†††

Then we had a stroke of luck. One of the small boats cast off from the jetty carrying a dozen men. It was being rowed by two boys who looked to be about fifteen or sixteen. Both of them were dressed in undyed coarse wool tunics and their heads had been shaved. Erik leaned across and said that both their dress and their lack of hair indicated that they were thralls.

For a moment I hoped that one might be Alric but, although they were too far away to distinguish individual features, neither looked as if they might be him. Their build and general appearance were wrong. However, they might know where he was or what fate had befallen him.

We watched as all but one of the men climbed aboard one of the longships which Tove told me was of a type called a drakkar, or dragon ship. This one had twenty holes a side meaning that it required forty rowers and he said it could hold eighty or ninety warriors. It was one of the largest moored in the lake and Erik added that it probably belonged to one of the jarls who led the Great Heathen Army. I would have liked to ask him to tell me about these leaders, but this was neither the moment nor the place.

Whilst the men set about getting the drakkar ready, the two boys started to row back whence they had come with one man sitting in the stern. He had grey hair and a long beard and was clearly quite elderly. The easiest way to explore the rest of the area was by boat and I suddenly had an idea; it was risky but I decided that it was better than trying to enter and work our way through Eforwic.

I knew that Erik had the best whistle and so I explained what I wanted. He put his fingers in his mouth and emitted a piercing sound which attracted the attention of the three in the boat. I beckoned them towards us and pointed to a small strand of shingle about two hundred yards north of where we sat on our horses.

From a distance, dressed as Danish warriors, the old man probably couldn't see how young we were. Later the two thralls told us that he was half blind anyway. They rowed upstream and met us at the shingle beach. We dismounted and Tove held the horses whilst we walked down to the boat as it grounded on the stones.

'What do you want? What's so important that you needed to call us over?' the old warrior asked in a querulous voice.

Suddenly his demeanour changed and he went to pick up the axe lying beside him on the thwart where he was sitting. I have no idea what had alarmed him, possibly our youth. Danish boys became warriors at fourteen, like us, but they didn't wear expensive byrnies and helmets, nor did they roam the countryside on their own. He got up surprisingly quickly for a man of his age, took a pace towards us and raised his axe. Then he staggered as one of the thralls rocked the boat from side to side.

He regained his footing and was about to cleave the skull of the errant thrall in twain when Tove's arrow took him in the throat and he toppled over the side and lay in a few inches of water as he breathed his last.

'Well, done,' I said in English as Erik and I climbed aboard. 'Wait here with the horses, Tove. Good shot by the way. I felt the wind of it as it passed my cheek!'

He grinned with pleasure as he pushed the boat off the beach.

'Help us,' I told the two thralls, 'and you'll gain your freedom.'

'The Danes hunt escaped thralls down and flay them alive to dissuade others from doing the same,' the elder boy said gloomily.

'He's right,' Erik said.

'You've signed our death warrants,' the other said with venom.

'What I meant was, you can come with us.'

'Who are you?' he asked panting with the effort of rowing whilst speaking.

'My name is Jørren and my eldest brother is the thegn of Cillium in Cent.'

The two boys looked at each other in delight.

'I'm Jerrik and this is my younger brother, Øwli. We come from Cantwareburh.'

Both names were typically Jutish. Many families living in Cent had started to use Saxon names, ever since we became part of Wessex, but some still stuck by the old traditions.

'Are your parents still alive,' I asked, thinking that perhaps they could accompany Alric back to Cent if we succeeded in rescuing him.

I knew that I couldn't return. I had stolen from my family and freed Cei, one of my brother's slaves. And that was quite apart from the men we had killed in Hrofescæster. Although no one there knew our names, they had our descriptions and by now someone might well have put two and two together.

'No,' Jerrik said sadly. 'The bloody Danes killed them when they sacked Cantwareburh and took us captive.'

'I seek my other brother, Alric. He was captured at the Battle of Salteode. Have you come across him?'

'There is an Alric from Cent amongst the captives, but he was injured,' Øwli said hesitantly.

'Injured?'

My heart sank.

'Yes, nothing really serious; his forearm was broken,' he tried to reassure me.

'And was it set properly?'

'Yes, there were several monks captured with us and one of them splinted it. It took some time to set, but Brother Abraham said it had mended well. However, the arm muscles are wasted.'

'Which arm?'

'The right one, unfortunately.'

I smiled. My brother was left handed, something my father had tried to correct, but without success.

'Where is he now?'

'With the rest of the captives on a small island further down this river.'

'Good! Let's get there before anyone becomes too suspicious.'

Chapter Five

Summer and Autumn 866

To call it an island wasn't quite accurate. It was connected to the rest of Eforwic by two narrow isthmuses; one in the north and one in the south. The Danes had built palisades across both to pen the captives in. A few guards manned each palisade but there were none in the captives' camp itself.

'As soon as the heathens have beaten off the Northumbrians, the Danes intend to take most of the captives overseas to the slave markets in Danmørk and Frisia,' Jerrik told me. 'They don't need that many thralls to serve the army.'

It sounded as if I had arrived just in time. As we went under the bridge and approached the so-called island I got more and more nervous. The two sentries on top of the northern palisade gave us no more than a cursory glance as we passed them but they seemed to take more interest when we pulled into the shore and Erik and I got out. Perhaps it was the fact that we had left the two thralls behind on their own that alerted them. As soon as I realised my mistake I told the two boys to tie the boat up and join us.

The four of us strolled into the camp, trying to look inconspicuous whilst searching for Alric. The place was devoid of tents or any form of shelter. The captives were fed, but not that well. Cooking pots, in which some form of porridge was cooking, were dotted here and there. Water came from the river but that was also where people defecated so it didn't surprise me to note that some people were ill. I shuddered to think that my brother had been living in these sort of conditions. We treated our slaves much better and I was amazed that the Danes didn't do so as well. Surely they were a valuable commodity?

Later I learned that the Danes weren't that fussed whether or not they died; there were plenty more thralls to be had in England

and, in any case, a glut of slaves depressed the market. As we meandered through the camp I glanced towards the palisade and, to my dismay, I saw the the gate open and two Danes wa;lked through it and headed towards us.

I didn't know whether we could brazen it out or whether we would be forced to kill them and run. My Danish was quite good by now, but I certainly didn't sound like a native. If we were going to have to talk to them I would have to leave it to Erik. We had become friends and I hoped that I could trust him, but I wasn't entirely certain that he wouldn't betray me in these particular circumstances.

As I watched the two warriors wending their way through the camp towards us Erik pulled at my sleeve.

'What do I say when they ask what we are doing here?' he whispered.

Had we found Alric I would have said we grabbed him and ran but, although the three of us sought him amongst the throng, so far there was no sign of him. Suddenly I saw someone who looked a bit like him, but the boy was much thinner and my brother had a ruddy complexion; this lad's was pale and wan. Alric had a shock of unruly which made him stand out hair but all of the thralls had shaven heads.

I was far from certain it was him, but then the boy stroked his nose with a bent finger, something Alric did when he was agitated. At that moment I was convinced that it had to be my brother.

He was standing by one of the cookpots and begging for some food. The woman stirring the glutinous mess inside the cauldron spat at him and told him to go away. That made me furious and I went over and struck the poor woman across the face with my open hand. I didn't mean to hit her so hard but she must have been weak from hunger because she fell backwards and passed out. Remorse hit me like a fist in the stomach and I went to see if she was alright. However her companions had closed around me threateningly and one had picked up a hefty looking lump of firewood. They might be about to be sold as thralls, but I was a mere boy and I had angered them. They wanted revenge.

I had no option. I drew my sword and waved them back. Then two things happened. Alric recognised me and Erik was asked by the two warriors what was going on. The crowd immediately slunk away and I grabbed Alric's arm and told him in Danish that he was to come with us.

The two Danes looked at me suspiciously. I had forgotten that my Danish would sound odd to their ears.

'Who wants him, and why have two whelps like you been sent to collect him.'

'Be careful Bjarke, the way they are dressed they are probably some jarl's sons,' the other one said nervously, looking us up and down. 'And they have their own thralls,' he added.

I could have hugged him. Bjarke looked unconvinced but evidently he wasn't about to risk offending someone more powerful than he was.

'Go on then, take him and get out of here before you start a riot.'

I had a feeling that Bjarke was more worried about that than who my father might be.

We didn't need telling twice. With Jerrik and Øwli half carrying poor Alric we made our way back to the boat. Once we had set off to row back upstream to the lake I nearly cried with relief. I went to examine Alric but, apart from his wasted frame and even more wasted right arm, he seemed to be alright. I scooped water up with my hands once we were clear of the fouled bank and washed the dirt from his face and body. What he needed now was rest and good food; and a lot of both. We had to find somewhere safe where he could recover.

ᛏᛏᛏ

We rode back to join the others, Alric riding with me. He was so weak that I had to sit him in front of me and keep one arm around him the whole way. Jerrik and Øwli shared a horse with the two

Danish boys but they were in much better condition than Alric and rode behind Erik and Tove.

By the time we reached our vantage point the battle was over. The army of Northumbria had been routed and were fleeing from the pursing Danes.

'What happened?' I asked Redwald after we had put Alric in the cart and Erik had explained who the two former thralls were.

'Some of the Danes pretended to flee back into the settlement and a third of the Northumbrians were foolish enough to follow them,' he said grimly. 'It was obviously a trap because none reappeared. Those who had gone after the Danes left a wide hole in the Northumbrian shield wall through which the Danes poured. They cut the left and right wings off from each other and half surrounded them. Then they started the slaughter. It didn't take long before the rear ranks broke and ran. Soon after that the rout was complete and the Northumbrians, what was left of them, ran for their lives.'

'I think both kings got away because I saw two mounted groups, each with a banner, riding away to the north just before the rest started to flee,' Leofflæd added. 'They were cowards. Had they stayed and encouraged their men they could have defeated the cursed heathens.'

I thought it unlikely but didn't say that to her. It would have only started a pointless argument. I remembered an old adage my father had been fond of: a man who flees when all is lost lives to fight another day.

I glanced at the three Danish boys, wondering how they were reacting to the phrase *cursed heathens* but they kept their faces neutral. At some point I would have to remind everyone that we needed to respect each other's beliefs if we were going to become a proper warband.

I wondered how I was going to get Alric, Jerrik and Øwli home to Cent. I couldn't go with them but there was nothing to stop the three of them returning. However, that was a problem for another day. First I had to get Alric fit again.

†††

My first priority was to get well away from the Danes. Having won and kept Eforwic they would undoubtedly ravage the surrounding lands once they had sobered up from celebrating their victory. We therefore travelled north on the Old Roman road; those without horses travelling in the cart. We made slow progress and by nightfall we'd only travelled a dozen miles.

The next day we made better time. We encountered several groups of Northumbrians making their way home but they gave us a wide berth and the further north we travelled the fewer people we saw. As twilight fell we found a spot in a hollow near a stream and away from the road.

We had eaten a cold meal the previous night as I daren't risk our campfire being seen. The hollow was deep enough for the light from a fire to be hidden and so we cooked up a stew of smoked ham, turnips, lentils, wild onions, crow garlic and chives. Tove had found the last three growing near the road as we journeyed north. I have to say it improved the flavour of the stew no end.

Alric had a better colour now and he ate ravenously. I had to ration his food to save him vomiting it all back up again. Ecgberht had said that his stomach would have shrunk and it would take time for him to be able to eat normally again. Jerrik and Øwli didn't have the same problem. They had been employed as ship's boys and, although they were treated harshly, they had been fed better.

We had only gone a few miles the next day when we saw a sizeable settlement over to our left. The countryside seemed peaceful this far north and there were a number of farmers and traders making for the place. We needed decent clothes for Alric and the other two and I would buy them weapons if I could find them. We also needed more horses but I doubted whether we would find them here.

I left the three former thralls with Ulf and the cart and the rest of us rode into the settlement, leaving our horses in the stable of the only tavern. We learned that the place was called Catræth and it was the base of the Ealdorman of the surrounding shire. He had been at Eforwic with his gesith and the shire's fyrd. However, none had returned so far. Word soon reached his wife that a group of boys and youths dressed as warriors had arrived and I was summoned to the ealdorman's hall.

As we rode up the lady was standing outside the hall with a boy aged about eleven and two girls of thirteen or fourteen at her side. I dismounted and bowed. Leofflæd also dismounted and took my horse. She was dressed like a boy and looked like one apart from her hair which hung halfway down her back. The others remained mounted.

'Have you come from the south? Do you know what has happened? Have we beaten the heathens?' she asked anxiously.

'We were at Eforwic when the army of the two kings attacked it, lady. I very much regret to say that the Danes won and those Northumbrians who escaped the slaughter will no doubt be making their way home.'

I had tried to put it as gently as I could but I fear that I only increased her level of anxiety.

'Oh dear, has Eforwic fallen then?'

'Yes, King Ælle and his brother expected the Danes to cross the Ðarcy at Tateshalla but they crossed the Hymbre instead. By the time that our army reached Eforwic it was already in Danish hands. We didn't arrive in time for the battle, unfortunately, and by the time we did it was all over.'

'You don't sound like a Northumbrian,' she said suspiciously.

'I'm not. I'm from Cent. The Danes captured my brother at the Battle of Salteode and I came north to rescue him.'

'Oh, I see. Did you succeed? Where is he?'

She sounded a little sceptical.

'He's in a poor way, half-starved and recovering from a broken arm. I left him and two others from Cent who we also rescued with the rest of our group outside the settlement whilst we came to buy a few essentials.'

She seemed convinced by my explanation and my reference to Ulf and the rest of our group was intended to give the impression that there were more of us than there were.

'Then I mustn't detain you any longer.'

'Lady, the Danes are busy ravaging the countryside around Eforwic. I have no idea whether they will come here but one of the youths we freed overheard a conversation which indicated that they intend to make the River Tinan their northern boundary.'

'Thank you for the warning,' she said, wringing her hands. 'God go with you.'

'And with you, lady.'

I remounted thinking she would need all the help she could get. I hoped her husband was on his way home safely as I didn't get the impression that she would be much good in a crisis. Certainly she didn't compare to Leofflæd, with whom I was becoming more and more impressed. I was convinced that she would have risen to the challenge brilliantly.

We managed to buy most of what we needed in Catræth except for chainmail and helmets for those without. Instead I bought several padded linen gambesons and leather hoods. We even manged to find bows. The one thing that wasn't for sale was horses. I was told that the horse fair took place once every three months and I'd missed the last one by a week. I asked if there were any breeders nearby and I was told that there was a farmstead at Malsenþorp that might be able to supply what we needed.

Our present stock of eight horses were a mixed bag: three rounceys, a pack horse and four nondescript farm horses that we had taken from the Danes. They were all tired and some were too large for their riders. My hope was that we could trade them plus a little silver for twelve new ones. I still had some money left but not a great deal. Thankfully we still had quite a lot of provisions in the cart, but not enough to see eleven of us through the coming winter.

I was told that Malsenþorp lay six miles north of Catræth. However, the Roman road divided before we got there and I debated which way to go.

'Do you know where the road that runs north-west goes?' Leofflæd asked, riding up beside me.

I shrugged. 'All I know if that we are still south of the River Tinan and therefore in the area claimed by the Danes.'

'Or so Jerrik and Øwli say.'

'You don't believe them?' I asked quietly.

'I have no reason not to,' she replied guardedly, 'but it was just a few drunken heathens boasting. How would they know their masters' plans?'

'I don't know, but it's all the information we have for now.'

'True,' she muttered, flashing me a smile. 'Come on then, Jørren, be a man and make a decision.'

She flushed me a radiant smile to rob her jibe of any insult and I realised what a pretty girl she was. I grinned back, but rather sheepishly I fear. I suddenly felt awkward in her company.

'Very well, we'll take the right fork and look out for a track off to the left after a couple of miles.'

Roman roads had marker stones every mile, although many were now missing. However, we were in luck. After passing two milestones there it was: a clear track leading off to the west. We hadn't gone far along it before we saw Malsenþorp ahead of us.

It was rather more than a farmstead, more like a small settlement. I counted seven huts in addition to a small hall and there were two barns and a long stable block. The land around it was pasture on which sheep and few cows grazed but what drew my attention was the herd of horses. There must have been at least thirty mares and stallions together with several foals between three and six months old.

As we approached men appeared armed with everything from rusty old swords to wooden pitchforks. What concerned me, though, was the three armed with bows. Two men and a boy of about fifteen had nocked an arrow to their bowstrings and the points were now pointing straight at me.

I told my little cavalcade to halt. Then I rode forward, dropped my spear, sword and seax to the ground. My bow and quiver followed, as did my helmet. Then I continued to walk my horse forward towards the man in the centre who looked to be the ceorl who owned the farmstead.

I stopped, held up my hand to indicate that I came in peace, and dismounted. A boy appeared from nowhere and took the reins of my horse as I walked up to the ceorl.

'What do you want, boy?' he barked at me.

'I'm hoping we can do business,' I said with a smile.

'You're not Danes?' he said with relief.

'No, at least I'm not. Three of my men are, but they are on our side. My name is Jørren of Cilleham.'

'Cilleham? Never heard of it.'

'No, you wouldn't have done. It's in Cent.'

He still looked at me blankly so I added 'part of Wessex.'

He evidently had only a vague idea of where Wessex might be, but at least he'd heard of it. He gestured for his men to lower their weapons and I felt much happier once the three bows were no longer trained on me. My byrnie was of good quality and the bows were the less powerful hunting variety but I had no wish to put my chainmail to the test.

'Your er, um men can stay there but you are welcome to join me for some refreshments in my hall.'

He was obviously puzzled by our youth and had sought the right word before deciding on men.

'May they have some water? And I would be grateful if the horses could graze and drink from the trough over there.'

He nodded and shouted across to one of his men before escorting me into the hall. It reminded me of the one in which I had grown up. It was dark and gloomy, a fire burned in the central heath over which a cauldron hung. A woman was adding ingredients for that evening's meal but she ignored us. The floor was of beaten earth and the place smelt of smoke, and unwashed bodies.

We sat down at the one long table in the room and a slatternly looking girl brought us two earthenware goblets filled with ale and a platter of bread and cheese. The ale was surprisingly good and the bread was freshly baked. The cheese was full of flavour too. It was a far cry from the stale bread and hard cheese that I had grown used to. I toyed with the idea of staying there but it was still south of the Tinan and a prosperous horse farm like this would be a draw to the Danes.

'Now, you haven't come here all the way from Cent for the pleasure of my company,' he said.

'No, the Danes have captured Eforwic and they intend to spend the winter there, raiding all of Deira,' I told him.

He immediately looked concerned. He knew as well as I did that Danes needed horses to move over the land as swiftly as their ships did over the sea and up the rivers.

'Thank you for the warning. It sounds as if I'd be well advised to move my stock up into the hills.'

'I was hoping to buy some of that stock off you in exchange for our horses and some silver.'

'Pardon me for saying so, but from the little I've seen of your horses they vary in quality somewhat.'

'Farmers need workhorses. I presume you sell those as well as riding horses for the thegns and rich ceorls,' I said with a smile.

'Yes, and I presume that you need strong working stock, not fancy palfreys, in exchange?'

'Yes, eleven riding horses and one cart horse.'

'I suggest we make it a dozen just in case one gets sick. Mares or stallions?'

'Mares. They are less feisty and not all my men are expert riders.'

'Good. Let me go and look at your stock and then we can talk money.'

He drove a hard bargain and when we left I had a mere forty silver pennies left in my pouch, but we had bought more oats and two barrels of root vegetables as well as the twelve mares and a proper cart horse. Now we needed a secure place to stay for the next few months whilst Alric recovered and I trained the various waifs and strays I'd collected along the way how to fight.

Chapter Six

Autumn 866

Alric had recovered sufficiently to ride a horse. However, he wouldn't be able to control it properly until his right arm had recovered its full strength, so Leofflæd rode beside him holding his reins. She had nursed him back to health and the two seemed to have grown quite close. I tried to repress my jealousy but it was no good. I cared for my brother deeply, but I was falling in love with Leofflæd. Of course I was being ridiculous. She was nearly seventeen and I wouldn't be fifteen for several months yet. I tried to put her from my mind, but seeing her every day and all day was eating away at me.

It cost me another two silver pennies for the ferry over the River Tes. Once over it we were in Bernicia, rather than Deira, but still in Northumbria. I was beginning to realise just how enormous Northumbria was. I was told that Bernicia was much longer from north to south then Deira was. Perhaps we would now be safe from the Danes but I wasn't prepared to risk it.

Two days later we came to another river – the Wejr. This time there was a timber bridge over the river; there was a toll but it was only half a penny. Upstream the river curved to the south from the bridge around a step sided hill on which there was a sizeable settlement. The toll collector told me it was called Dunholm and it was the seat of the local Ealdorman.

Dunholm was surrounded on three sides by the river. That coupled by the steep slopes leading down to the water made it difficult to attack. The only way into the settlement was via a narrow isthmus across which a palisade with two narrow gates had been built; one for entry and one for exit. The sentries on the entry gate demanded a tax of a silver shilling to take the cart in and a smaller charge for each horse. So we left Redwald and the three

Danish boys to guard the cart and our horses and the rest of us walked in for nothing.

I was well aware that we would need shelter for us and the horses during the coming winter and reasoned that we might have to build a hut and stables ourselves. We therefore sought carpentry tools. I also wanted everyone to have a shield and there were other items I thought might be useful. By the time we had bought everything we needed I had exactly nine silver pennies left.

We camped that night a little way north of Dunholm. Halfway through the night a thunder storm woke us and we spent the next few hours calming the horses and getting thoroughly soaked in the process. I planned to spend the next morning drying everything out but we never got the chance. Just before dawn we heard the distant sounds of fighting.

Erik and I rode back to see what was happening and stopped just inside the woods near the bridge over the Wejr. Danes were crossing the bridge and already there were several hundred on the isthmus in front of the gates. The sounds of battle came from the top of the palisade where the garrison of Dunholm was fighting off Danes with scaling ladders who were already in possession of part of the walkway on top of the palisade. It seemed that the Danes hadn't stopped at the River Tes after all.

'We need to get out of here,' Erik whispered and I nodded.

My decision not to relax after we had crossed the Tes had been vindicated.

We hurriedly decamped, although I was fairly confident that none of the Danes would venture north of Dunholm for a day or two. They would be too busy sacking the place, celebrating and then recovering.

We stopped in a clearing after five miles. I was confident that we were safe but I put out two sentries just in case whilst we built a fire to dry our clothes and then polished the rust off our byrnies, helmets and weapons. We rubbed the horses down with straw and broke our fast. Three hours later we were on the move again.

The next night was incident free and early the next morning we reached a wide river which I thought must be the River Tinan. What I wasn't expecting was to see a wall on the far bank. This was built of stone and stretched from east to west as far as the eye could see. Sections of it had collapsed but the rubble effectively blocked our way through it. However, the first problem was crossing the river.

We were still following the old Roman road and there had been a bridge here at one time. Now all that remained were the first spans on either bank. There was a large ferry capable of carrying four horses or a cart at a time across the river, but it was moored on the north bank and no one in the nearby hut responded to our shouts.

'What do we do?' Leofflæd asked after several minutes of fruitless calling.

'Head upstream and see if we can find a bridge or a ford, I suppose,' I answered.

I consoled myself with the thought that at least I wouldn't have to part with anymore silver pennies.

There was a track of sorts along the south bank but it was slow going with the cart. It took us three hours to cover ten miles and then we came to a timber bridge over the river that was just wide enough for the cart. On the far bank there was a small settlement of a few huts and a stone built church. There were a few strips of arable land and a pasture on which a few sheep and cattle grazed. The whole was enclosed by a thorn hedge. It looked for all the world like a monastery, but on a much smaller scale.

As we crossed the bridge two men in monk's habits came out of the enclosure and greeted us. They said that this was a priory, a daughter house of the monastery at Hagustaldes. I asked about the wall which ran a few hundred yards behind the priory and I was told that it was built by the Roman Emperor Hadrian many hundreds of years ago. At this point the wall was just a pile of rubble and I presumed that the monks had used the stone to build their church.

We paid the silver penny they asked and rode north a little way. A hundred yards behind the remains of the wall there was a road running east to west which appeared to follow the line of the wall.

'Which way do you think?' I asked Redwald.

'The wall seems to be in better repair in that direction,' he replied, pointing to the west. 'Perhaps we could built our hut and stables against the wall there?'

Knowing that we had heathen Danes with us I wanted to be a little further away from the good monks, but Redwald's idea of using the wall to build against was a good one. We turned westwards and followed the overgrown road.

After two miles we came across the ruins of what must have been a large fortress once upon a time. A few hundred yards further on there were remains of a tower. There was another one in better repair a third of a mile or so further on. I considered using it as our base, but it was too small. Then we struck lucky. About a mile away from the ruins of the fortress there was a small fort which was almost intact.

We dismounted and walked in through the gateway. It measured perhaps eighteen yards deep by twenty yards across. The walls were twenty feet high and ten feet thick. There was a walkway all the way around the top of the wall with what looked like teeth with gaps to protect the defenders on the walkway. Some of the teeth had fallen away but most were intact. The paving of the walkway had disappeared in one place, revealing the rubble that filled the gap between the outer and inner walls. In time rain and frost would erode that corner and inevitably the walls in that area would collapse. I determined to find suitable slabs somewhere to repave the section, but I had no idea how to make the mortar the Romans had used to join the slabs, which protected the interior of the wall from the weather.

The stone steps leading up to the walkway had also deteriorated quite badly and I decided to replace them in timber. We could use the stone from the original steps elsewhere.

There was a second gateway on the north wall. Unlike the southern gate this one was protected by a tower, probably to give the sentry a better view looking north. Inside the fort there were the foundations of two buildings either side of the road running between the two gateways. All that was needed were new wooden gates and two timber buildings constructed on the existing foundations: a hall for us to live in and a stables for the horses. We would also need a storehouse and a smoke house but the latter could be built outside the fort.

†††

I was still growing, as were the others, so that meant new clothes. More importantly our byrnies were now rather tight. Redwald had appointed himself as our carpenter and he pointed out that, although wood was plentiful locally, we would also need a lot of iron nails. From what the monks had told us about Hagustaldes I was certain that we could get what we wanted there. The problem was going to be paying for it all.

It was Cei who suggested the solution.

'Jørren has paid for everything so far but we all benefit from what he buys. I appreciated it when he gave me a pouch of silver but I have spent very little of it. I am quite prepared to give it back to Jørren so that we can make this place fit to live in over the winter and to buy clothes for us all as well as put extra links in our chainmail.'

He looked around the others and one by one they handed me the silver I'd given them what seemed like an age ago now. I counted it out. We now had thirty four silver pennies. It should be more than enough for what we needed.

I took Redwald, Cei and Ecgberht with me. Cei drove the cart and the rest of us rode. There was no palisade around the settlement but there was a thorn hedge around the nearby monastery. As it sat on the north bank of the Tinan the thought crossed my mind that it would be easy pickings for the Danes if they rowed this far upstream. We found everything we needed and left our byrnies with the blacksmith for him to insert rows of extra rings in accordance with the measurements I gave him. I had allowed a few inches extra for future growth as well. We left after arranging to pick up the byrnies the following week.

The rest of September and most of October was filled with hard work. Initially felling and preparing timber and then making the gates and erecting the buildings. Alric was eager to help and did what he could. Gradually he rebuilt the wasted muscles of his right arm and by the end of the month he looked much more like the brother I used to know.

I had tried to ask him about his time with the Danes but he was reluctant to talk about it, so I dropped the subject. He and I had been very close when we lived at Cilleham but now he was withdrawn and reserved. Oh, he was grateful to me for rescuing him, but our relationship had changed. When we were younger he was always the leader and I basked in his shadow. Now he readily accepted the fact that our little warband was mine and never tried to interfere.

When I thought about it, it was remarkable that Redwald, Jerrik, Øwli, Leofflæd or Ecgberht had never challenged me either. All were older than me, a couple by two years or more, but everyone seemed to accept my leadership quite happily. Of course, there were tensions, particularly between Jerrik, Øwli and the three Danes. I suppose it was inevitable after being mistreated when they were thralls. Strangely Alric had accepted Erik and the others readily and could often be found improving his Danish whilst he corrected their English.

Leofflæd was the centre of attention, of course. Ten boys on the verge of manhood around one attractive girl was bound to create problems. I believed that the interest the others had in her was purely sexual, whereas I fancied myself in love with her. It never became a problem, however, because she was adept at keeping them at a distance. The only one she seemed interested in was Alric but I came to realise that that she was merely mothering him. As he recovered she paid him less and less attention.

The hard work involved in building our accommodation for the winter bound us closer together as a group but there were times when I felt lonely. We were all a team but there were three distinct groups within the whole: the Danes and Alric; Leofflæd, Ecgberht, Redwald and Cei – probably because they were all older than the rest of us; and Jerrik and Øwli.

As October passed I realised that we needed to stock the larder for the winter. We had survived so far on what we had brought with us from Lindocolina, supplemented by trout from the Tinan and small game we had hunted. We probably had enough flour, barley and lentils to last us but we needed a lot more meat.

As soon as the smokehouse was completed we chopped up a lot of the leftover oak into chippings to feed the fire and went hunting for deer and boar. We had no dogs to track the animals so we had to rely on our own skills. Alric and I were the best trackers and so we walked ahead of the rest, who were mounted. There was only a strip of woodland, now somewhat depleted after our construction work, before the river and so we set out across the wild landscape to the north.

We came across several spoors but they were all old. The day was nearly over before we found fresh tracks. It was of a boar, a sow, and several piglets. The ground became rocky and they were difficult to track but I saw a small lake below us and I guessed that was where they were headed. Dusk is a favourite time for animals to drink.

I sent Erik, Ulf, Tove, Jerrik and Øwli ahead to cut the boars off whilst the rest of us chased them down. I had deliberately chosen the Danes and the former thralls in the hope that forcing them to work together might overcome any animosity between them. It could have been a mistake and it came close to being so.

We soon caught the boars up and they ran squealing straight towards where the five were waiting. They had dismounted and, leaving Tove to hold the horses, they strung their bows and waited with one arrow knocked and three others placed in the ground in front of them ready for quick use.

Their first volley wounded the sow and killed two of the piglets. A second volley quickly followed killing the last piglet, finishing off the sow and wounding the boar. There wasn't time for a third volley before the boar charged straight at Ulf. He dropped his bow and grabbed for his spear but he fumbled it. It fell to the ground and he stood there mesmerised as the enraged animal aimed its wicked tusks at his stomach. Had he reached Ulf the boy would have been disembowelled.

Jerrik was standing a few yards to one side of Ulf, who was the last in the line. He had been quicker to discard his bow and grab his spear but he stood there making no attempt to go to Ulf's aid. From where I sat a hundred yards behind the killing zone I had a perfect view but I was too far away to do anything. Suddenly Jerrik seemed to make his mind up and he thrust his spear into the side of boar just as it launched itself at the petrified Ulf.

Either it was expertly aimed or Jerrik was lucky and the point of the spear penetrated the thick hide just behind the foreleg and lodged in the boar's heart. The spear was pulled out of Jerrik's hands as the now dead animal's momentum carried it onwards. His head hit Ulf's chest and the boy went flying backwards to end up on the ground with the dead boar on top of him.

Apart from a gash to his chin made by one of the tusks, he was uninjured. Jerrik and the other two pulled the heavy carcasse off Ulf and the boy got shakily to his feet, helped up by Jerrik. Ulf pulled Jerrik towards him and hugged him. At first Jerrik stood there rigid, his arms by his side, but then he hugged Ulf back and they parted smiling at each other. I breathed several sighs of relief, not just because Ulf had survived practically unscathed, but now perhaps the animosity between the two brothers and the Danes was at an end.

We took the dead swine back in the cart and inexpertly butchered them. We hung the joints from the boar, the sow and two of the piglets in the smoke house but we feasted on the smallest piglet that night. Ulf and Jerrik were the heroes of the day and many toasts were drunk to them, using up the last of our ale but no one seemed to care.

I woke with a splitting head the next morning and decided to drink more moderately in future. Then I remembered that we had no more ale and so that wouldn't be a problem.

✝✝✝

We were nearly ready for winter when Jerrik, Øwli and Ecgberht came riding back. They had been looking for wild onions, garlic and herbs to dry and use for seasoning but they brought dire news as well. They had seen smoke in the distance to the east and had gone to investigate. There was a Viking longship moored at the bridge over the Tinan and the crew were pillaging the priory.

It was only a small longship of a type called a snekkja with a crew of between thirty and forty. It was far too many for us to tackle and so we prayed that the longship would return whence it came rather than venture further upriver. We were destined to be disappointed.

I had stationed two of us to watch out for the snekkja, just in case it came our way. The next day Cei and Alric came riding back to say that the ship had lowered its mast to pass under the bridge and the Danes were now rowing slowly towards us. We hadn't lit the fire in the central hearth that morning and we had left the gates open so that the fort looked as deserted as it had when we had found it.

Our hope was that the Danes would pass us by. I knew that would mean that they would inevitably discover Hagustaldes and I had sent Redwald to warn the ealdorman. There was little more we could do.

However, the Danes didn't pass us by. Presumably the stumps left by the timber we had felled attracted their attention. They moored below us and a party of a dozen came ashore to investigate. They looked around the gap we had left in the wood and scanned the old wall. I thought that they were about to return to their ship when one of them pointed towards our fort and said something to the Dane who appeared to be their leader.

'We must close the gates,' Øwli whispered urgently to me.

We were crouched behind the battlements on top of the wall and I risked a quick look down at the curious men who were now making their way up the slope towards the fort.

'Not yet,' I replied.

Erik and Ulf were in the courtyard waiting for my order to shut and bar the gates but I wanted the Danes to be well within range first.

'Ready your arrows but wait for my order. Pick your targets when I say so. Pass it on,' I whispered to Øwli and to Ecgberht on my other side.

When the enemy were less than fifty paces away I stood up yelling 'now.' I pulled back and released in one swift movement. My target was the man I thought must be their leader. He was wearing a chainmail byrnie but that didn't protect him at that range. The arrow struck his chest and he fell.

We had been practicing archery for the past month or more and, although some were better than others, everyone was now a reasonably accurate bowman. Even so two missed completely, no doubt due to nerves, and of the other seven arrows two struck the same man, so we had managed to take only seven warriors out of the fight.

The other five looked stunned for a moment, then they turned and ran. It did them no good. We got off two volleys at them before they'd gone twenty yards and hit every single one; most were dead but the cries from two of them indicated that they were only wounded. Another volley of arrows tore into their bodies and the screams ended abruptly.

Everyone jumped in the air yelling jubilantly, but there were still another score of Danes left in the ship. I half expected them to cast off and row back downstream. If so, we would have had to quit our winter quarters because they would undoubtedly return with enough men to take the fort. Luckily the ship's captain was more intent on revenge than taking the sensible course of action.

Leaving two men and what looked like a couple of thralls aboard, he led the rest ashore. At least he had the common sense not to make a frontal assault. He led his men over the rubble and thorough a collapsed section of the wall two hundred yards away and then they crept along close to the far side of the wall, thinking that they would be safe from our arrows.

'Come on. Up to the top of the gatehouse,' I yelled, sprinting along the walkway.

I climbed up to the platform on top of the north gate from where I had a good view down towards the Danes. As the others joined me and we drew back our bowstrings the Danes raised their shields above their heads to protect themselves.

I whispered to Leofflæd what I proposed and she grinned back at me. It caused my heart to leap but now was hardly the time for romantic thoughts. I took careful aim at the leading man and put an arrow in his foot. He yelped in pain and lowered his shield. As soon as he did Leofflæd put an arrow in his chest. At that range it would have penetrated chainmail; as the man was only wearing a leather tunic the arrow went through his ribs and deep into his heart. He was dead before his body slumped to the ground.

The others halted uncertainly and we did exactly the same thing to the next man in the line. The captain tried to rally his men but they had had enough and they turned to flee. He struck one man with the flat of his sword to try to get him to obey and in doing so exposed his torso. Leofflæd and I both aimed at him and he went down with two arrows in him. One in his neck and one in his chest.

That did it. The rest fled. A hail of arrows followed them and four more men fell before they were out of range. Not all were dead but we had no time to deal with those who were only wounded. I counted eleven men running back to their ship. We had done much better than I could have hoped, but I couldn't let them get away to tell other Danes about us.

'Get mounted,' I shouted as I headed to the stables.

It took us five minutes to saddle up and ride out of the gates. By this time the last Dane had boarded, the snekkje had cast off and they had started to row back downstream. Thankfully the current behind them was sluggish and they only had enough rowers to man five of the fifteen oars on each side. By the time that they were halfway back to the bridge near the priory we had passed them.

We leapt off our horses, grabbed our bows and quivers and raced onto the bridge. I was so focused was I on the task in hand that I scarcely noticed the blackened ruins where the priory had once stood.

By the time we had reached the centre of the bridge and had taken a couple of deep breaths to quieten our breathing the snekkje was less than a hundred yards away. The steersman had spotted us and was urging the rowers to put their backs into it. I took aim and lodged my first arrow in his fat belly. The man fell against the steering oar, pushing it sharply to the right. The longship lurched to the left and headed towards the bank where Tove was holding our horses.

One of the rowers jumped up to grab the steering oar but someone put an arrow in his back. The rest released their arrows as I grabbed my second one from my quiver. Eight arrows hit home, killing or wounding six of the rest. That left four. They let go of their oars and grabbed their weapons and their shields. When the bows rammed into the bank they ran forward to jump ashore.

'Back to the horses' I shouted.

Tove stood rooted to the spot as the four warriors charged towards him. Suddenly he hauled himself into the saddle and, leading the rest, he headed onto the bridge. We ran to meet him and grabbed our shields and whatever weapon came to hand: spear, sword or axe. Then we formed a shield wall two deep facing the four men.

We had practiced fighting in a shield wall but, of course, we had never done so for real. Those of us in the front rank held our shields so as to protect our bodies and thighs, whilst the rank behind lifted their own shields so as to protect both our heads and

93

theirs. We held our swords ready, the blades poking through the gaps between our shields whilst the men in the second rank also pushed their spears through the shield wall. It looked for all the world like an angry hedgehog.

The four warriors yelled insults at us whilst we stood silently waiting for their charge. This seemed to infuriate them even more. Suddenly they charged and my world shrank to the one man heading directly for where I stood.

'Brace,' I yelled, and the second rank put their shields against our backs and pushed to prevent us being forced back.

A moment later I felt an axe strike the shield above my head and the inside of the shield struck my helmet a heavy blow. I was slightly stunned, but not so much that I couldn't thrust my sword forward into the belly of my opponent. At the same time Øwli, who was holding his shield against my back, shoved the point of his spear into the Viking's face. He fell away and I found myself looking at a group of horsemen sitting and watching us on the north bank.

I prayed that they weren't more Danes before I became aware of another of the raiders to my left. I pushed his shield to one side so that I could thrust my sword into his side. Before I could do so, he turned towards me and raised his two-handed battleaxe on high. Then Alric, who was to my left, thrust his own sword into the man's eye and he fell back, crashing onto the timbers of the bridge.

It was over. The four warriors were all dead. Our only casualties seemed to be Alric's broken shield and Erik, who had a bad headache and a dented helmet. However, there were still the six horsemen who had sat watching us without helping either us or the enemy.

'Who are you?' I called across to them.

'More to the point, who the hell are you?' one of the horsemen called back.

They were a strange looking group, as I suppose we were in their eyes. There were three boys aged from perhaps twelve to fifteen and three warriors. Thankfully they were dressed like Anglo-Saxons, not Danes.

'I'm Jørren of Cilleham in Cent,' I called back, 'and these are my friends and companions.'

It sounded a bit too pretentious to call ourselves a warband, even though we had just killed the crew of a Viking longship all by ourselves.

'You are a long way from home, Jørren of Cilleham,'

'I came to rescue my brother, who was a captive of the Great Heathen Army.'

'Oh, did you? And did you succeed?' he asked derisively.

'As I'm standing here,' Alric said, 'I suppose he must have done.'

The man's jaw dropped and two of the boys with him sniggered, which earned them a sharp look from their leader.

'We have also just killed the entire crew of a snekkje,' I added. 'That brings our tally to around fifty.'

'I'm impressed,' the man said in a tone which indicated that he meant it.

'You know who we are but I have no idea who I'm talking to.'

'I'm Wigestan, a member of the gesith of Edmund, Ealdorman of Bebbanburg.'

'Nice of you to help us then,' I said sarcastically.

'You didn't look as if you needed much help, but I hadn't realised that you were just boys.'

'We're not,' Leofflæd said with a sweet smile, taking off her helmet and letting her long brown hair fall down her back. 'But I've killed more Danes than anyone here except Jørren.'

'They weren't Danes, they're Norse Vikings,' he said dismounting and walking towards us.

'Nothing to do with the Great Heathen Army then?' I asked dumbfounded.

'No, they come from Orkneyjar and have been raiding all down our coast. We're a scouting party who have been sent to find them. We knew that they'd come up the Tinan but not exactly where they were. There is a party of fifty mounted warriors waiting for us to report back. It's seems that they won't be needed after all.'

He paused, counting the dead in the ship and on the bridge.

'Where are the rest of them?'

'We killed them when they attacked our base.'

'Did you now. Well, I'll know not to mess with you, Jørren of Cilleham,' he said with a grin. 'I didn't know that they trained their warriors so young and so well in Cent.'

'They don't. We've learned the hard way; in any case only four of us are from Cent.'

I regretted that as soon as I'd said it.

'Oh, where are rest from then?'

'They joined us on the way,' I said evasively. 'Besides you have three boys with you as well.'

'They are scouts, not warriors.'

'As were some of us, originally.'

'I had better get back to our camp and report so I'll take my leave. I suppose that all the Norsemen's plunder should rightfully be yours?'

He said that slightly wistfully. I hadn't thought about that until he mentioned it. It would solve my immediate money problems, but I didn't realise then that it would actually make us rich.

He rode away and I watched them go wondering if I should have asked if we could go with him. It would have given us more security. However, I had no idea what this Edmund of Bebbanburg would have made of our motley group, especially the Danes. Besides, I had got used to being my own man and didn't fancy somebody else ordering me around. On balance I think I preferred to remain with our little group. Perhaps I should have asked the others, but was fairly certain that I knew what they would have said.

There were two young thralls who had stayed with the snekje when it ran aground. They turned out to be Picts from the far north. They didn't speak either English or Danish, but they did understand Norse, which wasn't too different to Danish: similar enough for us to communicate at any rate. The two were brothers called Cináed and Uurad and they claimed to be Christians, much to our surprise. They belonged to the Celtic Church, unlike the rest of us who were followers of the Church of Rome; but still, they weren't heathens, as I had supposed.

Their settlement had been raided and they were the only survivors. They had only been spared because the Vikings had lost three ships' boys in a storm and, being fourteen and fifteen, they were old enough to replace them.

The longship proved to be a veritable treasure trove. Each sea chest, and there were thirty one of them, contained the owner's share of plunder. We also found pouches of silver coins and hacksilver on the bodies. I put aside those items that obviously belonged to the Church, intending to hand them over to the abbot at Hagustaldes. However it wasn't something that the three Danes understood. They maintained that these items were legitimate plunder.

It was the first time that there was an argument caused by our different religious beliefs. They didn't understand that these objects were sacred to our religion. I didn't know whether they had buildings in which they worshipped and whether those places had sacred objects, or not. From their attitude I suspected not.

The conflict over the division of the spoils got serious and I had to intervene.

'These items belong to me as your jarl' I said as forcefully as I could. 'I determine who deserves what reward; it's not a matter for general discussion. If you don't like my decision then you are welcome to challenge me for the position as your leader.'

I glared around me but no one met my eye except Leofflæd, who mouthed 'well done' at me. I felt as if I was walking on air.

'Well then, items stolen from a church go to the abbot. I will take half the rest to pay for future expenses and we will divide the rest up between us equally.'

It wasn't that simple to determine the relative values of items other than silver, which was determined by weight. No one even knew the value of the few gold coins, let alone gold broaches encrusted with jewels. Anything difficult to value I put in my pile to save further argument. To be honest there were times when I wished we hadn't discovered so much plunder. It wasn't as if they had anywhere to spend it; at least, not until the spring came.

As we began the journey back to the fort a few flakes of sleet stung our faces. Winter was coming.

Redwald was waiting anxiously for us when we got back. The ealdorman had called out the local fyrd and women and children had fled up into the hills. Disappointingly he sent no one to our rescue and so it was a good job that we had managed to eliminate the Norse Vikings on our own.

The next day I rode to Hagustaldes to hand back the Church's property. Now it was the abbot's problem to sort out which church or monastery owned what. I also told the ealdorman about the Norse Vikings. I doubt if he would have believed me, thinking me a lying braggart, if it wasn't for the items I'd returned to the abbot for safekeeping.

Chapter Seven

Spring 867

The winter passed uneventfully. The Danes had grown curious about Christianity and between us we managed to satisfy their curiosity. In return they told us about their beliefs. It was far more complex that I had imagined with so many gods and goddesses, a world tree called Yggdrasil, and the various realms including Niflheim, Hel and Asgar, which included Valhalla.

When probed about the details they became defensive and I thought it best to abandon the discussion. Later Erik, Ulf and Tove came to me separately to ask about becoming Christians and I explained about baptism.

We also passed the time by teaching Cináed and Uurad how to fight, use a bow and to ride. We couldn't go far – the snow was too deep – but they grasped the basics. They also learned to speak both English and Danish after a fashion.

When the snows melted and the roads were passable again I took the three Danes to see the abbot and he arranged for them to be baptised. I think it was more to do with feeling more included in the group than it did with religious conviction. In practical terms it made little difference as we had no priest, nor did we observe fast days or saint's days.

They exchanged their Mjölnirs for simple silver crucifixes which I had bought for them but, contrary to normal practice, they decided to keep their original names instead of adopting Anglo-Saxon ones. Whilst I was in Hagustaldes I also managed to purchase two docile mares for the two Picts to ride, a second pack horse and more leather tents.

In late March we sat down to discuss where we should go next. Ecgberht thought that we should stay where we were, go hunting, plant crops and fish, much to his sister's disgust, but the rest craved a more exciting life. I spent some time thinking about the future but came to no conclusions. If we ventured south we would inevitably run into the Great Heathen Army; if we travelled north we could ask to join Ealdorman Edmund's warband, but that didn't have much appeal as I doubted that he would accept us as fully fledged warriors, given our youth.

One other option was to use the longship we had captured. Most of us knew little about ships, but the two Picts knew how to sail her, as did Jerrik and Øwli from their time as ship's boys. What we lacked was a steersman and the numbers and strength to row her. If we could overcome those problems we could sail down the East Coast and land Alric, Jerrik and Øwli somewhere in Cent. They could then return home.

When I tentatively suggested this one evening all three said that they would rather remain with the group. The idea of using the longship was met with some enthusiasm, however.

One idea mooted was to sail up the River Uisge pretending to be Norsemen eager to join the heathen army and then set fire to as many of their fleet as we could. That would restrict their freedom to operate. If we could burn a significant number of longships they would be largely confined to the land, and thus be prevented for striking wherever they pleased without warning.

'But where will we find enough rowers and a steersman?' Redwald said. 'The eldest of us could learn to use an oar, I suppose, but that would give us five or six at most; and we would need training.'

'Was there a port at the mouth of the Tinan,' I asked Cináed, the elder of the two Picts.

'No, not as such' he said shaking his head, 'only a fishing settlement.'

'Nevertheless, I think we should go there and see if we can recruit the crew we need.'

†††

I'll never know whether we could have done so. The thirteen of us packed everything we had into our saddlebags and onto the two packhorses, including two small chests containing our silver, and set off into a rainstorm. We left the cart behind as being too cumbersome and it was with a certain amount of regret that I bade farewell to the old Roman fort that had been our home for the past five months.

We were teaching the two Picts how to act as scouts and Cináed was riding ahead with Erik as we approached the bridge over the Tinan. Suddenly Cináed came galloping back.

'Jørren, there's an army crossing the bridge,' he panted.

'Going north to south or south to north,' I asked, my heart sinking.

If the Danes had decided to invade northern Bernicia we would have to turn around and hope to avoid them by heading west.

'They're coming from the north,' he replied and I breathed a sigh of relief.

It seemed most likely that it was Edmund of Bebbanburg, though where he was going was a mystery. I didn't know much about Bernicia but I was well aware that it was now sandwiched between the Danes and the Picts. If the army of Deira had been eliminated what chance did he have of defeating them on his own, especially as to do so would leave his northern border undefended?

I realised later that I was being naïve. Although the Deirans had been scattered outside Eforwic and many had been slain, most had escaped. Ælle and Osbehrt had spent the autumn and winter sending messages to every ealdorman and thegn to gather their men for another assault on Eforwic. This time they had summoned Edmund and the other ealdormen of Bernicia to join them. It was pure chance that we had arrived at the bridge over the Tinan at the same time.

'What should we do, Jørren?' Alric asked. 'Join them?'

'Let's go and see what is happening at least,' Redwald said eagerly.

'No, I think we should wait for them to pass and carry on with our original plan,' Leoflæd urged me.

I nearly gave into her, but the others clamoured to join the Bernicians and so I gave way. I nearly changed my mind when I saw the look of disappointment in her eyes, but to vacillate like that would lose me the respect of the others so we rode on to the bridge.

When we got there Erik told me that he estimated the numbers of those already across the river and those waiting to cross at about two thousand, not much more than half the heathens' numbers.

We attracted curious stares from the men marching past us, but they didn't stop and so I couldn't ask where they were going. Then a party of warriors on horseback appeared. The leader was dressed in expensive chainmail and wore a helmet with a gold circlet around it. Behind him a warrior held a yellow banner but I couldn't see the device on it as it hung limply in the rain.

'Lord,' I asked him as he drew level, 'do you go to fight the Danes?'

He stopped, as did his escort, but before he could answer another voice spoke up.

'Lord, this is Jørren of Cilleham in Cent who I spoke about.'

I looked at the banner bearer in surprise, but then I recognised him; it was Wigestan.

'Greetings Jørren of Cilleham, have you changed your mind? Do you now wish to join my warband?' Edmund said with a smile.

'Do you go to fight the Danes on your own, lord?'

He gave me an amused look and then laughed.

'You'd like to know if I'm mad before you join me, is that it?'

'We saw the army of Deira routed, lord. I fear you will need more men than this to beat them.'

'No, we go to join King Ælle and his brother. Well, it's raining and I'm anxious to reach somewhere dry before nightfall. What's your answer?'

I was greedy in those days and I thought only of the plunder to be had when we beat the Great Heathen Army, so I nodded.

'Yes, lord, if you'll have us.'

'Are your boys good scouts?'

'Yes, lord, the best,' I said proudly.

'Good. It's what I lack. Join us and tomorrow we'll see if you're as good as you say you are.'

And so we joined the army of Bernicia.

✝✝✝

Eforwic looked the same as the last time I'd seen it, except that the breach in the palisade had been repaired. My group had left the vast camp housing nearly four thousand men at dawn to go and recce the task that the two kings and Edmund had set us. Although Edmund was called the Ealdorman of Bebbanburg, in reality he was the sub-king of all Bernicia from the River Tes in the south to Dùn Èideann on the Linne Foirthe in the north.

We had joined Edmund's own group of scouts – the three boys we had seen last year and seven more ranging in age from twelve to twenty. I had been given command of the group, much to the disgust of the twenty year old – an Angle named Ceadda. I had just turned sixteen and he felt that he should be in charge as he was four years my senior. However, few of the original ten scouts supported him and, of course, my original group sided with me. Ceadda was forced to accept my leadership but I didn't trust him. He would need watching and I gave that task to the twelve-year old, Sæwine.

As the youngest member of the group he was something of a talisman. He was cheeky, but not in a malicious way, and everyone liked him; even Ceadda tolerated him.

We wouldn't make much difference in the coming battle with the Danes but we could still play an important role in their defeat. Our task was to destroy as much of their fleet as we could. We hoped that it would be poorly guarded, but even so it was a lot to ask of us. There were ten longships and several knarrs moored along the banks of the Uisge and another forty anchored out in the middle of the river.

I had decided to ignore the knarrs. They were merchant ships used for freight and transporting horses which relied on the wind for propulsion. Most only had six oars for manoeuvring them in harbour and so they were unsuited to raiding. If we could sink or burn the bulk of the longships, the Danes would be trapped on land where they could be hunted down; at least that was the theory.

I studied the area where the fleet was kept and the ships themselves for some time before devising a plan. Meanwhile the rest of my scouts familiarised themselves with where everything was so that they could find their targets in the dark.

Back at the camp I explained what I proposed. Everyone thought that it could work; everyone except Ceadda and his friend, Hroðulf that is. They kept trying to pick holes in the plan and were thoroughly negative. Hroðulf was eighteen and, like Ceadda, resented me. They were also openly xenophobic when it came to the three Danes and the two Picts. Leofflæd also came in for a lot of scorn. They obviously thought that a girl had no place alongside warriors. That didn't stop the two of them lusting after her.

The first problem I had was to eliminate the watch who guarded the fleet. This seemed to be provided by the ships' boys, who helped to man the longships at sea, men with grey beards who were long past their best fighting days, and the steersmen. All told there were some two hundred Danes in total; far too many for my little band of twenty three to handle.

Luckily each of the forty ships out in the river had an anchor watch aboard, which reduced the numbers ashore. It was difficult to count how many as the ships were rafted together. Some appeared to be deserted whilst on others sizeable groups were playing games of chance, drinking or doing maintenance work. I estimated that there were probably the best part of a hundred of them all told. However, that still left odds of four to one on shore for us to tackle.

We returned some four hours after sunset and I divided my boys into four groups, one for each of the camp fires burning below, putting Leofflæd, Redwald and Wealhmær, one of the Bernician scouts, in charge of the other groups.

I led my group towards the easternmost fire. I had chosen Alric, Cei, Tove, Ecgberht and Hroðulf. The latter was there to split him from Ceadda. I had put Ceadda and Sæwine in Redwald's group.

There were four Danes, all greybeards, sitting around the campfire. I guessed that another twenty or thirty were asleep in a nearby store hut. We strung our bows and I pointed out their targets to Alric, Cei and Ecgberht. The other two - Tove and Hroðulf - were there to take out any of the four we missed or only wounded. I took aim at my man and hissed 'now.'

I hit my man in the throat and two of the others died without a sound. However Ecgberht's arrow only wounded his man. The other two released their arrows almost immediately and finished the job, but not before the wounded Dane had uttered a cry of alarm. Thankfully it didn't wake anyone in the store hut but someone on one of the anchored longships called across to ask if anything was wrong. Sound travels a long way over water at night but there was nothing that the watch out in the river could do in time. That didn't stop them from raising the alarm on shore, of course.

Thankfully Tove had the presence of mind to call back that one of the silly old fools had burnt himself in the fire. That evinced a laugh and I clapped Tove on the back to congratulate him. He hardly sounded like an old man but perhaps they thought that one of the ships' boys had joined the men.

My main worry was the Danes who sat around the other camp fires. Two men at the next one along got to their feet, but they were cut down by arrows before they could do anything. There were sounds of alarm from the other two groups but, again, they were quickly silenced by other archers.

We listened for any sounds from within the buildings where the rest slept but there was nothing. I eased open the door to be greeted by a waft of fetid air and the sound of snoring and the odd fart. There must have been thirty Danes asleep inside, mostly men

105

but there were quite a few boys as well. We set about our grisly task, starting with the boys.

They ranged from twelve to fifteen. Some would have been thralls and some the sons of warriors. I hated killing them like a thief in the night, especially the thralls, but if we spared any we would all be dead. I put my hand over the mouth of the first one. His eyes shot open in alarm as I slit his throat, then closed his lifeless eyes as he still looked at me with reproach. I dreamt about those eyes for months afterwards.

I moved onto the next one and this time I avoided looking at his face as I drew my dagger across a throat still devoid of an adam's apple. When he was dead I closed his eyes and looked at him. He was probably eleven or twelve and I felt worthless. I had to grit my teeth, however, and I moved onto the next one. This was an old man with a grey beard that covered his throat in thick hair. I couldn't risk trying to saw through it and so I stabbed him in the eye. The point entered his brain and he died instantly.

I glanced around me. The others were finishing off the last few and we all sat there when we were done morosely contemplating the slaughter we had committed. I was sick of killing and very nearly vowed to become a monk at that point in my life. However, I couldn't afford to let my emotions overcome me. This was only the start of what we had to do that night.

††††

The rest of the task was easy after that. The other groups had been just as successful as we had been but an aura of melancholia hung over us as we piled anything flammable we could find against the masts of the ten longships tied up alongside. Once everything was ready I gave the signal and ten of us lit two torches each from the four campfires. We threw them onto the pile of debris around each of the masts and, as soon as we were sure that fires had caught, the others cast the longships adrift.

We watched as they drifted out into the centre of the river and then headed downstream towards where the rest of the fleet was moored. The tarred rigging was burning brightly by this stage and we could hear alarm bells ringing in Eforwic. By the time that the fireships reached the anchored boats the debris on deck and the masts themselves were well alight and then the fire spread to the rigging of the rest of the longships.

By now warriors would be streaming out of Eforwic to investigate the fires. It was time to retreat and I gave the order. I stopped to look back before we crested the ridge between the river and our encampment. Practically the whole fleet was burning merrily. Then I saw that perhaps ten ships had managed to get away. Presumably the anchor watch had cut them free and let them drift downstream and away from the general conflagration. It didn't matter. Eighty per cent of the fleet had been destroyed.

Then I saw something else silhouetted in the flames. Four people were struggling with each other and one of them had hair down to their waist. Leofflæd was fighting someone off and I had a pretty good idea who it was.

By now the others had disappeared into the darkness and so I headed back down the slope, pulling my sword from its scabbard as I ran. I was about twenty yards away when I saw one of the larger figures lunge at a smaller one. It was difficult to make out faces in the darkness against the amber and yellow of the burning ships but the silhouette was unmistakably that of Tove. The latter fell and I knew that either Ceadda or Hroðulf had stabbed the young Dane.

The three remaining figures fell to the ground and seconds later I reached them. Hroðulf was trying to hold a struggling Leofflæd down whilst Ceadda was busy ripping her trousers down. I didn't hesitate. I thrust my sword into Ceadda's back with such viciousness that it nearly went all the way through his body and into Leofflæd. Thankfully the point struck a rib and stopped just in time. Hroðulf eye's opened wide in horror at his dead friend and then ran away into the darkness. I was about to go after him but Leofflæd was convulsed by sobs and I couldn't leave her.

I rolled the dead Ceadda off her and took her in my arms to comfort her. She hugged me back so fiercely that I thought she was going to break my ribs. I stroked her back, not knowing what to say to comfort her. She relaxed and looked into my eyes as they glistened, reflecting the dancing flames several hundred yards away across the water.

'Come on,' I managed to croak, 'we need to get away before the Danes find us.'

She nodded but pulled me to her again, kissing me fiercely on the lips. Suddenly nothing else counted; not the slaughter I had taken part in, nor the death of Tove. All that mattered was the feeling of bliss as I lay there in Leofflæd's arms as her lips made love to mine.

It was the sound of Danish voices nearby that brought us down to earth with a bump. We lay there, hardly daring to breath, as the voices receded.

'Come on,' she hissed urgently, 'we need to get out of here.'

'Wait a moment,' I whispered, pulling Tove's corpse upright and slinging him over my shoulder. 'He deserves a proper burial. Ceadda can stay here as food for the carrion crows.'

I staggered under the weight and thought inconsequentially how much the boy had grown in the time I had known him. He was the first of our little group to die and I felt his loss keenly.

†††

It had never occurred to me to report what had happened to Edmund and so it was a profound shock to be rudely awakened the next morning by someone kicking me hard in the side. I was dragged out of the tent I shared with Alric wearing nothing but my night tunic and hauled before Ealdorman Edmund. There at his side stood a smirking Hroðulf. On his other side there was a man dressed ready for war who glowered at me. I wondered what the hell was going on. Was I having some form of hallucination? The pain in my side told me that this was all too real, however.

'Let Jørren go,' Edmund barked at the two warriors who had manhandled me to stand in front of him. The two glanced at the man at Edmund's side who nodded. They released me but still stood either side of me. From that I gathered that they were the stranger's warriors, not Edmund's.

'You were sent to tell him I wanted to see him, not to mistreat him. This is the boy who destroyed the Danish fleet last night. We owe him a debt of gratitude, not abuse. Get out of my sight!'

The men looked at him resentfully, but left his tent. Edmund sighed and looked me in the eye.

'I'll keep this short because there are more important things afoot today,' Edmund barked at me. 'Did you or did you not kill Ceadda last night?'

'I did but he ...'

I got no further before both the unknown man and Hroðulf gave a cry of triumph.

'I'm sorry Jørren. We are all grateful to you for what you and your boys did, but you have admitted to killing Thegn Cynemær's son. You must pay him the weregild due, which is six hundred shillings, or be sold into slavery.'

It was a great deal of money but I could afford to pay it – just. However, I didn't see why I should. Ceadda was a rapist and probably a murderer. If he wasn't the latter, then that grinning loon, Hroðulf, was the guilty party and Ceadda was his accomplice.

'Have you anything to say?' he added, almost as an afterthought.

'Yes I have, lord. This is a farce of a hearing. I demand to be heard at a proper trial and to call witnesses as to my character. Furthermore Ceadda was in the process of raping Leofflæd when I killed him and either he or Hroðulf murdered Tove.'

'Tove?'

'A Danish boy, lord, not worth more than a slave,' Hroðulf sneered.

I wished at that moment that I'd managed to kill him as well.

'He was one of my men, a Christian and free, not a slave.'

'Very well, does he have a family?'

109

'No, lord but he was sworn to me.'

'Then I will reduce the wergeld you must pay to four hundred shillings.'

It was poor recompense for the death of loyal Tove but I still had no intention of paying Cynemær a single penny.

'And what of the fact that he was raping one of my scouts at the time?'

Cynemær went puce in the face and I had difficulty in supressing a chuckle when I realised that he thought that I was accusing his dead son of sodomy.

'He is not here to answer the charge,' Edmund said.

'Lord, your father-in-law asks you to take the field without delay,' a man said urgently after bursting in on us.

I didn't know who he meant at the time; later I learned that Edmund's daughter was King Ælle's wife.

'We will continue this after our victory,' Edmund said, rising from his chair. 'Stay here. You and your scouts have done enough.'

Edmund went through a curtain, presumably to put on his armour. Cynemær shoulder barged me as he left, whispering in my ear 'you are as good as dead, boy. I don't want your money, I want your head.'

Hroðulf followed him with a silly grin still fixed on his face. However, it disappeared when I punched him hard in the groin and he doubled over in agony. Leaving him to recover, I walked past the openly grinning sentries just inside the entrance and went back to our part of the camp.

'What happened,' someone asked as everyone crowded around me.

'The ealdorman said I must pay six hundred shillings for Ceadda's death, less two hundred for the death of Tove. However, Ceadda's father, Cynemær, has sworn to kill me.'

'What are you going to do?' Redwald asked anxiously.

'I'm leaving, but you don't have to. None of you have done anything wrong, far from it. You're all heroes.'

'Nonsense,' someone else said. 'Where you go, we go.'

To my surprise I saw that it was Sæwine, the boy who had meant to be watching Ceadda. He hadn't been with Tove when he'd been killed and I made a mental note to tackle him about it later.

'You can't leave. You're sworn to serve Edmund,' I told him.

'Now we'll swear to follow you,' he said simply. 'He was wrong to fine you for killing that swine.'

Wealhmær and the other Bernician scouts murmured in agreement.

'Very well, get packed. We're leaving.'

'Er, and where exactly are we going, Jørren,' my brother asked, looking perplexed.

'Mercia. Hopefully it's free of Danes and other people who want my head.'

Chapter Eight

Summer / Autumn 867

As soon as I got a chance I cornered Sæwine and demanded to know why he hadn't kept an eye on Ceadda as I'd asked.

'He threatened to kill me if I didn't disappear. He would have done it too. There was nothing I could achieve by defying him and so I ran for help. The first person I encountered was Tove so I told him what was happening and he went to confront Ceadda; the rest you know.'

I breathed a sigh of relief. I liked Sæwine and so I was pleased that he'd acted sensibly and not dishonourably. I blamed myself for what had happened; I should have picked someone older and more capable of standing up to Ceadda for the task.

It was over a month before we heard what had happened on that fateful day after we'd left. We had avoided settlements, only a few of us entering to buy essential provisions, until we were well inside Mercia. Even then we proceeded with caution. The next place we stopped at was Snotingaham. We thought ourselves safe, from both the Danes and the vengeance of Cynemær. We were wrong on both counts.

The settlement was abuzz with various rumours about the fate of Northumbria. What was clear was that the two kings, Ælle and his brother Osbehrt, had lost the battle against the Great Heathen Army outside Eforwic and both had been killed. It was said that Ælle had been captured and had suffered the agonising death known as the blood eagle. If true, it was a horrible way to die, as Erik explained to me.

'He would have been held face down whilst his ribs were severed from his spine, probably with a sharp axe,' he said with rather too much relish for my liking. 'His lungs would then have been pulled through the gaps to create what looks like a pair of wings. It's a ritual usually reserved for a man of noble birth who has murdered the father of the man carrying out the ritual.'

'Who would have done such a grisly act and who was the father that Ælle was supposed to have killed?' I asked, appalled by the barbarous death he'd suffered.

'Probably Ívarr the Boneless and his brothers. Their father was Ragnarr Loðbrók, the famed king of Norweġ and Danmǫrk, who Ælle murdered by throwing into a pit of snakes.'

'I see; and this Ívarr is the leader of the Danes?'

'One of them, yes. There are many jarls who have rallied to the call for revenge against Ælle and the Northumbrians, but the main leaders are three of the many sons of Ragnarr: Ívarr, Halfdan and Ubba.'

I would have liked to have learned more about our enemy but Erik didn't know much. He'd been the son of a bondi, what we called a ceorl or freeman, and only knew what his father had told him - which wasn't much - and what he gleaned from listening to men talking around the campfire. He did add that revenge might have been the motive for Ívarr and his brothers, but the rest were there solely for plunder.

I asked him about Ívarr's curious nickname and he said that it was because he was incapable of getting an erection. He'd been given the nickname by a girl he'd tried to bed against her will but then failed to rise to the occasion, as Erik quaintly put it. Ívarr had killed her in revenge for the ridicule which followed, but the name had stuck. However, no one ever used it to Ívarr's face.

I was curious as to the fate of Edmund of Bebbanburg, but no one seemed to know if he'd survived. I heard later that he'd been injured and he'd died of his wounds. The new lord of Bebbanburg was Ricsige, Edmund's sixteen year old son.

Sæwine, Wealhmær and their friends were naturally upset when I told them of their previous lord's death, but I thanked the Lord God that they had decided to join me. If they hadn't, they would no doubt be dead as well.

We had camped in a peaceful glade just to the north of Snotingaham whilst we sourced what we needed for our journey further south. I had no clear vision of the future, except to get as far away from Northumbria as possible. I had a hazy notion that we would be safe in Wessex but that was all. I was still nervous that Cynemær would have sent his men to track us and so I sent two of our group to watch the road from the north during daylight. On the day in question it was the turn of Ulf and Alric to stand watch.

I had planned to leave the next day so when the two scouts came galloping back into camp we were just about ready to leave anyway.

'Danes, Jørren,' my brother panted.

'And hundreds of them, about three miles away,' added Ulf.

'Are you…'

I was about to ask them if they were sure, but it would have been a fatuous question. They knew only too well what Danes looked like. Instead I yelled for everyone to get everything loaded onto the horses. Ten minutes later we left the glade and, as I looked behind me, I could see the dust cloud kicked up by the Danish army. I debated whether to warn Snotingaham. It would be a risk as I feared being trapped there, but I couldn't leave without raising the alarm.

'Alric, take everyone to the south and don't stop until you are well clear of the place. I'm going to warn Snotingaham; I'll catch you up.'

At first he looked as if he was going to argue but then he nodded his head and I cantered away towards the settlement on top of the cliff. I heard hoof beats behind me and glanced around to see Sæwine close behind me. I was tempted to stop and send him back, but time was of the essence and so I allowed him to join me. Later he told me that he still felt guilty about Tove's death. I got the impression that he thought that appointing himself as my unofficial bodyguard somehow atoned for it.

Riding through the narrow streets shouting that the Danes were coming wouldn't have achieved anything, except to induce hysteria and panic. Instead I rode up to the ealdorman's hall and told the sentry, urging him to tell his lord without delay.

'Why should I believe you?' the man asked belligerently, presumably thinking I was trying to make him look a fool.

'I don't care if you do or not. The Danes are only a few miles away so, unless you want to be responsible for the deaths of everyone here, I suggest you run and tell your master.'

I rode away with Sæwine, not looking back to see if he had gone up to the hall as I'd suggested. I had no idea what the ealdorman could achieve in the way of evacuation in the short time available, but I had salved my conscience.

✝✝✝

That night we camped well away from the road. It was the middle of September and the nights were drawing in and the temperature was cooling. When it started to rain as we sat around the campfire, I realised that the time was coming when I'd have to think about winter quarters.

Leofflæd sat across from me that night and I watched the firelight dancing on her face and in her hair. I was mesmerised by her and, at the same time, incredibly frustrated. Our brief period of intimacy after firing the Danish fleet had convinced me that Leofflæd was as much in love with me as I was with her, but there was no repetition; indeed she seemed to avoid me whenever there was an opportunity for us to be alone. Consequently I felt hurt and confused. For my part I took refuge in treating her with coldness and indifference. I knew that it hurt her but I didn't seem to be able to stop myself.

My misery was compounded when Erik, who was sitting next to me, dug me in the ribs and whispered something that convinced me that I had to act instead of brooding.

'Jerrik and Leofflæd seem to be getting close to each other, don't you think?'

I looked across and the two of them were sitting alongside each other and muttering something into each other's ears. Suddenly Leofflæd giggled and hit Jerrik's arm, but in a playful manner. I was on the point of making a fool of myself by reacting like a jealous lover when the first spots of rain fell. A minute later the heavens opened and we all sprinted for our tents. Spending a night soaking wet was no one's idea of fun.

I shared a tent with Alric and decided that I would have to risk being mocked and ask for his advice. I'm glad that I did. Instead of deriding me as a callow youth besotted with a girl more than two years older than me, he went quiet whilst he thought about what I'd told him.

'I'm no expert so I could be wrong, but have you talked to her about the way you feel?'

'No, we haven't talked much at all. Those few kisses outside Eforwic are all I have to go on; that and the fact that I've caught her watching me when she thought I wasn't looking her way.'

'You're our leader, for better or worse, so you must avoid causing disharmony amongst us. If you try to claim the only girl as your lover, and ride roughshod over the feelings of others, you'll do untold damage. You need to talk to her and see how she feels. If she prefers Jerrik, you'll just have to accept it. If she really does love you, as you say she does, than she must be the one to let Jerrik down lightly.'

I lay awake for a long time, listening to the patter of the rain on the oiled leather of our tent and the gentle snores of my brother before I came to the conclusion that he was right.

The rain had passed over by dawn and the next day we headed south-east under a grey sky until we met the old Roman road known as the Fŏsweg. I decided that we needed to put out scouts before we travelled further and I chose myself and Leofflæd in the hope that, once we were away from the others we might be able to talk, although whether I could pluck up the courage to do so was another matter.

We overtook a few carts as we travelled but there didn't seem to be any traffic heading the other way. No doubt news of the Danes incursion into Mercia had already reached here.

'Leofflæd,' I began tentatively, 'I've been meaning to have a word with you.'

'Yes, well, now is not the time or place,' she retorted. 'We're meant to be making sure that the road is safe for the others.'

'I doubt very much whether the Danes have managed to get ahead of us,' I replied sarcastically, immediately regretting it. This was not how I envisioned the conversation going.

'I'm sorry. I didn't mean to snap,' I added a few moments later.

'If it's about the time I kissed you, I'm sorry. I don't know what came over me. I can only apologise,' she mumbled contritely.

'Why? Why would you feel you have to apologise? It was the most wonderful moment of my life.'

'It was?' She sounded amazed. 'I thought that you; well, that you didn't feel the same way about me as I did about you.'

'Why would I think that?'

She thought about he answer to that, but the shrugged.

'You're young and, not to put too fine a point on it, naïve and inexperienced when it comes to women.'

'So you feared that I would be filled with lust and just wanted to sow a few wild oats?'

'Something like that. I didn't want to lead you on just because I was in love with you. I know that you don't feel the same and well, it could have been awkward.'

'You're in love with me?'

'Yes. Sorry. I didn't mean to say that; please forget that I did.'

'But I feel the same way!'

'No, you just think you do because I kissed you.'

'No, I've had strong feelings for you ever since we met, and don't say it's just a crush. I know it's a lot deeper than that. I can't stop thinking about you and I want to be with you all the time. Every time I've got a problem, which is most of the time, I want to discuss it with you, and…'

117

My voice trailed away as I realised that I was gushing.

'You're not joking? You really are in love with me?'

'Get down off that horse and I'll prove it to you,' I said with a broad smile.

'Whoa, down boy! Save it until we're alone tonight.'

My heart started beating much faster as she gave me an impish grin. Then the grin faded.

'What about Jerrik?' she asked unhappily.

'Is he in love with you?' I asked, trying to ignore the butterflies in my stomach.

'No, I don't think so. He started by being a friend but I think he would like to take it a lot further than that.'

'And have you encouraged him?' I asked, uncomfortably aware of the jealousy in my voice.

'No! Of course not,' she replied, glaring at me. 'I just don't know how to let him down lightly. The last thing you or I need is someone who's bitter and resentful; especially if others take sides.'

I nodded. If I wasn't careful we could end up tearing our little group apart.

'Perhaps I could ask Alric to have a tactful word?'

I realised then that my brother's idea of getting Leofflæd to put him off wouldn't be a good idea; but perhaps he could be the one to tell him that he was fishing in a pool where the only fish had already been hooked.

✝✝✝

'Where are we going to spend the winter?' Jerrik asked two nights later.

We were now in southern Mercia and he had asked the one question that was on everyone's mind. Alric must have raised the matter of Leofflæd and me tactfully because he had come up to us the previous evening and wished us both well. He did whisper a crude comment in my ear but I let it pass, grateful to know it wasn't going to be an issue. When the others saw us holding hands and then heading off to her tent together we attracted a few more ribald suggestions, but everyone seemed genuinely pleased for us.

'Well, I doubt if we'll find a deserted fort this year,' Wealhmær, one of the Bernician scouts, said gloomily.

'But there's nothing to stop us building one, or a fortified hall at least,' I pointed out. 'The question is where?'

'Nobles are always short of money, aren't they?' Ecgberht asked. 'Why don't we buy some land? Then we'd have a permanent base.'

'Or we could seek a powerful lord who's looking for experienced warriors to add to his warband,' Cináed suggested.

'But that would mean losing our independence,' Uurad, the other Pict, objected.

'Perhaps the most important thing is to find somewhere safe to over-winter,' Alric said. 'Then we can look for a permanent base in the spring.'

This seemed to meet with general agreement but we were still no nearer finding a place to spend the winter months.

The next day we reached Coventre, a settlement which had sprung up around the monastery founded a hundred and sixty years ago by St Osburga, or so we were told in the tavern where seven of us stopped to buy ale whilst the rest set up camp.

We no longer attracted as much attention as we were all that much older, but people were wary of well-armed young warriors. Four men wearing padded gambesons that had seen better days seemed to take a special interest in us and I saw one of them speak to a scruffy urchin. The man slipped him a coin and shortly afterwards the lad slipped out of the door.

'Those four in the dirty gambesons have just sent for reinforcements, if I'm not mistaken,' I whispered to the rest. 'I think we should have a word with them to see what their problem is. Redwald, you and Cei keep watch outside and give a shout if you see anything suspicious.'

We went over and surrounded the men sitting at the table in the corner. One went for his dagger but Uurad put a knife at his throat before he could draw it.

'Now, now, men; no need to get excited. We are just curious why you sent for your friends as soon as you saw us.'

'No, you're mistaken. We're just here enjoying a quiet drink,' one of the other men blustered.

'You had better watch your step, boy,' another of the men said. 'This is our territory. You've obviously got money, judging by your fine clothes and weapons. Just give us that pouch you've got at your waist and we'll let you go.'

'Do you think that just because we're young that we're wet behind the ears?'

'Careful, lad. You may look pretty with your swords but we know how to use them.'

'Really?' Redwald asked with a grin. 'Well then, tell me how many Danes have you killed?'

'Danes?' the man asked, surprised. 'Don't make me laugh. There are no Danes near here. They're all in Northumbria.'

I shook my head.

'A week ago they arrived in Snotingaham.'

'You're lying!' the fourth man said.

'No, I'm just telling the truth. However, we don't want any trouble so we'll leave you to your drinking.'

Just at that moment Cei appeared to say a dozen armed men were coming down the street. The last thing the tavern keeper wanted was a fight in his premises and so he ushered us out through the back door and we made our way back to the stables where we'd left our horses.

I was fuming at being forced to leave without our ale, and for no good reason. Perhaps we should have stayed and showed them just how well we could fight, but there was no point. They didn't look as if they had a silver penny between them.

That night I reached a decision after talking to both Leofflæd and Alfric. We would leave Mercia and find somewhere in Wessex to buy a farmstead. At least there we should be safe from the Danes.

How wrong I was.

Chapter Nine

Winter 867 / Spring 868

It was late October before we found what we were looking for. By that time we had travelled as far south as Silcestre, a vill in Hamtunscīr, one of the shires of Wessex. We had avoided the larger settlements after the incident in Coventre and replenished our supplies by hunting and by buying vegetables and staples like flour from small settlements. Silcestre was one such settlement.

We arrived there on a sunny but cold day. We rode through the fields in which weeds had been allowed to grow and pasture land in which long grass and wild flowers predoiminated. I was certain that it could support twice the amount of livestock grazing there at the moment.

The settlement itself consisted of a hall surrounded by over two dozen huts and a small wooden church that had fallen into disrepair. It had evidently been a Roman camp at one stage, and an important one. The ditch had been filled in over time and the walls had fallen into disrepair. Some of the stone had been used as the foundations for the huts and to build the hall.

As we approached the latter through what had once a gate into the fort people ran inside their huts, but not before I'd noted the poor quality of their clothing. Of course, some would be slaves but the rest would be ceorls – freemen who owned the neglected fields or rented them off the thegn. The whole place reeked of poverty and lack of care.

I dismounted outside the hall and a portly man emerged with a boy of about twelve at his side who scowled at me.

'Good day, are you the thegn?' I asked with a smile.

'The thegn is dead,' the fat man replied tersely.

'Oh, I'm sorry to hear that. Who is the new thegn? You?'

'No, I'm Dudda, the reeve. There is no heir. We're waiting for King Æthelred to appoint a new thegn.'

If the thegn had held his land directly from Æthelred, he would have been a king's thegn; an important man and a member of the Witenaġemot – the high council of the kingdom.

It appeared that the last thegn had been ill for some time before he died. Dudda, a name which meant *round* – most appropriate given his rather portly state – was evidently lazy and had let things slide.

We bought most of what we needed but the settlement didn't have a great deal to spare. I found that surprising as I was told that the vill consisted of eight hides: that is to say it could support eight families of ceorls.

We wasted no more time and fifteen minutes later we were on the road to Wintanceaster where King Æthelred was normally to be found. The principle settlement of Wessex wasn't as large as Lundenwic, but it was just as crowded and just as smelly.

We were stopped at the entrance to the compound containing the king's hall by a surly sentry dressed in a leather coat sewn with iron scales, wearing a helmet and armed with a spear.

'Who are you, boy; what's your business here?' he demanded gruffly, looking me up and down.

'My name is Jørren of Cilleham and I wish to discuss the purchase of Silcestre with the king,' I replied.

He looked at me dubiously and for a moment I thought that he was about to send me on my way, but evidently the way I was dressed made him think twice. He looked to his left where I could see two boys dressed in good quality blue woollen tunics and red trousers playing a game of cyningtaefl just inside the gatehouse. When the man shouted at them, the younger one got up from the table on which the board was set and came over.

'Go and tell the steward that there's a young noble here who wishes to see the king.'

'But the king's not here,' the boy replied in a high treble.

'You know that and I know that but the little lordling here evidently doesn't.' the man sneered.

I moved my horse closer to the sentry so that he had to step backwards and leaned down from the saddle so that my face was a foot away from his.

'Then I will see whoever is in charge,' I hissed.

'I'll go and tell the steward that you want to see the Ætheling Ælfred, the king's brother,' the boy squeaked before disappearing.

I backed my horse up and dismounted. Leofflæd did the same and I looked at her quizzically.

'I'm coming with you; that is if you want me to be the Lady of Silcestre?'

'Does that mean we are betrothed,' I asked, slightly bemused by this turn of events.

'Yes, I suppose it does,' she said with a grin.

'Don't I get a say?'

'No,' she replied with an even broader grin.

Just at that moment the boy returned and we divested ourselves of our weapons before being allowed into the compound. Leaving the rest of the warband to find fodder and water for the horses, we followed the boy over a series of duckboards laid over the mud, past a stone built church and up the steps that led into the hall. Although hall was hardly the way to describe the king's accommodation. It was also built of stone and consisted of various chambers leading off a central passageway. At the end stood a pair of doors guarded by two more sentries.

One of them opened the right hand door and our guide led us through it, standing to one side once inside. I had expected to be taken to see the steward, but instead the boy had shown us into the main hall which was crowded with people. I didn't pay much attention to them or to my surroundings. My eyes were fixed on the raised dais at the end of the hall.

Ælfred must have been about nineteen at the time but he was small and thin and looked as if he was two or three years younger. I would be sixteen the following spring but already I was taller and broader in the shoulders than he appeared to be. Then I noticed the woman sitting on a smaller throne beside him. I assumed that must be the Lady Wulfthryth, Æthelred's wife. Beside her stood a boy of about nine who looked bored out of his mind.

'Who is the boy?' I asked our guide.

'The Ætheling Æthelhelm, the king's elder son. His younger brother is Æthelwold, but he's only six so he's spared having to attend the daily audiences. I will let the chamberlain know that you are here then I must get back to my post at the gate.'

'What are you,' I asked him as he was about to leave. 'A messenger?'

'No, I'm what is called a page, a member of the king's household. I'm ten, but when I'm fourteen I'll train to be a warrior and hope to become one of the king's gesith.'

The gesith were the king's companions, all nobles or the sons of nobles, who acted as the king's bodyguard.

'So you're a nobleman's son?'

'Yes, I'm the third son of the Ealdorman of Dorset. I don't stand to inherit land so the choice is either the church, which doesn't appeal at all, or become a warrior.'

With that he disappeared back through the door and we were left standing there, not knowing what to do or what was expected of us.

Eventually another boy, older this time but dressed in the same way as the boy who'd said he was a page, led us forward to the dais.

'I'll say your name and you kneel; wait for Lord Ælfred to tell you to rise and then state your grievance or plea, whatever you've come here for, as briefly as you can,' he explained.

By that time we'd arrived in front of the throne and he left us. I knelt and was conscious of Ecgberht kneeling beside me.

'Please rise,' Ælfred said in a kind voice, but one that sounded tired. 'What is your plea?'

'My name is Jørren, lord. My eldest brother is the Thegn of Cilleham. I understand that the vill of Silcestre is now in the king's gift, the last thegn having died recently without an heir, and I would like to purchase it.'

Ælfred looked amused and even Æthelhelm looked slightly less fed up.

'And what will you use to purchase the vill? Is your brother so wealthy that he can buy it for you?'

'No, lord. I have silver and even some gold and jewels of my own.'

The smile left his face and Ælfred now looked suspicious.

'And how did you come by this treasure?'

At that moment a man I hadn't noticed before mounted the dais and whispered in the ætheling's ear.

'I'm told that you have an escort of a score of well-armed youths mounted on good horses. Are you brigands? Is that how you came by your wealth?'

He seemed to notice Leofflæd for the first time.

'Your warband even includes girls, so it seems,' he added, looking slightly affronted.

'Leofflæd is my betrothed, lord. We rescued her and her brother from the Danes at Lindocolina. My wealth, such as it is, comes from the Danes we have killed.'

'What were you doing in Lindocolina?'

'Seeking the Danes in order to rescue my other brother, who was captured by them at the Battle of Salteode.' I paused, then added 'in Cent.'

'Yes, I know where Salteode is,' he said testily. 'And did you succeed?'

'Yes, lord. He is with the others outside the gates of the royal compound.'

The distrust evident on his face up to now disappeared; Ælfred now looked intrigued.

'You must tell me more, but this is not the time or the place. There are others waiting their turn to be heard. Dine with me later and bring your brother and your betrothed. I want to know as much as possible about this Great Heathen Army.'

'Then shall I bring Erik and Ulf as well, lord? They are members of my warband. You may be interested in what they have to say as they're Danes, but ones who've been baptised as Christians.'

'No!' the Lady Wulfthryth almost shouted, speaking for the first time. 'I will not eat with filthy Danes!'

'Then you need not grace us with your presence, sister-in-law,' Ælfred said frostily, earning him a glare from both Wulfthryth and her son, which Ælfred blithely ignored.

'Come, lord,' a voice said at my elbow. 'No doubt you will both wish to bathe and change your clothes before you dine with Lord Ælfred,' the man who had whispered in Ælfred's ear said, guiding us away.

✝✝✝

Our first problem was finding something a little more ladylike than trousers and a tunic for Leofflæd to wear. Thankfully Alric managed to buy something suitable from a clothier that was near enough the right size. He also purchased new tunics for me and the two Danish boys made of fine wool and embroidered at the hem, neck and sleeves. We already had trousers, ribbons for our calves and shoes that would pass muster.

Slaves bathed us in warm water - a real treat as normally we had to make do with freezing cold streams - and untangled and trimmed our hair. I was surprised how rank Wealmær smelled when he came to tell me that they would be sleeping in the warriors' hall if I needed them. He also assured me that our money was safely stowed in the royal treasury.

Both Ælfred and his other guests – the captain of his personal gesith, the Ealdorman of Hamtunscīr and Bishop Asser – listened intently and were full of questions. Everyone accepted what they heard as true; everyone that is except Asser. He plainly thought that we were either braggarts or out and out liars.

I had a feeling that we might need some proof and so I emptied the contents of my pouch onto the table. It contained gold and silver Mjölnirs – the Thor's hammer emblem worn by many of the pagans – silver pennies from East Anglia, Mercia and Northumbria, and other coins from Danmørk, Norweġ, Orkneyjar and even Sweoland. That was enough to silence his scepticism.

'It sounds as if you could be very useful to us next spring,' Ælfred said thoughtfully. 'You say that all your warband can ride well, can follow a trail and are proficient with sword, spear and bow?'

'Yes, lord. More importantly, they can all kill. Most boys their age haven't done so and are hesitant the first time.'

'They certainly lack the killer instinct your boys possess,' the ealdorman said thoughtfully.

'Lord, may I ask? What campaign is planned for the spring?'

Ælfred glanced at Erik and Ulf before continuing.

'King Burghred of Mercia is determined to eject the Danes from his kingdom and my brother thinks that we should help him. I agree; if Mercia falls, then Wessex will be next.'

'Yes, I can see that. Northumbria was conquered because it stood alone and, of course, it was previously weakened by the struggle for the crown between King Ælle and his brother.'

Ælfred nodded and then changed the subject.

'You mentioned the vill of Silcestre when we first met.'

I was glad that he'd raised it. I'd sought to do so all evening but hadn't wanted to seem self-seeking when there were more important matters to discuss.

'Yes, lord. What payment would the king be expecting, if I may ask?'

'I will need to discuss it with him, of course, so I can't promise anything, but I intend to recommend that he accepts your bid subject to one condition.'

'Yes, lord,' I said expectantly.

'That you and your score of warriors serve him as scouts whenever the need arises. That's on top of the payment you will have to make, of course, but if you agree, it will be less than it would have been otherwise.'

'Can you give me an indication of the money I will need to find?'

He was about to rebuke me for my persistence but Bishop Asser, who was sitting on Ælfred's other side leaned across and whispered something in his ear.

'Quite so, thank you bishop.'

He turned back to me and smiled.

'Bishop Asser has reminded me that Silcestre is without a priest and the church has fallen into disrepair. Normally the king would expect a payment of ten silver shillings per hide but, if you undertake to employ a priest and repair the church as well as providing scouts for the army, then I think something in the region of half that amount might be appropriate. However, it is up to my brother and you can't tell him I suggested any figure.'

'I understand Lord Ælfred. Thank you.'

The weight of a silver penny varied, depending on where it was minted, but it averaged three ounces. Forty shillings would therefore equate to ninety pounds of silver in weight. If I traded some of the looted gold and jewels for silver I probably had enough to pay the king and still have some left over to repair the church. The priest's stipend would have to come out of whatever my income from the vill proved to be.

Not only would we have a permanent base now, but there would doubtless be more opportunities to kill Danes and take their possessions in the years to come. Furthermore, I would be a king's thegn which was higher up the social scale than my eldest brother. That made me think of Alric. He would never resent my good fortune, but the least I could do was to find him a farmstead of his own somehow.

✝✝✝

Leofflæd and I were married in the newly repaired church at Silcestre at the end of March, just before I had to leave to join the king's army, which was mustering at Suindune. The priest had been sent by Bishop Asser. He was young, well-educated and seemed pleased to have been appointed. He said he was a distant cousin of the bishop's but I suspected that he was, in fact, one of his bastards.

My new bride was furious at being left behind but I insisted that she stay and run our new vill. There was another reason. It didn't show much yet, but she was pregnant and I wasn't about to risk losing the child.

Redwald would also be staying behind. One of my first actions after Æthelred had agreed to Ælfred's recommendation was to dispense with Dudda's services and support Redwald's election as his replacement. Dudda owned a farmstead near the settlement and he retreated there uttering dire threats and promising retribution. I dismissed them as empty bluster at the time. I should have been less cocksure.

There were twenty five ceorls over the age of fourteen in the vill. They were obliged to bear arms when required, however five of the men were really too old to fight so I left them to defend the settlement.

I departed from Leofflæd with great reluctance. We were in love but that didn't mean we didn't row. Hers was a feisty temperament and when she disagreed with me she wasn't backward in letting me know. However, when we did fight we soon made up and our lovemaking was all the more passionate afterwards.

Dudda was one of the twenty men who was obliged to come with us as part of the fyrd. I enjoyed watching him sweat as he heaved his bulk along the road, but I soon heard rumours that he was spreading dissent amongst my ceorls. The rumour had spread that we were heading for Mercia to help their king to fight the Danes. The men weren't happy on either score: they were only obliged by law to fight in defence of Wessex and the Danes' fearsome reputation frightened them.

On the day we were due to reach Suindune a delegation came to my tent and asked to speak to me. Dudda stood in the background and said nothing, but I knew that he was behind it all.

'Lord,' the eldest of the ceorls said nervously, wringing his woollen hat in his hands as he spoke. 'We don't think it's right that we should be asked to fight the Danes in Mercia. We are Saxons and they are Angles; let them fight their own battles.'

There was a chorus of agreement from the rest.

'Is Æthelred king of the West Saxons?' I asked.

'Yes, lord,' the man replied, evidently puzzled by the question.

'And do we follow him as our liege lord?'

'Yes, lord, but not outside…' he started to say.

'And why do you think he is going to aid the Mercians, who have been our bitter enemies in the past?'

'I don't know, lord.'

'Because it is better to fight the Danes on Mercian soil than it is to allow them to enter Wessex, which would mean that the heathens would be able to burn our homes, rape our women and enslave our children. Do you understand now why we are going to aid King Burghred instead of waiting for the Danes to invade our kingdom?'

'Yes, lord. Sorry, lord,' he said contritely. 'It was Dudda who said…'

'Yes, I know who has been stirring up trouble only too well. Don't worry I'll deal with him.'

When the men had dispersed I sent Cináed and Uurad to fetch Dudda, but they came back empty handed.

'He has deserted us, Jørren, taking one of the horses with him.'

'Go after him and bring me his head,' I said angrily.

I had said it in the heat of the moment and almost immediately regretted it, but it was too late. The two Picts had already left.

Darkness fell and there was still no sign of Cináed and Uurad and I began to hope that Dudda had somehow eluded them. It was a vain hope. It was midday before they caught us up. They were grinning triumphantly and leading the missing horse. Uurrad had a blood soaked sack in his hand and I didn't have to be told to know what was in it.

'You should have given him a fair trial, lord,' one of my fyrd told me reproachfully.

'Mind your manners, ceorl,' Ecgberht scolded him.

131

'No, he's right. I acted hastily. I will naturally pay his family the appropriate amount of wergeld.'

My heart sank. It was the right thing to do and it would save further trouble with my men, but the fine for killing a ceorl was two hundred shillings. I had nothing like that amount left in my coffers. I could only pray that the coming campaign was immensely profitable.

✝✝✝

We spent a week at Suindune waiting for the rest of the contingents to arrive. On the third day I was summoned to meet the king. Æthelred was nothing like his brother. Whereas Ælfred was small and looked young for his age, his brother was six inches taller, broad shouldered and, instead of the thin, wispy hair that Ælfred sported on his upper lip, the king had a thick moustache whose ends reached his chin.

Most Anglo-Saxon men favoured a moustache; it was one of the things that distinguished them from the Danes, who took pride in their beards. I was now seventeen and my facial hair had been growing for the past couple of years, but I preferred to keep my face clean-shaven so that I could pass for either Saxon or Dane.

Like Ælfred, the king had hair the colour of wheat. Whilst his younger brother had hair down to his shoulders, Æthelred's was longer and worn in two plaits. There was a third man in the king's tent who I hadn't seen before. He had dark hair and a face which was scarred from his left eye to his mouth.

'Good morning Jørren. Cyning, this is Thegn Jørren whose warband is to scout ahead of the army,' Ælfred said by way of introduction.

'And what will my huntsmen be doing, Ælfred? Scratching their arses? They are perfectly capable of making sure that we don't walk into a trap,' the dark haired man objected.

'Yes, Pæga,' Ælfred said patiently, 'but as I have already explained, Jørren had a score of young men who are mounted and well armoured. They've fought the Danes before and are much more mobile than our foresters and huntsmen. Their task will be to guard our flanks as we advance into Mercia whilst Jørren's warband scout ahead of the vanguard.'

'We are not here to bicker anew, Pæga,' the king said impatiently, 'we've been through all this. Ælfred has faith in Jørren's men and I can see the sense in employing mounted scouts.'

'At least let's have a look at these rascals before you make a final decision, cyning.' Pæga suggested.

I learned shortly afterwards that Pæga was the king's hereræswa. He was to command the vanguard and wanted his own foresters and huntsmen as pathfinders. I could understand his caution; after all, we were an unknown quantity. In truth I was surprised by Ælfred's confidence in us.

That afternoon we paraded in front of the king's tent. We might be young – the eldest of us was only nineteen – but we looked the part. Everyone wore a chain mail byrnie, a leather hood under a good quality steel helmet with a nose guard and each had a sword and a dagger hanging from his belt. Our horses were all rounceys; they looked well fed and had been groomed until their coats shone.

Each warrior had a quiver full of arrows and a war bow hanging from his saddle, together with an axe or a mace. We also carried a spear and had a round shield painted red and displaying a blue lion's head slung on our backs. We were better equipped than the king's own gesith, something that Æthelred commented on with a frown.

'Are you all Saxons?' Ealdorman Pæga asked, looking distinctly put out.

'No, lord. None of us are. Four are Jutes from Cent, one is from Wales, one from Mercia, two are Christian Danes, two are Picts and the rest are Northumbrians.'

'Ha, I thought so!' he exclaimed triumphantly. 'How then can we be certain of your loyalty to Wessex?'

'The last time I heard, Cent was ruled by the King of Wessex,' I replied caustically. 'Everyone here has sworn an oath of fealty to me and I am King Æthelred's liege man. Are you questioning my honour?'

'No, of course not,' he replied with a scowl. 'You all look very pretty but there is a world of difference between looking the part and being able to fight.'

'You are right, of course, lord. Tell me Cei, how many Danes have we killed?'

'Over a hundred and fifty, Lord Jørren,' he replied with a grin.

He didn't add that ninety of them had been killed whilst they slept.

'How many Danes have you killed, lord?' I asked Pæga sarcastically.

'That's enough Jørren,' the king barked. 'You've made your point. Your men will scout ahead of the vanguard.'

We left four days later. Some two thousand men had answered the king's summons. I'd wondered whether my brother Æscwin would be there, but I learned that only the fyrds of Hamtunscīr and the three adjacent shires had been called out. Although I would have dearly loved to see him again, I did wonder how he would have reacted to Cei's presence. I was also worried whether he knew that it was Cei and I who had killed those four robbers in Hrofescæster. It seemed like a lifetime ago now, but the law has a long memory. Owing one lot of wergeld was quite enough for me to deal with.

Initially we followed a broad valley heading north east, camping near Oxenaforda inside Mercia on the third night. From there it would take us another ten days to reach Snotingaham but we would be linking up with the Mercians at Ligeraceaster, which was around a six day march at our present slow pace.

The weather had been cold but fine at first, but on the day we left Oxenaforda dark clouds covered the sky and a strong wind blew from the west. Two hours later the rain started and it poured down incessantly from then on. Everyone's instinct was to huddle inside their cloaks and keep their heads down and that's exactly what we couldn't afford to do. Scouts had to remain alert, even in friendly territory. We had stopped to refill our water skins from a stream and allow our horses to graze when the one of the sentries I had put out came riding in from the north.

Jerrik slid from his horse and came running up to me.

'Danes,' he panted. 'A dozen of them on this road about two miles away.'

'Right, this is what we do,' I shouted. 'Erik and Ulf, take the horses. It's too wet to use our bows so our best chance is to hit them before they know we are here. Wealmær and Cei, you head back up the track behind us to cut off any Danes who manage to get past us. Cináed and Uurad, work your way behind them through the woods to stop any of them fleeing back the way they've just come. The rest of you get into the trees on the left of the road and wait for my whistle. Pick your man and make sure that you kill them before they realise what's happening. Oh, and I want the rearmost man captured alive for questioning. Now move!'

We were evenly matched as far as numbers went, once the six in the cut-off groups had left, but I was relying on surprise to tip the odds in our favour. My heart was pounding and I tried to calm myself as the tension mounted. It seemed forever before we heard them coming. Although they were deep inside southern Mercia, they weren't alert. Their heads were down to keep the rain off their faces and they hadn't put scouts out ahead. This was going to be easier than I thought, or so I hoped.

†††

It wasn't. The tactic was to bring down the horses with our spears and then kill the dismounted riders. The first part worked well but four of the Danes managed to jump clear of their horses before they collapsed. Several were trapped under their dead steeds but two managed to wriggle free and escaped to the north. Three more were thrown from wounded animals, but then the panicked beasts ran into us, disrupting our attack. Two of the

Northumbrians were injured: Cola suffered a blow to the head when one of the horses reared up in pain and a hoof landed in his helmet and Swiðhun a dislocated shoulder when he was barged out of the way by another animal.

I didn't discover this until later. I was too busy fending off an attack by a big Danish axeman. I blocked the first blow with my shield but the axe bit into it, splitting it. Thankfully the axe was stuck fast and, when the Dane tried to pull it free, he ripped the shield from my arm. I didn't feel anything for a moment then an excruciating pain hit me. When I'd lost my shield my radius, one of my forearm bones, had snapped.

I struggled to overcome the agony as my opponent went for me with his dagger. I just managed to block his first thrust with my seax but he smashed his fist into my jaw and my vision clouded. I fought to remain conscious but the combined effect of the pain in my arm and the punch meant that I was quite unable to defend myself. I was convinced that I was about to die when another of the Northumbrians, Stithulf, chopped into the Dane's neck with his sword. The head was half severed from his body and he sank to his knees. I gave a sigh of relief before the world went black.

When I awoke my arm felt as if it was on fire. My jaw hurt as well and I thought it might well be broken. As my blurred vision cleared I saw Erik kneeling by me, binding a splint to my forearm.

'I've set it, Jørren, but we need to get you to a healer as soon as possible. The same goes for Cola, but I don't think there is much hope for him. His skull is cracked; the helmet robbed the blow from the hoof of some of its impact but he's still unconscious.'

'I've pushed Swiðhun's shoulder back into its socket,' Ecgberht added, 'and strapped it up so he should be alright in a few weeks.'

'What about the Danes?' I asked through gritted teeth.

'All dead bar one, as you wanted,' Alric said from my left. 'We've collected a useful amount of coins, arm rings, hack silver and weapons as well.'

He pushed a young Dane who looked to be about fifteen, judging by the wispy beard he was trying to grow, into my field of vision.

Just then Øwli held a leather flask to my lips and drippled some fiery liquid into my mouth. It felt as if it was burning my insides as it went down but, after a few mouthfuls, the pain receded a little.

'Found it on that big hairy man who nearly killed you,' he said with a grin.

I gingerly felt my jaw with my other hand and was relieved to find that, although it was badly swollen, it wasn't broken. After drinking more of the contents of the flask than was perhaps wise I lapsed back into blissful unconsciousness. I was dimly aware of being hauled up to sit in front of Alric and of being bumped around but my next memory is of waking up back in my own tent.

Alric had taken Swiðhun and me back to the main army and, when the king heard about the Danish patrol, he decided to set up camp early that day. One of the many priests and monks travelling with the army, who was an infirmarian, had checked my forearm and said that it had been set well. He rebound it into a proper splint whilst I was still unconscious and Alric had set up our tent for me to rest in.

The next morning I was still in pain, but it was bearable, so I went to check on Swiðhun before reporting to the king. I found Æthelred with Ælfred and several ealdormen, including Pæga, outside the king's tent. The rain had stopped although the air was still full of moisture. The Dane we'd captured was on his knees in front of the king with Erik standing beside him acting as translator.

The boy was evidently terrified but Erik was making a hash of both the questions addressed to him and his answers. No doubt he was overawed at being in the company of so many nobles.

'Ah, Jørren,' Ælfred said, with evident relief. 'Your man is making a poor fist of interrogating this heathen, I fear. How is your arm by the way?'

'The infirmarian says that it will take a month or more to heal and then another month before I can build up its strength again.'

'I see.'

'I'm grateful to you for intercepting that patrol, Jørren,' the king added. 'Hopefully the Danes still don't know where we are or in what numbers.'

He smiled at me and even the obnoxious Pæga nodded and muttered something that sounded like 'well done'.

'I'm puzzled that there are Danes so far south of Snotingaham and, I must confess, a little concerned as to the fate of the Mercian army at Ligeraceaster.'

I questioned the terrified Dane and learned that, according to him, the main body of the Great Heathen Army had entrenched themselves at Snotingaham for the winter. They had planned to march south and conquer Western Mercia until they heard that King Burghred had mustered a large army to oppose them. When rumours began to circulate that Wessex was marching to join the Mercians Ívarr, Halfdan and Ubba had decided to stay put and improve their defences.

However, they had sent two patrols south; one to ascertain the strength of the Mercians and the other to bypass Ligeraceaster and find out how strong the army of Wessex was. In the meantime they had sent forage parties far and wide to gather provisions for a siege.

'So presumably the heathens still don't know where we are or in what numbers,' Æthelred said with satisfaction. 'Thank you Jørren. Who will lead your scouts until you've recovered?'

'Oh, I'll still ride with them, but I won't be killing any more Danes for a while,' I replied with a smile. 'My brother, Alric, will take command if there is any fighting to be done.'

We buried Cola in the graveyard of a nearby settlement. It was a long way from Northumbria and we all felt depressed for some time afterwards. We had been lucky I suppose, to have only lost two of our number; I didn't count Ceadda and Hroðulf as ever having been part of our group. One was a rapist and a murderer and both were traitors as far as I was concerned.

I can't say I was comfortable riding with a broken arm but I managed using my left hand and my knees to control my horse.

Thankfully there were no more incidents until we linked up with the Mercians a few days later.

Chapter Ten

Summer 868 to Spring 869

The Danes had built a palisade around much of the settlement, the rest of the perimeter being protected by a steep cliff. Although our combined armies outnumbered the Danes by two to one we had no siege engines and so our only alternatives were to attack the defences using ladders or starve them out. The palisade was fifteen feet high and we would have lost too many men in an assault, so we sat outside the three gates and waited.

I used the time to improve the training of my men, both in scouting and tracking and in fighting with bow, sword and spear. We also went hunting and were mostly successful. Consequently we ate better than most during the dreary months of April, May and June. The fyrd were not only bored but they were increasingly concerned about harvesting, which began in late August. Without a good harvest they and their families would starve this coming winter.

When the Danes asked to parley it came as great relief to everyone. Some of the fyrd had already started to slip away, although I'm glad to say that none of my men did so. They had been incorporated with the rest of the fyrd of Hamtunscīr until recently. Now they had been returned to me at my request so that I could improve their fighting skills.

I made a gift of the Danish byrnies and helmets we had taken off the patrol to those who they fitted best and awarded the enemy's weapons to those who proved most skilled at using them. If there were any lingering doubts about their loyalty to me, this put an end to them. They were most appreciative and inordinately proud of the fact that the fyrd of Silcestre were now better equipped than anyone else; better even than some of the professional warriors.

'Your skills as interpreter are required again, Jørren,' Wealmær, who was one of the sentries on guard in our section of the camp, told me early one afternoon in June.

I made my way through the mud and slime to the king's tent. Predictably the interior of the encampment had quickly become churned up and, even though duckboards had been laid down, they had eventually sunk below the surface. I tried to remove as much mud from my boots as possible but inevitably traipsed some filth inside the tent. I'd given up wearing shoes as soon as I'd lost one in the mud. Now I wore expensive leather boots made by some itinerant cobbler who accompanied the army, and no doubt made a fat profit from doing so.

'Ah, Jørren, good. How's the arm?' Ælfred asked me as I handed my cloak to a servant.

'Thank you, lord. Much better. The splints can come off next week, or so I'm told. Then I'll be able to concentrate on building up the wasted muscles.'

'Good, let's get on,' Æthelred said impatiently. He turned to the Mercian king who theoretically we were here to support. I had met Burghred twice before and hadn't been impressed by either his foppish appearance or his rather weak character.

'The Danish leaders, Ívarr, Halfdan and Ubba, have asked for a meeting,' he began. 'No doubt their food supplies are running low. We need an interpreter as none us speak Danish well enough.'

Or at all I thought to myself.

'Will you translate for us Thegn Jørren?'

'Of course, cyning. However, Ívarr and Halfdan are from Norweġ and therefore speak Norse as their mother tongue.'

'Are they not Danes?' Æthelred interrupted.

'No, cyning,' I explained patiently. 'The Great Heathen Army is a mixture of Vikings from Danmǫrk, Norweġ, Orkneyjar and Irlond. The last three all speak Norse, not Danish, as their mother tongue. There are also a contingent of Sweonas as another of the Ragnarsson brothers is Björn Ironside, King of Sweoland,'

'Then how on earth do they communicate with each other?' Burghred asked, somewhat bewildered.

'The languages are similar and Norse is probably the common tongue, amongst the leaders at any rate. No doubt the two Raganarsson brothers also speak Danish fluently, but my point is that they can converse amongst themselves in Norse and I probably wouldn't know what they were saying.'

'Ah, and you think it would be useful if we had someone present who could listen to their private conversation?' Ælfred said, nodding in agreement.

'Precisely, lord. That way we might have a good idea how far we can trust them.'

'Who do you have in mind?' Æthelred asked.

'Ulf. He's a Dane but his mother was Norse. He might be a bit out of practice but he's the only one I know who was brought up speaking both Danish and Norse.'

'You want him to translate instead of you?' Burghred asked.

He seemed slightly annoyed that the King of Wessex and his brother seemed to have taken over the meeting.

'No, cyning. I suggest he stands behind King Æthelred's chair and whispers anything they say in Norse to him.'

'Good idea, thank you Jørren.' Æthelred said, earning himself a scowl from his fellow king.

It was the first time that Æthelred had smiled at me and I felt elated that, at long last, he might be warming towards me.

†††

The three Danish leaders were quite dissimilar in appearance. Ívarr was the youngest and the fact that he was beardless added to that impression. His long dark hair was well groomed but otherwise he looked unkempt. His clothes looked greasy and were made of rather coarse wool. He had charisma but there was also an aura of menace about him. There was no doubt that he was the leader of the three.

Halfdan had similar facial feature to his younger brother but they were partly hidden behind a full beard. It was well groomed but he had tied various gold, silver and jewelled rings into it. His hair was fairer than Ívarr's and he was dressed in a good quality tunic and the baggy trousers favoured by the Vikings.

Ubba was a head taller than the other two. He was a bear of a man with muscular arms. He was the only one to wear a chain mail byrnie over a short-sleeved tunic. His beard was trimmed close to his face and his long blond hair was also cut short. I doubted if I could get my hands more than half-way around his bull-like neck.

All wore soft leather boots like mine and, like us, none wore even a dagger at his waist. There were three chairs set out for them but they remained standing. Behind them stood three of Ívarr's hirdmen, just as three of Burghred's gesith stood with us. None were armed but the two groups of bodyguards looked as if they only needed the smallest excuse to lay into each other.

'Thank you for coming,' Burghred began. 'We are here to listen to what you have to say.'

'We are safe behind our walls and your farmers must be getting anxious about their crops,' Ubba said with a sneer. 'We want to give you the chance to withdraw with honour before your men desert you.'

The two kings looked at each other in surprise when I translated this.

'If you want us to withdraw, why don't you come out and fight us in the open instead of skulking inside Snotingaham like a load of fearful old women?' Æthelred asked before Burghred could reply. 'Your supplies must be running low, many of you will be ill and I imagine that your men are getting bored with doing nothing.'

The three Vikings looked at each other when I translated what Æthelred had said and started to converse fiercely in Norse. Ulf told me later what they were arguing about. It was evident that Ívarr wanted to leave to pillage elsewhere, Halfdan was in favour of returning to Eforwic and Ubba wanted to stay put until they'd extracted a sizeable bribe to leave.

'How much do you want to leave Mercia?' Burghred asked, fastening onto the latter.

'Five tons of silver,' Ívarr replied without hesitation.

Æthelred and Ælfred immediately protested that it was a ridiculous amount, but Burghred held up his hand for silence and so I waited for his reply.

'Two tons,' he told me to say, but I hesitated.

Even that was enough to give every heathen warrior about fourteen ounces of silver each; not that it would be shared out equally, of course.

'Offer one,' Æthelred whispered to me.

'You won't be paying it,' Burghred told him angrily. 'It's my kingdom and my money!'

'No, but you are setting a precedent here. They have hardly lost a man yet and so this is easy money for them. It gives them a reason to come back again next year and demand more.'

King Æthelred was right, of course, but Burghred wouldn't listen.

'Offer them two,' he insisted.

I looked helplessly at Æthelred but he looked away. I looked at his brother instead and he nodded after a pause, so I offered two tons.

They discussed it and Ubba pressed for acceptance but Ívarr shook his head.

'Not enough; four tons. Accept it or we will ravage Mercia next year.'

I thought that they probably would anyway but Burghred nodded.

'Tell them that it will take time to collect it.'

I did so and Ívarr told him he had two months to deliver it.

In fact it wasn't until the end of August that the final shipment was delivered and the Danes returned to Eforwic. By then we had returned home. It was with mixed sentiments that I rode back into Silcestre. I noted with pleasure that Redwald had completed the

144

repairs to the gaps in the defensive wall with timber and the settlement now had a proper gate.

I couldn't wait to see Leofflæd again but, despite the loot from the score of Danes we had ambushed, I still didn't have enough to pay Dudda's family the wergeld that was due to them.

✝✝✝

The summons to appear in front of the ealdorman's court came on the day that Leofflæd gave birth to a little girl. It seemed that my offer to Dudda's wife and son to pay the two hundred shillings to them in instalments hadn't worked. They had appealed to the Ealdorman of Hamtunscīr for immediate payment. My euphoria at the baby's birth and, more importantly in a time when many mothers died in childbirth, the relative ease of the birth, evaporated immediately.

There was only one solution. I would have to borrow the rest of what I owed. It would mean mortgaging my vill but I could see little alternative. I asked Alric to choose two others to accompany us and to get the ostler in charge of the stables to saddle the horses. I was getting impatient and went to the door of the hall only to find the whole warband coming towards me.

'Jørren, we've collected what we have and I think it will be enough to make up the difference,' my brother said.

'No, I gave that to each of you as your share of the spoils. I can't accept it, although the gesture is greatly appreciated.'

'Then look at it as a loan,' he replied. 'We won't demand a punitive rate of interest either, unlike the usurers in Wintanceaster. There is one thing we ask in return, however.'

'What's that?'

'That you end the tenancy of Dudda's family. We won't suffer Ailwin's jibes and enmity any longer.'

Ailwin was Dudda's thirteen year old son. He'd been an arrogant and spiteful little sod when his father was still alive; now he was insufferable. I had given some thought to the tenancy of

Dudda's farmstead but hadn't reached any conclusion. Normally it would have been inherited by the dead man's son after the payment of the appropriate inheritance tax. This hadn't yet been paid, or even agreed with me.

A further factor was Ailwin's age. He wasn't yet an adult and couldn't therefore take on the tenancy. His mother could have done, but I would have to agree. What I didn't know was whether I had the right to end the tenancy. I needed advice and the best person to give me that was the shire reeve.

His name was Tunbehrt. Like me, he was a king's thegn, but his holding was much greater than mine, being thirty hides or three tithings. Ten tithings made up a hundred and there were forty-four hundreds in Hamtunscīr. He was therefore an important man and only the ealdorman was senior to him in the shire's hierarchy.

I took Alric, Redwald and Wealhmær with me as escort and rode to Tunbehrt's principal hall just outside Wintanceaster but he wasn't there. He was away hunting a band of outlaws who were robbing merchants and farmers travelling along the road through the forest to the south. As it stretched from Wintanceaster to the south coast and covered an enormous area I had little option but to await his return.

The one thing I did manage to do was to register my daughter's birth with one of his clerks. We had decided to name her Cuthfleda, meaning *gift of God*.

Tunbehrt's wife invited us to sleep in the hall but I decided to go and see the ealdorman and settle the business over the wergeld whilst we were waiting. Wintanceaster was also the seat of the Ealdorman of Wintanceaster as well as being Wessex's capital.

Ealdorman Merewald was an old man, which explained why he hadn't accompanied the army to Snotingaham the previous year. I gathered that he only had daughters, one of who was Tunbehrt's wife, who I'd met earlier. It didn't take a genius to work out who the next ealdorman would be.

He received me sitting in a chair in his bedchamber being fussed over by another daughter, a pretty girl called Guthild who appeared to be about fourteen. Alric had accompanied me whilst the other two waited outside with our horses. I could sense his interest in Guthild as soon as we were shown into the room by Merewald's steward. She smiled shyly at us and I was conscious of the fact that her eyes lingered rather longer than was seemly on my brother. I groaned inwardly. She was far above him socially and I had enough problems without Alric falling in love with the unattainable.

'Lord, I am sorry for intruding on you when you are unwell.'

'Please don't apologise. I may be old and bedridden but there is nothing wrong with my brain. What can I do for you?'

I explained about Dudda and his wife's plea to him for immediate payment of the wergeld.

'And I assume that you cannot pay her at the moment?'

'No, not without borrowing part of the sum, lord.'

'It seems to me that you had just cause for punishing this man, but not to kill him, of course. My bedchamber is not my court but, if you want my advice, I would recommend offering half now and half next year. It's a reasonable compromise that I could probably agree to,' he said with a smile.

'Thank you lord; that is most helpful.'

'Now I think you had better take your leave before my daughter and your brother make fools of themselves.'

Alric looked abashed at having been caught making cow's eyes at the girl but Guthild seemed not in the least perturbed.

'Father, you grow fanciful in your old age,' she reprimanded him.

I glanced behind me as we left the chamber and I caught Guthild looking thoughtfully at Alric's receding back. I'd heard of love at first sight but I didn't believe in it. The love between Leofflæd and I had taken time to blossom and grow. We went back to Tunbehrt's hall but he hadn't yet returned. I was about to give up and go home, intending to try again in a few days' time, when a harassed looking messenger arrived.

'I've been seeking you for two days, lord,' he said handing me a letter.

It was an invitation for Alric and myself to dine with the king that evening. It came as rather a surprise and I wondered what we had done to deserve such an honour. My next thought was that we were dressed for riding, not dining in the king's hall, and there was no time to ride back to Silcestre and return in time. There was no alternative but to spend some of my precious silver on new clothes for us both.

Leaving our weapons with the gatekeeper, we strode into the king's hall wearing our newly acquired robes that reached the ground and more or less hid our riding boots. Frankly we were rather young to wear such clothes – they were normally the garb of older nobles and wealthy merchants – but they were cheaper than buying new embroidered tunics, fine wool trousers and shoes.

I'd expected to eat in the main hall along with the royal household but we were shown into a side room where there was a table and seven chairs. This was obviously going to a more intimate affair. I was intrigued.

Ælfred and Pæga entered the room shortly after we had and we were served a goblet of mead by two pages, one of whom I recognised as the boy who had met us at the gate of the royal compound what seemed like ages ago, but was in reality only nine months. The king and the Lady Wulfthryth joined us and I was so busy bowing my head that at first I didn't see the girl with them. To my utter astonishment it was Guthild. She kept her eyes demurely on the ground but every once in a while she would look at Alric under lowered lashes.

'Stop gawping,' I hissed quietly at him. 'You look like a stranded fish.'

He had the grace to blush and I didn't think anyone had noticed until I saw Ælfred glancing speculatively at the two of them. Thankfully Guthild was seated at one end of the table and Alric at the other. I sat beside my brother with Ælfred on my other side. The king sat in the centre with his wife on his other side and Pæga was between her and Guthild.

It was a simple meal with two meats, various root vegetables and bread to mop up the juices. Æthelred and Pæga ate with gusto whilst Ælfred pecked at his food sparingly. The two ladies ate nearly as much as the king and his hereræswa but did so in a manner that made it less obvious. I was nervous and ate more than Ælfred but I can't say I enjoyed it. Alric consumed barely anything.

Once the platters were cleared away and we had cleaned our fingers in bowls of water brought by the pages Æthelred cleared the room and even the two sentries left us.

'I have asked you all here because of the continuing threat posed by the heathens,' the king began.

'I thought that they were still at Eforwic,' Pæga said, looking surprised.

'And so most of them are, but it doesn't mean that they'll stay there,' Æthelred pointed out. 'In fact, I received tidings today indicating that Ívarr may have already left, heading north-west with about a third of the pagan horde.'

'That's good news isn't it, cyning?'

'Not necessarily; he may be linking up with more Norsemen from Irlond. There are also reports that some groups of Danes have been seen heading south-east back towards the Kingdom of the East Angles.'

'More good news,' Pæga said, looking pleased. 'The further they are away from Wessex the better.'

'The land of the East Saxons and Cent aren't far away from there and they are part of Wessex,' I pointed out.

'Besides,' Ælfred added, 'we can't allow them to pick off the other Anglo-Saxon kingdoms one by one or we'll end up being isolated.'

'That's why I have decided to strengthen our alliance with Mercia,' the king said. 'My brother has been betrothed to the Lady Ealhswith, daughter of a prominent Mercian ealdorman and a descendent of King Coenwulf of Mercia. That's where you come in, Jørren.'

'Me, cyning?'

'Yes, I need a good escort to bring the Lady Ealhswith here to Wintanceaster from Torksey in Lindesege where she is at the moment. If the rumours of Danes in that area are true, then they are probably the vanguard of the main heathen horde. I'm not sending a larger group to escort her because I don't want a confrontation with the Danes. Your job, and that of your men, is to sneak her out of there and bring her safely back to Wessex. Can I rely on you?'

'Yes, cyning of course.'

'You won't want a load of hysterical women as well but Ealhswith will need a lady with the appropriate status as a companion and as a chaperone. I have therefore asked the Lady Guthild to perform that function. There is no one I know with a more level head on her shoulders, except of course my beloved wife.'

If Wulfthryth felt patronised, she hid it well. I could feel Alric getting excited at the prospect of being in Guthild's company for weeks, perhaps months. I groaned to myself.

'But what about Guthild's father? Doesn't he need her love and care, cyning?'

'It was Ealdorman Merewald who suggested his younger daughter to me,' the king replied with a smile. 'But it is good of you to show such concern for him, Jørren.

'Of course,' he went on. 'I don't expect you and your men to undertake this task for nothing. Would two hundred shillings seem an appropriate reward?'

I started. Had the king chosen the same amount as the wergeld I owed Dudda's family by chance? His next remark answered that.

'And if I were you, I would hesitate to grant his wife's request to take on the tenancy of Dudda's former farmstead.'

Chapter Eleven

Spring to Autumn 869

My first problem was Leofflæd. She insisted on coming with us and nothing I said could dissuade her. I had to agree that having another female along on the mission made a lot of sense but, not only was I worried about her getting hurt, but I needed someone to stay and look after the vill; and, of course, our baby daughter.

Redwald had recently got married to a girl in the settlement and, as reeve, he would be staying anyway. He and his bride moved into the hall pro tem and, as the baby had a wet nurse, that seemed to solve the problem. It didn't stop me worrying though; both about Leofflæd and about Cuthfleda. I'd heard too many tales about babies and infants dying suddenly to be entirely happy. Leofflæd didn't seem to share my concerns and so I tried to push them to the back of my mind.

I set off with Guthild, my wife and seventeen other warriors on a cloudy day in late March. We needed to travel swiftly and so we took no carts, only pack horses. There would be no grand pavilion for the Lady Ealhswith either. We only took small leather tents with us that could sleep two people. She would have to share with Guthild on the return journey. I took a spare tent as well on the assumption that Ealhswith would have a maid.

We stayed that first night in the monastery at Oxenaforda having covered just over forty miles, with which I was pleased. We were now inside Mercia but there was still a long way to go; another one hundred and fifty miles if my information was correct.

We were able to use the old Roman roads as far as Lindocolina. From there Torksey was only ten miles to the north-west. However, I decided to leave the Roman road known as the Fŏsweg at Newercha and follow the River Trisantona north to Torksey.

As we had reached the area where Danish patrols had been reported a few weeks ago, we advanced with even more care than usual; and it was just as well that we did.

My warband were a pretty tight-knit group. We had been through a lot together, some of it pretty harrowing for young men our age, and each of us had our own demons to fight. However, we trusted each other and seldom fell out. The one exception was Wolnoth. He was an orphan who had trained from the age of eleven to be one of Edmund of Bebbanburg's scouts. He had joined me, along with the late Ealdorman Edmund's other scouts two years ago.

Wolnoth always kept himself to himself. He was a good tracker, hunter and pathfinder but he seemed to prefer his own company to that of others. We had camped for the night beside the Trisantona some ten miles south of Torksey. I intended to approach the vill on foot with the utmost caution early the next day. The others had teased Wolnoth because he seemed aloof from the jovial comradeship around the campfire and he had stormed off. I had followed him intending to have a private conversation with him. It was evident that something was bothering him but I couldn't think what it could be.

He walked past the sentry hidden in the edge of the trees and went deeper into the wood, muttering something to himself. I was fifty yards behind him when he froze and dropped silently to the ground. I took cover beside a bush, drawing my dagger as I did so, and tried to see in the poor light cast through the canopy by a new moon what had alarmed the lad.

I was still peering into the gloom when I sensed a presence beside me. I turned and nearly thrust my dagger into the person beside me until I realised it was Wulnoth. I knew he was a good scout, but to have moved so close to me without me realising meant that he was exceptional.

'Danes,' he breathed almost inaudibly into my ear. 'Perhaps forty or fifty of them camped two hundred yards that way.'

We withdrew as quickly as we could without making a noise. When we got back to our encampment I gestured to everyone to be quiet and kicked dirt over the fire to put it out. When everyone had huddled close enough to hear my muted voice I told them about the Danes.

'What do we do? Leave quietly?' Alric asked.

'No, that would just risk running into them later. We need to eliminate them.'

'Eforwic,' Sæwine muttered, spitting to show his distaste for what we had had to do that night.

'Precisely. We do the same now as we did then. We kill the guards and then kill them as they sleep. I know it is asking a lot of you. Some still have nightmares about killing defenceless men, but it's the safest course of action. I won't think badly of anyone who wants to stay here and guard the horses.'

To their credit no one did, so I decided that Sæwine and Wulnoth should stay. Both protested but I told them firmly that it was an order. I also asked Leofflæd to stay behind but she said that she could kill a sleeping Dane just as ruthlessly as anyone else and wouldn't hear of it.

We left our armour and weapons behind. Leofflæd and I took our bows, just in case, but all we would need, hopefully, would be our daggers.

The Danes were laughing and drinking around five separate campfires. At first I couldn't see any sign of sentries but then they changed over. There were four in all, assuming that they all changed at the same time: three at the edge of the trees around the campsite and one by the horse lines. Their horses were tethered to three long ropes tied between trees in a patch of open grassland so that they could graze. As we watched several boys brought leather buckets from a nearby stream and watered each horse in turn. When they'd finished they lay down to sleep in front of the horses, watched over by the sentry.

'They're thralls,' Erik whispered in my ear. 'We can't kill them.'

I agreed, but I couldn't risk them giving the alarm either.

'Did you see how many there were?' I asked him.

'I counted seven. Wait; I'll check with Ulf.'

A few minutes later he returned.

'He agrees, there were seven.'

'Right. As soon as the warriors turn in take seven men with you. You deal with the sentry and tell the others to keep their hands over the mouths of the thralls to keep them quiet until you and Ulf can explain to them that we've come to set them free. Select who you want to take with you and warn them, but wait for three owl calls in quick succession before you move. Clear?'

'Have you got enough to deal with so many Danes?'

'No, once you have finished bring the boys here and leave them with Ulf. Make sure they move quietly though. We'll have taken care of the other sentries by then. All of us, less Ulf, can then move in and cut the throats of the sleeping men.'

It sounded alright in theory, but it didn't work out like that. Uurad made a botch of killing his sentry and the man was able to shout a warning before Uurad cut his throat. Unsurprisingly, that alerted the sleeping Danes.

Thankfully my men did what they'd been instructed to do if my plan failed; they melted back into the woods and headed for our campsite. We'd left everything packed and ready so all we had to do was to ride away. My only concern was how quickly the Danes could mount up and pursue us.

That is, everyone did what I'd said except for Erik and Ulf. Erik had the presence of mind to tell the thralls he'd set free to grab the leading reins of as many horses as possible whilst he and Ulf cut through the ropes to which they were tied. Erik then led the boys and the horses away into the woods whilst Ulf stayed and cut the throats of the three horses that the boys hadn't managed to lead away.

We were just about to leave when Erik arrived with the herd of horses. Now that the Danes were afoot we had a little more time and so we waited for Ulf. When he arrived I congratulated him and Erik on their initiative and, with the former thralls each riding

154

behind one of my warriors and the rest leading a number of horses, we retraced our steps upstream. We were just in time as we heard the angry Danes crashing through the woods looking for us as we left.

✝✝✝

Once we were five miles away we stopped and headed deeper into the woods beside the river to catch a few hours' sleep before dawn. I now had a problem. There were now some fifty angry Danes between us and our goal of Torksey. Moreover, if they managed to return to the main body of the Viking horde there would be a lot more than fifty searching for us. We had to find them and kill them, and do it as quickly as possible.

The boys we had rescued from servitude were a mixture of Northumbrians from Eforwic and Mercians from Lindesege. All were orphans, or thought that their parents must be dead or enslaved. They were aged from ten to thirteen and so too young to be trained as warriors. I had no idea what to do with them, but that was a problem for another day.

They told us that there were thirty eight Danes. Having killed four, that left thirty four. It was still a lot, but it was better than fifty.

Leaving the boys and all the spare horses with Leofflæd, Guthild and Alric, I rode off with the rest in search of the Danes. It didn't take long to find them. They were walking disconsolately along the track downstream. We headed eastwards into the scrubland that lined the river at this point until I was sure that we were out of sight and sound from the Danes. Then we raced north to rejoin the riverside track some three miles north of where we'd last seen them. We couldn't be far from Torksey by now and so time was of the essence.

The terrain here couldn't have been better for our purposes. It was wooded again, but the trees were well spaced with shrubs growing under them. We left Jerrick who was probably our worst archer, with the horses and each climbed a tree from where we had a good view of the track but which was a good fifty to a hundred yards back. Then we waited, but not for long.

The Danes were strung out, walking along in small groups with no scouts out. They all looked to be young and only one was wearing a byrnie. I hooted thrice like an owl and arrows rained down on the column. A few seconds later, whilst the Danes were still wondering what was happening, a second volley tore into them, then a third. By this time nearly half of the enemy were dead or wounded and the other half were running in all directions.

'Concentrate on the ones heading north,' I yelled, taking careful aim at the man in the byrnie.

He was older than the rest and presumably their leader. My arrow took him in the back and he fell on his face, but the chain mail had robbed my arrow of much of its penetrating power. However, his helmet had come off when he fell. I let another one fly and this time I hit him in the back of the neck as he struggled to rise. He fell back to the ground and didn't move again.

I glanced around me. Several more Danes were down, including all those who had tried to escape along the track. The dozen or so who were left had finally got themselves organised and had formed a shield wall to protect themselves from our arrows. Holding their shields in front of them and over their heads, they started to edge sideways, heading north. We came down out of the trees and formed up facing them. Although we now outnumbered them, I wasn't about to lose men attacking them directly.

'Aim for their lower legs,' I said, putting another arrow to my bow.

Their shields were similar to ours, apart from the pagan symbols painted on them. They were three foot in diameter, made of lime wood, banded in bronze or iron and with a central metal boss. On most men they covered from the lower face to the knees. That left their shins and feet exposed. Arrows that hit the shin bone cut the skin but did little other damage. However, puncturing the calf muscle behind the shin bone or the feet could immobilise a man, at least partially.

After several had been wounded in this way, the Danes became so infuriated that they abandoned their shield wall and charged straight at us, yelling like berserkers.

'Swords and shields,' I shouted, dropping my bow and swinging my shield around from by back to my front.

We formed one long line with shields overlapping and sword points protruding above our shields. The Danes crashed into us individually and paid dearly for their uncoordinated attack. We thrust into their virtually unprotected torsos and, although the ferocity of their attack forced us back a step or two, our line held.

I felt a blade strike my helmet but it slid off the surface and thwacked my shoulder. The chainmail held, although I would have a nasty bruise there tomorrow. I disembowelled my attacker before he could do any more damage.

A minute later it was all over. Those wounded in the foot or calf tried to get away but they were easily overtaken and killed. Over a dozen were badly wounded, rather than dead, but I needed this patrol to disappear. So we killed them before hauling all the bodies deeper into the woods. We collected their helmets, weapons and anything of value, which wasn't as much as I'd hoped, and went back to where we'd left our horses.

All that was left to show that the skirmish had taken place was flattened vegetation and dark patches in the mud where blood had seeped into the ground. Of course carrion birds quickly gathered in large numbers to feast on the bodies, but I hoped that they wouldn't be visible from any distance.

I breathed a sigh of relief as we rode back to join my wife and our captured herd of horses. At least they should fetch a pretty penny.

✝✝✝

Torksey was surrounded by a vast encampment of Danes. Tents made of leather or untreated woollen material had been erected on three sides of the settlement with the river on the fourth side. I could see the ealdorman's hall in the centre surrounded by huts and a timber church, but they were lost in the sea of tents.

I estimated that the encampment must have housed between fifteen hundred and two thousand Vikings. Various banners hung from spears thrust into the ground outside some of the huts and the larger tents and I counted fifty or so of these. Erik told me that each jarl and hirsir would have his own banner and so they indicated the presence of the crews of fifty ships. That confirmed my estimate if most longships were crewed by thirty men and a few of the larger ones by sixty or seventy.

A black ram's head on a red background flew from the top of the hall which, Erik said was the Ubba's banner. Alongside it was another, smaller, banner with a black raven with its wings spread wide on a faded yellow ground: Ívarr's banner, which disproved the reports that he had taken his men north-west into Cumbria. Halfdan's banner was missing, which probably meant that he had remained in the north to hold Eforwic.

The Danes had constructed a ditch and earthen rampart around their camp with a single gap for access in the west. The two ends of the rampart rested on the river where the remains of the Viking fleet was moored. I counted fourteen longships, all that was left of the ships we had burned at Eforwic.

During the day two groups of Danes of a similar size to the one we'd ambushed rode back to their camp. The next day another patrol returned and this seemed to cause great excitement. That afternoon there were evident signs that the Danes were about to leave Torksey. I had been about to attempt a swim across the river to try and ascertain whether the Lady Ealhswith was held captive there. Instead I decided to wait and see whether the heathen horde left.

At dawn the next day the exodus began. It took a long time to bring the horses in from pasture and so the last Danes didn't leave until midday. Once they had gone, heading upriver, the settlement was eerily quiet. Just before dusk small groups of people started to return to the settlement and I surmised that these were the inhabitants who had fled when the Danes came.

Early the next morning I rode into Torksey with Alric and Leofflæd. We had divested ourselves of armour, mainly so as to appear less threatening but also because we had to cross the river, which we did sitting on our horses and letting them do the work. The inhabitants surrounded us as we entered the settlement, their mood ugly. We had to keep reassuring them that we were friends until we reached the hall.

A man came out of the hall and demanded belligerently to know who we were and what we wanted. By the way he was dressed I assumed that he was either the reeve or the steward; certainly not the ealdorman.

'We have been sent by Ælfred, Ætheling of Wessex, to escort his betrothed, the Lady Ealhswith to Wintanceaster.'

That seemed to reassure him but he told me that Ealhswith's father and the whole household had moved to another vill the ealdorman owned at Gæignesburh weeks before the Danes had arrived.

'Where is Gæignesburh?'

'To the north on this bank of the river, about a three hour walk from here.'

My heart sank. That was only eight or nine miles away. Even if the main body of the heathens hadn't come down the river, their fleet would have passed Gæignesburh.

'Do you know where the Danes have gone?'

'No, but they appear to have had patrols out for the past week or so, perhaps seeking the whereabouts of King Edmund's army.'

'The East Anglians? I thought they had a truce with the Danes?'

He shook his head.

'It's rumoured that the heathens sent a demand for King Edmund to provide more money and more horses and he refused.

It's said that he has mustered his army at a place called Hægelisdun, and is determined to fight the Danes.'

'Thank you. Where is the best crossing place as the rest of my men are on the far bank?'

'There is a bridge at Newercha; that's the nearest.'

We swam our horses back to the others and, once we had changed into dry trousers, we set off south for Newercha. I did consider swimming everyone across the river but, as the former thralls were novice riders and with so many horses, I decided against it.

Luck was with us. There was a fair at Newercha when we got there and both horses and livestock were being auctioned. I sold twenty five of the horses that day, which added significantly to my wealth, even after giving my men a small pouch of silver each. That still left us with enough horses to mount the boys as well as more pack horses to carry the extra tents and equipment that I bought for them. I also purchased better clothes, shoes, a cloak and a dagger for each one.

We camped that night just outside the settlement and in the morning we set off for Gæignesburh.

✝✝✝

As soon as I saw the settlement I could understand why the Danes had left it alone. It was quite sizeable and protected by a moat, earth ramp and palisade on all four sides. There was a wooden tower at each corner and two more besides each set of gates.

We found the Lady Ealhswith safe and well at the hall but, when I said that we would be riding back to Wintanceaster both she and her father rejected the idea. They insisted that it wouldn't be seemly for a lady of her standing to ride all that way.

I had been dubious about taking Guthild with us, not least because I feared that it would encourage Alric to develop a relationship with her that was doomed to end in disaster. In fact they had never been alone and, although they spent a lot of time talking together, I was certain that nothing unseemly had taken place. The only downside had been the absence of Leofflæd in my tent as she was sharing with Guthild until we collected Ealhswith. Now Guthild proved her worth.

'Nonsense, there is nothing wrong with a lady riding. I'm Guthild, daughter of the ealdorman of Hamtunscīr and companion for your daughter until we reach our destination. I've ridden all the way here because it's necessary if we want to avoid trouble and travel swiftly,' she told Ealhswith and her father in her forthright way.

'It may be all very well for a Saxon noblewoman,' Ealhswith replied, her eyes flashing, 'but we Mercians behave with more decorum. After all I will be marrying the heir to the throne and one day I may be your queen.'

I disliked Ealhswith at that moment and nothing caused me to change my mind in subsequent years.

'You may become the king's wife in due course, although we all wish Æthelred a long life I'm sure, but we don't have queens in Wessex,' Guthild replied with equal asperity. 'Besides the king has two sons who may grow to adulthood before their father dies. It will then be up to the Witenaġemot to choose who will become the next king.'

'Lady,' I said diffidently. 'What the Lady Guthild says is correct. A carriage would slow us down, restrict us to certain roads, and make our journey more than twice as long as it needs to be. You can ride I take it?'

She gave me a withering look.

'Of course, better than you I daresay.'

'Then it's settled. We won't need the carriage then.'

'What about my clothes, jewels and maids?'

'I have brought spare horses.'

'I may be an excellent rider but my maids aren't.'

'Then they will have to stay here.'

'That's not acceptable!'

'My wife and Guthild can look after you.'

'Wife?' she said studying my warband and the boys, who were still sitting on their horses as we conversed outside the hall.

Leofflæd dismounted and took off her helmet, allowing her long hair to fall down below her shoulders.

'I'm the wife of Thegn Jørren,' she said with a smile. 'Despite my appearance I can assure you that I'm quite capable of looking after you.'

'You don't even look like a woman,' Ealhswith said disparagingly.

'I assure you that I am. I even have a daughter to prove it,' Leofflæd said sharply. 'Not all of us are useless at anything bar embroidery and looking pretty.'

'That's enough,' I cut in before any more damage was done.

I turned to the affronted lady and her parents.

'Lord, if you wish your daughter to wed Lord Ælfred then I fear that the only safe way of reaching Wessex is on horseback. Otherwise I shall have to return empty handed.'

'Wait here,' the ealdorman said brusquely before disappearing back into the hall with his family.

'Dismount,' I ordered everyone, fed up with being treated so inhospitably.

I entered the hall to be greeted by the sight of the family huddled in argument a few feet from the door.

'At least have the courtesy to send for ostlers and servants to tend to my men and our horses, instead of leaving them outside in the sun,' I said to the ealdorman, not bothering to hide my annoyance.

He flushed and his wife muttered 'impudence' loud enough for me to hear.

'Very well, but please wait outside,' he said stiffly.

A minute later ostlers and stable boys appeared to take our horses away to water them and servants came out of the hall with bread, cheese and ale. We went and sat in the shade to eat and drink and wait for the ealdorman's decision. I had cooled down enough to realise that the King of Wessex and his brother might not be very pleased with me if I returned empty handed.

Ten minutes later a servant appeared and invited my wife, Guthild and me into the hall.

'We have agreed that riding, whilst unusual, might be appropriate in the circumstances. However, my daughter is unhappy at the prospect of travelling to a strange land with people she doesn't know on her own. My youngest son, Ulfrid, will therefore accompany her.'

A boy who appeared to be eleven or twelve stepped forward and gave me an unfriendly look. I sighed. The sooner this journey was over the better, I thought. But at least we wouldn't be lumbered with a carriage and a cart carrying Ealhswith's belonging.

My men and the boys we'd rescued slept in the warriors' hall that night whilst my brother and I shared one room and my wife and Guthild another in the hall. Conversation during the meal was somewhat stilted at first but relations thawed somewhat later, probably helped by the mead and ale we'd consumed. I tried to stop Alric boasting about the Danes we'd killed a few days previously but the ealdorman seemed impressed and Ulfrid listened agog.

Our return was uneventful, although we took a different way back. Lady Ealhswith had agreed to ride, but drew the line at sleeping in a tent. We therefore rode from monastery to monastery in a more circuitous route. When we got to the one dedicated to Saint Alban at Verulamacæstir we heard what had happened in East Anglia.

The two armies had met outside Hægelisdun but King Edmund's nobles had urged him to negotiate with Ívarr and Ubba. They had agreed to do so but, when Edmund and a few of his nobles had arrived to meet the two heathen leaders, the Danes had killed the nobles and had taken Edmund prisoner. The East Anglian fyrd had subsequently dispersed and the Danes had taken possession of East Anglia in a relatively bloodless campaign.

It was grave news. Now only Wessex and Mercia stood firm against the Danes and their allies.

Chapter Twelve

869 - 870

Immediately after I returned to Silcestre I paid Dudda's wife and son the wergeld I owed them and then evicted them from their farmstead, giving it to Alric, not as my tenant but freehold. He still owed military service as and when required but he didn't have to pay me any rent. He took three of the boys we had rescued from thraldom to help him work the farm promising to train them as scouts and warriors over the next couple of years. Little did we know at the time but we didn't have years before they would be needed to fight for Wessex.

Gunhild and he had grown ever closer over the months we had been away. I thought that they stood no chance of ever becoming betrothed but my brother and Ulfrid had become quite good friends during the journey home and the boy persuaded Ealhswith to speak to Ælfred about them.

Of course, Ealhswith had other, more important things to worry about, such as her forthcoming marriage, and I thought that she would forget her promise. Whilst she also liked Alric, she made it clear on numerous occasions that she didn't care much for me. I don't think she ever forgave me for making her ride all that way instead of travelling in a carriage with her two maids.

I was therefore surprised when Leofflæd and I were invited to her wedding. Alric was also invited, a singular honour for a ceorl, even if he did own his own farmstead now.

The wedding was very much like every other one, except for the grandeur and the crowded church. Every ealdorman who was able to attend was there with their wives and older children. Guthild came with her sister and her husband, who was a wealthy thegn in Dorset, but her father was absent. I was one of a small group of thegns who were invited and I was grateful to Ælfred for the honour.

My wife was almost unrecognisable from the girl who had ridden with my warriors and Ealhswith told her later than she had hardly recognised her. I was consumed with pride but slightly worried when Alric made a beeline for Guthild when we walked from the church back to the king's hall.

As befitted our status, Alric, Leofflæd and I were sat with a few other thegns and their wives at the end of one of the long tables, well away from the king, the groom and his bride. I was therefore surprised when Ælfred beckoned me.

I made my way around the hall until I was behind his chair. He made a gesture for me to lower my head so that he could whisper in my ear.

'I haven't had a chance to thank you for escorting my bride safely to Wintanceaster. I hear it was a profitable expedition for you, but nevertheless I wish to reward you. There is a vill within my gift at Basingestoches. It is much larger than Silcestre and it will make you a wealthier man.'

'Lord, I am most appreciative and don't wish to offend you, but would it be possible to give the vill to my elder brother Alric?'

He looked at me in surprise, then smiled.

'Ah, would that be because then Alric could legitimately ask for the hand of Guthild?'

'Partly, lord, but also because he is my senior and yet I am a thegn whilst he remains a ceorl.'

'Your sentiment does you credit, Jørren, but the king has already agreed to the match between Alric and Guthild. She will inherit five vills when her father dies, as will her sister, and that will make Alric much wealthier than you. So you can keep Basingestoches with a clear conscience.'

'Thank you, lord.' I paused then asked 'what does Guthild's brother-in-law make of the match?'

'Oh, as he'll be the next Ealdorman of Hamtunscīr he'll be happy enough.'

I returned to my place feeling bemused and euphoric at the same time.

††††

Leofflæd and I visited Basingestoches for the first time in October that year. I took the four boys who I was training as scouts together with Erik, Ulf, Cei and Swiðhun. Guthild's father had died in September and Alric was now betrothed to his daughter. They were away visiting the five vills that she had inherited and my brother had given his farmstead to Leofflæd's brother, Ecgberht. Life seemed to have treated us very well. It couldn't last, and it didn't.

Basingestoches was about three times the size of Silcestre and consisted of twenty one hides, including three outlying farmsteads. Much as we loved Silcestre, it was obvious that we would need to move our home here. The reeve was of a very different calibre to Dudda, but I didn't take to the priest. He was an austere man who looked down his nose at us and chided Leofflæd for dressing and riding like a man. Needless to say she gave as good as she got, but I decided that I would have to ride to Wintanceaster and see Bishop Asser about replacing him as soon as possible.

I left a few of my warband at Silcestre under Wealhmær's command to guard the vill, collect taxes and continue with the fyrd's training. Cei, Erik, Ulf, Jerrick, Øwli, Cináed and Uurad would accompany us to Basingestoches, together with the four boys we had rescued. Redwald and Ecgberht would also be staying at Silchester, of course.

It was a sad moment when our warband split up just after Christmas but, should the need arise, they would reunite and fight together in the future.

That need came rather sooner than I had expected. I should have known that there was another motive behind Æthelred's and Ælfred's generosity in giving me such a fine vill as my reward for bringing Ealhswith safely to Wessex. I had just emerged from a somewhat unsatisfactory meeting with Bishop Asser when a page asked me to go with him. With a start I realised that the page was

Ulfrid, Ealhswith's youngest brother. I had assumed that he would have returned to Mercia, but apparently not.

'Good morning, Jørren. I assume that Basingestoches is to your liking?'

I nearly replied that it was, save for its priest, who Asser had just refused to move, but I bit my tongue.

'Yes, Lord Ælfred, very much so. I am forever in your debt.'

'Well, there is something you can do to remedy that, if you're willing.'

My heart sank and I wondered what else I would be expected to do in return.

'Have you heard that the wretched heathens have murdered poor King Edmund?'

He went on to tell me that Ívarr the Boneless and Ubba had tortured Edmund of East Anglia and finally killed him by using him as target practice by the few archers the Danes possessed. What made it even worse was that he'd been killed in a church and then beheaded. His corpse had been dumped in a wood for the carrion birds and animals to feast on and his head had been disposed of separately.

Ælfred had been told that local people had recovered the body for Christian burial but no one could find the head until their thegn heard someone calling to him. He went to investigate and found the head. It was impossible for a severed head to call out, of course, but the tale circulating was that Edmund had summoned the thegn himself. The martyred Edmund was already been talked of as a saint.

'The Danes are overwintering at Theodforda. Having overrun Northumbria and East Anglia, the king is worried that they may turn their attention to Wessex next. East Seaxna Rīce is an obvious target, but they may also cross the Temes into Cent after that.'

I immediately thought of my brother Æscwin at Cilleham. Instead of regarding whatever Ælfred was about to ask of me as a chore, I now wanted to help in any way I could.

'We still have perhaps two months before they move. It's important to know where their next target is.'

I was puzzled.

'How can we find that out, lord?'

'Can Erik and Ulf still pass as Danes?'

I was impressed that Ælfred had remembered their names.

'Yes, lord. We still speak in Danish once a week to keep our skills in the language up. They would need to exchange their crucifixes for Mjolnir, of course. Presumably there is someone in Wintanceaster who can make them Viking clothes? When would you want them to leave?'

'As soon as possible. You're certain that they'd be willing to undertake such a dangerous task?'

'I will have to ask them, of course, but I'm fairly certain that they will do it.'

Erik said yes straight away but Ulf was less certain.

'What if we are recognised?' he asked.

'You are much older and bigger now,' I replied. 'Trim your moustaches and let your beards grow. That will make you look more like Vikings and it will hide your faces better. Some of the others and I will come with you until we are close to the encampment, so all you have to do is to ride the last ten miles or so on your own and keep your ears open.'

The two nodded and I went to tell my wife that I would be leaving the next day.

✝✝✝

It snowed that night and by morning it was a foot deep and still coming down in flakes the size of a silver penny. It seemed that we wouldn't be going anywhere for a while. It was the end of January before the thaw started. Of course that brought its own problems with roads that were quagmires and flooded rivers whose fords were impassable. We set off eventually in the second week of

February. It was dry with weak sunshine that did little to warm the ground or the air.

It might have been bitterly cold but at least the going was easy on the paved Roman roads. Even those sections where the cobbles had been taken for use elsewhere didn't slow us down as the mud was frozen solid. Leofflæd had perforce stayed at home this time as she was expecting our second child, so I had taken Cei, Jerrick and Øwli in addition to Erik and Ulf from Basingestoches. I had also sent for Swiðhun and Wolnoth from Silcestre. To bring our number up to ten I had decided to take two of the older boys we had rescued the previous year along for the experience. They were called Hunulf and Ædwulf; both were thirteen and had showed promise, both as hunters and as archers.

We made good progress, staying for the first two nights at monasteries in Certesi and Lundenwic. The cold snap had ended by the time we left on the third day but, although it was warmer, drizzle permeated everything, making us cold and wet.

It took us two more days to reach Grantebrycge where we would leave the Roman road network and head north-east for the final thirty miles or so to Theodforda along muddy tracks. By now the weather had improved and so I decided to camp off the main thoroughfare some eight miles short of the Danes' encampment. The next morning Erik and Ulf changed clothes and helmets and we prayed together before I took their crucifixes from them and handed them two Mjolnir in their place.

When they had left for the final leg of the journey, I went into the wood to be by myself. I don't think I have ever felt so apprehensive in my life. They had become like brothers to me, as had many of the others, and I knew I would fret until they returned safely.

They didn't come back that day and my anxiety increased. I was on the point of doing something stupid, like going to look for them, when they returned, smiling and laughing as if they didn't have a care in the world. I could have cheerfully killed them for putting me through the most miserable twenty four hours of my life. However the news they brought made me worry all over again.

'We selected a camp fire with a few young warriors like us around it,' Ulf began. 'As you know, we took the four trout we'd caught earlier and we gutted these and put them into the cauldron with the grain and the vegetables already in there. We gathered that food was running short and so our contribution was welcomed.'

'Anyway,' Erik interrupted, 'they asked us why we had joined them instead of eating with our own companions. We said that we'd had an argument with our jarl and thought it best if we made ourselves scarce until he'd calmed down. They laughed and that was that. I'd expected more questions and had more details prepared, but in the end it wasn't necessary. I think they were just glad to have the fish.'

'They started moaning about the cold and the wet. They are really looking forward to being on the move again,' Ulf continued.

'Did they say what their target is in the spring?' Swiðhun asked impatiently.

'I was coming to that,' Ulf said, aggrieved at being interrupted.

One thing that Erik and Ulf liked, like all Scandinavians, was a good story and they took exception to being rushed.

'They started talking about how rich Wessex was,' Erik said, taking up the tale. 'So I asked them if they didn't think Mercia was a better target. They laughed at me and said that there was more plunder to be had in Wessex.'

'Then one of them said that it was a pity that Ívarr had fallen out with Ubba. I said that I hadn't heard about this and he told me that Ívarr and a thousand men would be returning to Eforwic before travelling north and crossing to Irlond.'

'You're sure about this?' I asked. 'That means that there will be less than fifteen hundred of them left if they do attack Wessex. Did you get any more information?'

'Unfortunately they were too junior to know any details, but one of them did say that he'd heard that Wintanceaster was full of gold.'

'Wintanceaster?' I said, surprised. 'So they don't intend to raid in Ēast Seaxna Rīce and Cent?'

'Ēast Seaxna Rīce, yes; it's on their route. They speculated whether they would be able to take Ludenwic on the way but their objective was definitely Wintanceaster.'

This was disastrous tidings, and not only for Æthelred and Ælfred. Both my vills lay in the path of the invaders.

†††

We made it back to Wintanceaster in four days. The weather stayed dry, if bitterly cold, until the last day when light snow started to fall. I sent my men back to their respective vills with instructions to speed up the training of the fyrd whilst I went on with Erik and Ulf to see the king and Ælfred.

At first Æthelred didn't believe us but, after Ælfred had questioned Erik and Ulf in detail, the king was convinced and gave them a pouch of silver each. They left us after thanking the king slightly too fulsomely for my liking. They had never thanked me like that, but then again I hadn't rewarded them so generously, judging by the weight of the pouches they'd been given.

The door closed behind them and I was left alone with the king and his brother.

'Which way do you think they'll come?' Æthelred asked me.

'Well if they do take Lundewic, or at least try, they will probably take the old Roman road to Silcestre and then take the road south-west to here.'

'Via Basingestoches?'

'Yes,' I agreed glumly.

'Then we need to stop them before they get too far into Wessex,' Ælfred said.

'We also need to warn King Burghred,' Æthelred added, 'so that he can defend Ludenwic.'

The boundary between Mercia and Wessex ran along the River Temes. The road crossed the Temes via a bridge at Stanes, which was therefore the point at which the road entered Wessex. It was there that Æthelred decided to make a stand.

Having decided to call an emergency meeting of the Witenaġemot to be held at Wintanceaster in ten days' time, the king let me go and I returned to Basingestoches to prepare for war.

In early June we received word that the Danes had overrun Ēast Seaxna Rīce and then in August we learned that their attack on Ludenwic had been repulsed by the Mercians. Unfortunately Burghred's hereræswa didn't follow up this success, but had stayed safe behind its walls. We had mustered some three thousand men near Stanes by early September, but most of them were members of the fyrd. Æthelred only had a few hundred proper warriors, including his nobles, their gesith and the garrison of Wintanceaster.

My warband had been tasked to find and shadow the enemy and so at dawn the next day we crossed the two bridges at Stanes, one about twenty feet wide over the Temes and a much smaller one over a tributary which joined the main river from the north. Once across both we advanced slowly towards Ludenwic. This was rich farming land and so there were few woods and little cover. We therefore stayed well away from the road, but I still worried that we were very exposed.

Luckily we saw the heathen army before they saw us. It was difficult to estimate numbers but I thought that there were more than the fifteen hundred we had anticipated. Perhaps the rumours about Ívarr the Boneless heading north from Theodforda had been wrong?

It had been overcast all day and for the past hour the clouds had got darker and darker. Suddenly the heavens opened and rain pelted down. It reduced visibility to a few hundred yards and so we were able to get closer to the road without being seen.

The Danes hadn't bothered to put scouts out and the leaders rode together in front of the column. We had found a dip in the ground in which to hide the horses whilst Erik, Ulf and I crawled forward to the lip of the hollow.

'That's Ubba,' Erik whispered excitedly.

'But Ívarr's not there, so the story about him heading north or to Irlond must be true,' Erik added quietly.

'No, but Halfdan is. Who's the other jarl riding beside him?'

'I've seen him before. I'm sure that's Brynjar, the senior jarl amongst the Norsemen.'

'If Halfdan has left Eforwic that might explain why there appears to be more of them than we'd thought. Come on, we need to detour around them and get to the bridge before they do.'

Although many of the enemy were mounted, a sizeable contingent were on foot and so the column was moving slowly. When we appeared ahead of the Vikings there wasn't much they could do about it. We clattered across the two bridges and I reported what we'd found to Æthelred.

The old Roman stone bridge over the Temes still existed jutting out from both banks but the centre section and the piers that supported it were now made of timber. We had intended to fire the bridge as soon as the Danes were halfway across its twenty foot span, but the heavy rain had put paid to that idea.

The enemy army came to a halt as soon as they saw our men drawn up to deny them the crossing. There was a flurry of activity before the whole heathen army moved off along the north bank of the Temes.

'Where's the next crossing point?' I heard the king ask his brother.

'I don't think there's another before the bridge at Readingum,' he replied.

I knew Readingum. It was a large settlement on the south bank of the Temes. If they seized it they would have a base just inside Wessex. What was even worse, Basingestoches was less than twenty miles to the south and Silcestre was even closer, being a mere eight miles to the south-west of Readingum.

✝✝✝

Only two hundred or so of our army were mounted, including my scouts. The enemy had over six hundred horses and doubtless they would race ahead to seize Readingum and its bridge. Nevertheless Ælfred was sent ahead with our horsemen in a vain effort to deny the Danes the crossing.

When we reached the southern end of the bridge we found we had just beaten the Danes to it. We started to erect a barricade across our end of the bridge whilst someone went to tell the inhabitants to evacuate Readingum.

The vanguard of the heathen army arrived shortly afterwards and saw what we were doing. A few hundred dismounted and charged across the bridge on foot and more were arriving on the far bank all the time. I thought it was hopeless but Ælfred was determined to deny them the crossing for as long as possible.

By now it had stopped raining and we were able to use our bows effectively. My men sent volley after volley at the charging Danes. However, they used their shields to protect themselves and only a few were hit. So we aimed at high trajectory to hit those in the rear instead. From the screams it seemed that our arrows were having an effect.

A minute or so later the leading heathens attacked the men manning the barricade. We shot volley after volley at the enemy pouring onto the bridge but we were now running low on arrows. Eventually Ælfred conceded that we were fighting a losing battle. The enemy's casualties were far greater than ours, but we were hopelessly outnumbered.

The horses were brought forward and we ran to them as the Danes climbed over the makeshift barricade. One or two didn't make it, but most of us, including all my men, were able to mount and gallop away through the deserted streets of Readingum.

Unless Æthelred could dislodge them, the heathen army now had a base from which they could raid at will into Wessex.

That night Æthelred and the rest of the army arrived at Silcestre and he called a meeting of all nobles in my hall. Redwald coped efficiently with having so many important guests and, although the meal he served us wasn't exactly a feast, it was adequate and appreciated by all.

'We have to attack the bloody heathens before they start to devastate our estates,' Ealdorman Ethelwulf of Berrocscir maintained.

The king was more cautious, however. It was one thing to defend a river crossing but quite another to meet the experienced Vikings in the open with an army largely composed of farmers and tradesmen.

'May I suggest something, cyning,' I said after half an hour of discussion that had got us nowhere. 'The Danes will no doubt ride out to plunder and pillage in groups, not en masse. I suggest that my scouts track them and then we attack these groups with overwhelming numbers.'

'Might they not leave Readingum and make for Wintanceaster?' someone asked.

'Unlikely, I would have thought,' I replied. 'It's late in the season for campaigning and, with so many mouths to feed over the winter, my guess is that they will overwinter here before invading Wessex in the spring. Their priority now will be to gather food to last them the next few months. We need to deny them that.'

'How?' Ethelwulf asked succinctly.

'By attacking their forage parties, lord.'

Ethelwulf grunted. 'Makes sense I suppose.'

Silcestre, being the only fortified settlement in the area, became our forward base. Ethelwulf was given five hundred of the kingdom's best warriors and he and I sat down to plan our strategy.

Chapter Thirteen

Winter 870/871

We had some successes in ambushing the Danes as they plundered the area around Readingum but we also had a few disasters. On one occasion they laid a trap for us. Whilst we were ambushing a hundred Danes several hundred more suddenly appeared and we were lucky to extricate ourselves without losing more men. Thankfully none of my scouts were killed but a few were wounded. I learned a valuable lesson that day: always keep some scouts deployed to warn of reinforcements in the area.

Christmas was a muted affair that year. Leofflæd had been safely delivered of a baby boy in December but it had been a difficult birth and she hadn't recovered sufficiently to travel up from Basingestoches. On the last day of the year Swiðhun and Wolnoth returned from a regular patrol only a couple of hours after they had left Silcestre.

'Jørren, the Danes have left Readingum and are moving towards Inglefelle to the west of their camp.'

'What sort of strength?' I asked after sending Hunulf to warn Ethelwulf that he needed to get his men ready to move.

'Several hundred, perhaps as many as five hundred.'

'Thank you, go and warn the warband to get ready to leave.'

We formed the vanguard for Ethelwulf's small army as we headed due north to intercept the Danes. I sent Jerrick, Ædwulf and Øwli to the north east, just to make sure that there wasn't another force of Danes waiting to attack us in the rear. To assault the Danes with only marginally greater numbers was a risk but, unlike most of the fyrd, our men had spent the past few months training and they were now more disciplined. Furthermore, many of them had faced the Danes in the many small skirmishes that had occurred. They therefore had some experience of real fighting.

We came across the Danes as they made their way along the bank of a tributary of the Temes. No doubt they were hoping to avoid us and sack Taceham. The river wasn't very wide but the winter rains and melted snow had swelled it until it was too deep to wade across.

Ethelwulf sent me with my warband and another score of archers to attack the enemy's left flank and to prevent them from retreating whence they had come. Meanwhile he formed his men into a shield wall whose own left flank curled around to meet the river. The Danes were now surrounded on three sides with the river on the fourth.

The enemy were flying two banners, one of which Erik identified as that of Jarl Sitric, the ruler of Jutland where my family had come from several centuries before. The other banner was probably that of a less important jarl.

It was a fine day, if somewhat chilly. The air was crystal clear and there was a breeze blowing from the east which would assist the flight of our arrows. Once we were in position we commenced firing volleys at the Danish flank. At first we caused severe casualties because we were firing into their unprotected side. As soon as they realised, they swung a hundred men around to face us so that they could use their shields to protect that flank. Of course, it that also weakened the line facing our own shield wall.

We changed our target and now aimed high to hit the warriors in the rear ranks of both those facing Ethelwulf's men and those in front of us. With a roar the men facing us broke ranks and charged towards us. Perhaps a hundred and fifty yards separated us. We sent one final volley straight at them, bringing down perhaps a dozen more before we threw our bows aside and picked up our shields, spears and axes or drew our swords.

I had forty men and a few boys but the Danes charging us no longer numbered a hundred. We had killed or wounded half of them and now they charged us as an undisciplined rabble, which gave us an advantage.

I stood in the centre between Cei and Erik, our shields overlapping. The first man to reach me was a big bearded warrior wielding a two handed axe. He screamed and raised it high. Had it landed, it would have probably cut my head in two. It didn't. I thrust at his eyes under the rim of his helmet whilst Erik on my right thrust his spear under his armpit and into his chest.

The big man fell, dragging Erik's spear out of his hands. For a moment he was left defenceless just as another Dane thrust his sword towards the gap between the bottom of his helmet and the rim of his shield. I knocked the blade up so that it scored along the side of Erik's helmet, doing little real damage. A second later Erik had managed to draw his seax and he chopped it down into the man's shoulder, sundering the links of his byrnie and breaking his collar bone. The man screamed in agony and Ulf, to Erik's left, finished him off with a thrust of his sword into his throat.

'Drop the seax; it hasn't got enough of a reach. Draw your sword,' I shouted at Erik as another warrior headed my way.

This one was easier to dispatch. He tripped over the corpse of my previous assailant and I thrust my sword down into the back of his neck. Then, all of a sudden, the pressure eased. The Danes had prised apart the join between my shield wall and the right flank of Ethelwulf's men. The rest of them fled through the gap, discarding helmets, shields and weapons in their haste to escape. The Danes had been routed.

Ethelwulf killed the wounded and a subsequent count of the dead revealed that there were over two hundred bodies. Scores more had been forced into the river and had to been swept away to be drowned, hopefully.

Of course, we had casualties of our own. I bitterly mourned the deaths of Jerrick, Swiðhun and especially young Hunulf. The fool had ignored my instructions that he should remain in the rear rank and he had stepped forward twice to replace a man who'd been killed or wounded. We were a sombre bunch on the way back to Silcestre, carrying our dead with us. That evening, whilst everyone else was celebrating Ealdorman Ethelwulf's great victory, we sat morosely remembering our three friends.

✝✝✝

We had only just buried them when King Æthelred and his brother Ælfred arrived with the main army of Wessex. Word of Ethelwulf's triumph had reached him in Wintanceaster and he'd come north to finish the task, as he put it. Only it didn't prove to be as simple as that. After Inglefelle we estimated that the Danes numbered no more than thirteen hundred men. There was a rumour that Ubba had returned to Lundewic with his men; if true, he now occupied the most important settlement in Mercia. Whether that was true or not didn't matter. As Æthelred had brought over two thousand to add to our four hundred and fifty, we now outnumbered the enemy by two to one.

The Danes had abandoned their camp outside the settlement and taken refuge within Readingum. Our only option was to flush them out so we entered the place in four columns. At first the place seemed deserted then our column was attacked from the side streets and the alleys. Before we could react the attackers had retreated into the maze of back streets. Then rocks were hurled down at us from roof tops. I managed to kill one of our attackers with an arrow but we had suffered a dozen dead in return and the fyrd were getting jittery. Eventually Ethelwulf, who led our column decided to retreat but, when we tried to do so we found the way out was blocked by a barricade.

We charged it only to find it was manned by axemen who chopped our men down with ease as they tried to scale it. When I saw Ethelwulf fall with his helmet and skull crushed I decided the time had come to get out anyway we could. Yelling for everyone to follow me I ducked into a narrow alley.

Of course it could have been a dead end but luck was with me and eventually we emerged into the barren fields that surrounded the settlement. We made our way to the nearest wood and treated our wounded as best we could. I sent some of my men to the edge of the trees to watch for any pursuing Danes but, thankfully, none chased us. Out of the six hundred men Ethelwulf had led into Readingum, less than five hundred made it to safety, and of those fifty were wounded.

It had been a disaster but the other columns had suffered even worse. Thankfully both the king and Ælfred had survived and we retreated to Silcestre. The next day we abandoned it, much to my sorrow, and retreated to Æscesdūn where we encountered the fyrd of Dorcesterscir led by Bishop Heahmund. Not only did that restore our numbers to well over two thousand but it was a great boost to morale.

The night after we arrived the Danes camped in the nearby old Iron Age hillfort and we spent a miserable night without hot food. That night the rain lashed down and we were soaked to the skin. On the morning of the eighth of January we took up a position astride the ridge below the hill fort. Unsuprisingly, the men were grumbling about being cold, wet and miserable. To make matters worse, the ground was sodden and even boggy in places and damp bowstrings meant that our arrows would lack any power.

We formed up with Æthelred commanding one half of the army and Ælfred the other. The dividing line was the ancient track known as the ridgeway, which ran down the spine of the ridge. Bishop Heahmund was with the king and proceeded to celebrate mass before the coming battle. That put the men in better heart, especially when the saw the advancing Danes slipping and sliding on the wet ground. Much to my amazement King Æthelred ignored the oncoming Danes; he proceeded to pray on his knees whilst Heahmund carried on with his service.

By the time the Danes reached Ælfred's wing the enemy were exhausted and their charge lacked any vigour. The two shield walls clashed and gradually we managed to push the foe back along the ridge. As we slowly advanced men fell on both sides but we had the greater numbers and they lost more than we did. Eventually they broke and ran. We were too exhausted to give chase and watched them go. Then I remembered the other wing of our army and I clambered up to the top of the ridge.

The king's division were still locked in a furious battle with the rest of the Danes and so I ran, slipping and sliding, to where Ælfred stood. I explained the situation, panting with exhaustion as I did so and Ælfred immediately yelled for his men to form up in wedge formation. Five minutes later we crested the ridge and charged down into the enemy's left flank. That was enough to decide the battle. I managed to hack down one man before the Danes were routed and fled.

Æscesdūn was regarded as a great triumph, but the truth is we lost as many men as the Danes did; it was only a victory because we were left in possession of the battlefield and, perhaps more importantly, one of the enemy dead was Jarl Brynjar.

†††

We needed to regroup and raise more men. I was thankful that my small warband hadn't lost more than we had. Two of the scouts who had joined me from Edmund of Bebbanburg's household had been killed and I regretted not getting to know them better. Two more were wounded but would recover in time, with any luck. They were Cináed the Pict, who had a shoulder wound, and Ulf. He'd suffered a stomach wound which eventually killed him. That left me with a warband of fifteen, six of whom were the boys we had rescued the previous year.

I missed Ulf the most, but not as much as Erik did. He was now the last of the three Danes. Fifteen of my ceorls from Silcestre and Basingestoches had also been killed or badly wounded and I was left with a fyrd of eighty men and boys over the age of fourteen. I felt depressed and, on top of everything, I was worried about Leofflæd. I hated being parted from her in these unsettled times.

The next day, whilst the army was collecting our dead for burial, I sent Erik, Cei and Ædwulf to shadow the heathen army and see what they were up to.

Erik and the others came back just before dusk with disheartening news. There were a dozen new longships at Readingum. They must have been rowed up the Temes all the way from the sea. No doubt these were new arrivals attracted to England by tales of plunder back in their homeland. It meant that the Danes had now replenished their losses and were as strong as ever.

Once the king and Ælfred learned of the enemy reinforcements they decided to withdraw further into Wessex and to send to shires that hadn't yet provided a contingent for reinforcements. The place they chose for our encampment was Basinges, barely two miles from my vill of Basingestoches.

I took the opportunity to ride over to Basingestoches with Ecgberht and his three boys as escort to find out how my wife and the children were. Leofflæd was in a bad mood when I arrived, which I put down to being confined to the hall. Much to my alarm, she announced that she was going to join me. However, her brother and I eventually persuaded her that care of the children was more important and I asked Ecgberht to take them, and everyone left in the vill, to Wintanceaster for safety.

I made a fuss of the baby, who we had decided to name Æscwin after my eldest brother, and played with little Cuthfleda until it was time for her to go to bed. Perhaps I should have sent them away immediately. I was worried that the Danes might arrive in the area but I wanted one last night with Leofflæd. Who knew when we would be able to make love again, if ever?

Normally our sex was passionate and exhausting; however, that night it was gentle and tender. The next morning I said goodbye to her, and to our three children, with a heavy heart. I watched them until they were out of sight and then returned to the settlement to carry out one other task; I buried the coffer containing all our wealth in the pigsty. Hopefully, if the Danes ransacked the place, they wouldn't find it there.

When I returned to Basinges I found out that the nobles and fyrd of Suth-Seaxe had arrived to swell our numbers. They were just in time. On the twenty first of January one of my patrols returned to say that the Great Heathen Army was camped five miles away.

The hall, the timber church and some of the huts at Basinges were located in a fort that dated back to a time before the Romans came. It was a simple circular structure with one entrance up a ramp. Beyond it there was a square of flat ground on which several more huts had been built which was bordered by a steep earthen rampart. It was a perfect defensive position which the king had improved by tearing down the huts and using the timber to improve the ramparts.

I was given command of the circular part of the fort, which was manned by my scouts, all the hunters who possessed a bow and the newly arrived men from Suth-Seaxe – the least experienced part of the Wessex fyrd. To my surprise and delight Æthelred made me Ealdorman of Berrocscir to replace the dead Ethelwulf. It also meant that I wouldn't be junior in status to my fellow ealdorman of Suth-Seaxe. Inevitably he was a great deal older than me. At the time I was nineteen but I had much greater experience of warfare than my fellow ealdorman, something which he thankfully acknowledged with good grace.

The rest of the army was drawn up at the top of the ramparts between my men and the advancing Danes. Our plan was to use the archers to rain arrows down on the heathens at high trajectory until the Danes succeeded in forcing our men manning the ramparts to retreat. They would then fall back and form up on the level ground either side of the central part of the fort. With the centre secured, we hoped that the two wings could hold the Danes until such time as they were exhausted and forced to retreat. That was the plan but, as so often happens in war, it didn't quite work out like that.

The Danes suffered significant losses, both from my bowmen and from those defending the outer ramparts, but their determination eventually drove Æthelred's wing back. When the king was wounded his wing lost heart and they fled, leaving Ælfred's wing and my centre to face the combined weight of the heathen army.

185

The king's gesith conducted a fighting withdrawal, defending the wounded Æthelred until they were safe inside the centre area of the fort.

Several of the monks with the army rushed over to tend to the king. He had been wounded in the thigh and an artery had been nicked. Consequently he was losing a lot of blood. One of the monks applied a tourniquet whilst another cleansed the wound with wine and sewed it up. They applied a poultice of moss and honey and then bound it up. The bleeding had been stopped but the greatest risk was one of infection.

My instinct had been to rush over and see how Æthelred was, but my duty was to organise the defence of the fort. My archers sent arrow after arrow into the packed ranks of the enemy. Many were killed or wounded but they reached the bottom of the ramparts and started to climb them regardless.

I left my fellow ealdorman in charge of our reserve of a hundred men and asked him to use his judgement to bolster any point where it looked as if the enemy were about to break through. I glanced around me. The weakest point looked as if it was where the ramp entered the fort. Although we had built a palisade there with a gate out of wood taken from the huts, it wasn't anywhere near as stout as I would have liked and the Danes were chopping at the gate with their axes.

I called my warband to me and we ran to the ramparts either side of the palisade. Whilst the boys held shields to protect us from thrown spears, stones, hand axes and the odd arrow, the rest of us shot arrow after arrow into the throng clustered around the top of the ramp. It was with some dismay that I realised that my quiver was empty and the other archers were down to their last few arrows as well.

However, God answered my prayers and the Danes suddenly withdrew. All along the ramparts they started to fall back, leaving behind a pile of dead and seriously wounded. The greatest number were piled in front of our makeshift gate and I felt that the burning sensation in my aching arms, caused by firing so many arrows in quick succession, had been well worth it.

Halfdan himself strode forward from the ranks of the enemy and shouted up to us, asking in poor English for a truce whilst they recovered their dead and wounded. I strode to the top of the rampart above the area where Ælfred's men had been fighting and called down, asking for the ætheling's instructions.

'It's barely two hours before dusk; allow a truce until nightfall,' he called back. 'We'll take our own dead and wounded to the rear as well. Then we'll fall back under cover of darkness.'

That night we withdrew, allowing the Danes to claim a victory as they'd been left in possession of the old fort. However, the truth was that many had died on both sides, but they had lost at least a hundred more than we had.

Chapter Fourteen

Spring 871

We took our dead and wounded to Wintanceaster; the former for Christian burial and the latter for treatment. I enjoyed a tearful reunion with Leofflæd and made a fuss of the children. She had rented a small hut but, as the Ealdorman of Berrocscir , I was invited to move into the king's hall, where we were allocated a small chamber. It wasn't as large as the hut we'd vacated but we ate in the main hall and we felt honoured to be guests of the king.

Æthelred's wound was taking a long time to heal and so, for the meantime, Ælfred took over the running of the kingdom. The heathen army had retreated to Readingum to lick their wounds and, as it turned out, to wait for reinforcements. As we learned later, they had come in the shape of Ubba and the men who had left to occupy Ludenwic.

The nobles and fyrds of Dyfneintscir and Sūþrīgedcir arrived to bolster our own numbers and we concentrated on training the new men to fight in a shield wall. Then on the tenth of March a patrol of my scouts came in to report that the Danes were on the move. This time they were heading straight for Wintanceaster and estimates of their numbers varied from two and a half to three thousand men. We had three thousand men fit to fight, so they had an advantage as eight hundred of ours were, as yet, unbloodied.

March had been a wet month and the roads were mired in mud, except for those stretches of the Roman roads which were paved. It took three days for the enemy to reach us and by that time everyone was inside the walls. The place was crammed with people and food would become a problem if the enemy besieged us for any length of time. A direct assault was less of a threat. The Danes had no siege engines and the walls were high. Using scaling ladders was unlikely as it would be expensive for them in terms of casualties.

It was frustrating to see smoke columns rising into the air indicative of a large number of settlements and farmsteads being torched in the surrounding countryside. King Æthelred was carried up to the walls to see what was happening for himself. He wept to see the wanton destruction of Hamtunscīr and ordered the army to sally forth and attack the perpetrators. To do so would have been a disaster, of course, as the Danes would have cut us to pieces as we emerged from the gates. Thankfully wiser counsel, including that of Ælfred, Pæga the Hereræswa and myself, prevailed.

On the twentieth of March the Danes appeared before the west gates with a battering ram which they had constructed from a large oak tree. It was mounted on four axles with eight solid wheels and it was covered by a wooden roof. It was crude, but it would have been effective had it been allowed to batter the gates unhindered.

Pæga took one look at it and sent for barrels of oil. As soon as the ram was in position we poured oil down onto the wooden roof of the ram, some of which splashed the warriors holding shields above their heads to protect those operating the ram from our spears, arrows and rocks. As soon as we threw lit torches onto the roof it erupted into flames which spread to those soaked in oil nearby. Soon the ram and a score or more Danes were burning merrily.

The screams of those unfortunate enough to be set on fire were enough to send shivers through the most callous man, but it had the desired effect. The next day the Great Heathen Army abandoned the siege and marched away to the south west.

I set off with my warband to trail them whilst Ælfred prepared the army of Wessex to march out to intercept the Danes. Leofflæd had insisted on coming with us and I had, perhaps unwisely, given in to her demands. The children remained in the king's hall with their nurses.

King Æthelred accompanied the main body, but he travelled in a small, specially adapted cart as his inflamed leg was now so painful that he couldn't ride.

I had included the hunters and archers and the members of my fyrd who could ride in my warband. The extra horses came from the royal stables and so I now had a mounted force a hundred strong. We caught up with the first group of Danish stragglers less than four miles from Wintanceaster. They were on foot and numbered fewer than us. We rode around them and dismounted, the spearmen forming a small shield wall with a group of archers on each flank. I commanded one group and Leofflæd the other. If anyone objected to being commanded by a woman they were wise enough not to say so. We commenced shooting at the Danes and brought nearly half of them down with our first three volleys.

That enraged the rest and they charged us, yelling insults and vowing to kill us all. Whilst the hunters and other archers continued to shoot over our heads, my warriors dropped their bows and joined the shield wall. Another dozen Danes were killed or badly wounded before they reached us. By then we outnumbered them by more than two to one.

I was worried that the fyrd would break but they didn't and, although a few of them were killed, we slaughtered the remaining Danes. I left Leofflæd and the younger boys collecting anything of value and pressed on. We repeated the tactic with the next group. This time there were less than fifty of them and we suffered nothing more than a few minor wounds.

By now word had reached the leaders that they were being harried from the rear and so they found a place called Meretum to make a stand. Once again it was an ancient British fort, but it wasn't nearly as good a defensive position as Basinges had been for us. It stood at the top of a shallow incline with trees growing around it on three sides. There was a single defensive ring and that had been eroded over time so that it was no more than five feet in height in most places.

Leaving my warband to watch the Danes, I galloped back to brief Æthelred, Ælfred and Pæga.

'A frontal assault would be costly, cyning,' the hereræswa said, addressing the king but, in reality, talking to the ætheling. 'Our best tactic is to creep up on them through the trees, if they provide the cover Ealdorman Jørren says they do.'

'I agree,' I said, 'but we need a diversion to keep their attention on the open ground to their front. Furthermore, if the Danes have any sense, they will have men in the woods to give warning of an attack from there.'

Pæga look surprised, and then nodded his agreement. I had gone up in his estimation. I think he had always mistrusted my judgement in the past because of my youth. He didn't have the same problem with Ælfred, although he was only three years older than I was.

'What do you suggest?' Æthelred asked before his brother could speak.

I sensed that his injury was not only causing him severe pain but it must have been exasperating to see Ælfred treated as if he was in charge.

'If all those except for the diversionary force attack through the woods on one side of the fort, my scouts will act as the vanguard and quietly dispose of any Danes we find beforehand.'

'Your men are that good?' Pæga asked sceptically.

'They've had plenty of practice at disposing of sentries quietly, although that's usually been at night.'

'Then why don't we delay, pretending we are about to launch a frontal assault until dark? Your men can take care of any groups guarding the woods at night; then we'll move into position ready to attack at dawn.' Ælfred said, tactfully looking at his brother for confirmation of the plan.

'They'll all get lost in those woods in the dark,' Pæga said disparagingly.

I nearly lost my temper and asked him if he had a better idea, but I took a deep breath before speaking.

'Have we got rope or cord with us?' I asked.

'No, but we can easily fetch it from Wintanceaster,' Ælfred replied, looking puzzled. 'What do you want it for?'

'To link each group together with one of my warriors leading. They will take them to the place they'll need to form up.'

The other three looked at each other in surprise. It wasn't something anyone else had thought of but I know that men get disorientated in the dark and become lost.

'Right,' Pæga said. 'We'd better make it look as if we're going to attack this afternoon. We don't want to let the heathens escape.'

✝✝✝

It went just as I had hoped, at first. There were several groups of Danes a hundred yards or so inside the woods in the sector we intended to attack from. Some stood together quietly talking, others watched the woods individually. Disposing of them was a task for my scouts, not the hunters or the fyrd, so I left the latter with our horses and fifteen of us cautiously worked our way forwards in a line.

When we saw a group we surrounded them and attacked together. Each man had a specific target. This was work for daggers and seaxes, not swords. I crept up on the first group with six others. They weren't paying attention to the woods but were chatting quietly amongst themselves. They never knew what hit them. I stood behind my target and grabbed his face with my left hand, yanking his head back. A split second later my dagger cut across his throat and felt his warm blood cascade over my hand as I sawed the blade to and fro until I was sure that he was dead. The others had had similar success.

Not every group was executed so cleanly and silently but any sounds that were made were unlikely to have escaped the dense woodland. The trees were full of sound at night anyway as animals hunted their prey and called to each other.

My next target was a lone sentry who stood with his hands in front of his mouth as he tried to blow some warmth into them. He was young, perhaps as young as Erik, Ulf and Tove had been when they joined my warband. However, I couldn't let that affect me.

Because he had his hands in front of his face I had to adopt a different tactic. This time I pulled his helmet from his head and quickly brought the pommel of my dagger down to knock him out. His beardless face stared sightlessly up at me in the gloom under the tree canopy. He was indeed very young, probably no more than twelve or thirteen and I hesitated.

I should have realised that a boy wouldn't be out here on his own. As I steeled myself to cut his throat I heard the merest whisper of movement behind me. My men who were nearest to me went to attack the Dane who had loomed out of the darkness but they would have been too late. Instinctively I dropped to one knee, turning as I did so. My reaction was unexpected and an axe blade cut the air where I had been standing a split second earlier.

I leaped up, ramming my dagger towards the man's chest under his ribcage. At the same time I brought my fist up into his jaw to prevent him shouting out. With dismay I felt the point of my dagger slide sideways over a good quality chainmail byrnie. However, my uppercut had stunned my opponent. In the time it took him to recover his wits I was able to thrust upwards with my dagger again this time with more success and the point entered his neck just below his jaw. He gurgled briefly and then his corpse fell against me.

Now covered in blood, but his, not mine, I breathed a sigh of relief before being violently sick. I'd been in many fights but none had shaken me to the same extent that this one had. After checking that he was dead I went back to the boy. He was still unconscious and I went to cut his throat, but then hesitated. Instead I told one of my men to bind him and gag him. We'd take him back and question him later. Of course it was an excuse; I was being sentimental, but I felt better about myself as a result.

Once we were certain that the woods were clear of Danes in that sector, I took most of my men back with me to guide the main body into position. I left Erik, Cei and Wealhmær in case there was a change of sentries, but it was only two hours before dawn and I thought in unlikely that they would rotate before then. On our way

I checked on the boy I'd knocked out. He was awake and stared at me wide eyed with fright. No doubt his head hurt like hell as well. I picked him up, surprised at how light he was, and slung him over my shoulder.

After leaving him with the baggage train I led the hundred men assigned to me forward into position. The plan was to attack with fifteen hundred men as the sun rose. The second wave would follow on. It would be light by then and they would have the sound of fighting to guide them in any case.

Once we had formed up just inside the wood I joined Leofflæd. We huddled together holding hands and waited for dawn to arrive.

✝✝✝

As the first rays of light struck the tops of the trees we got up and stretched our limbs, stamping our feet to restore circulation. I picked up my shield and drew my sword ready for the signal to attack. A minute later a hunting horn blared out three notes in quick succession and we walked forward to the edge of the trees. Another long blast rang out and we advanced in four long lines and climbed the low ramparts of the fort.

The enemy had all slept inside the fort and as I reached the top of the rampart I was greeted by confusion and alarm all over the level ground in front of me. Some of the enemy had slept in the open around camp fires that were now no more than embers, some had erected tents and some slept under their animal skin cloaks. The sound of the horn had woken most of them and they were busy grabbing their weapons. A number had taken off their byrnies to sleep and were still trying to put them on.

The camp was guarded by about two hundred men but they were standing on the ramparts beside the entrance to the camp watching the diversionary force from Dyfneintscir and Sūþrīgedcir some four hundred yards to their front.

We swarmed down the far side of the rampart and tore into the unprepared Danes. I cut down the first man I reached, who was still searching for his shield, and a second later used my own shield to deflect a spear thrust. I chopped off the head of the spear and then drove my sword into the spearman's belly. I was still pulling it out when a Dane came at me with a two-handed battle-axe. I threw up my shield to deflect the blow and, as the man raised it to try again, Leofflæd shoved her sword into the man's armpit. He screamed and dropped the axe. A second later I had severed his spine and we moved on.

The speed of our assault had prevented the Danes from forming a shield wall and individual fights were developing all over the interior of the fort. Then the second wave of our army appeared on top of the ramparts. We forced the enemy back until they were confined in about a quarter of the fort. They had little room to manoeuvre but they had at last been able to form a shield wall.

We withdrew to form our own shield wall, but the rear ranks of the enemy started to climb the rear of the ramparts behind them and flee into the woods on that side. I had anticipated this and our plan was for the fyrd of Dyfneintscir and Sūþrīgedcir to move up to block their retreat. Unfortunately, the Danes had been routed so quickly that the former diversionary force were still en route to the blocking position.

Less than half an hour later we were left in possession of the fort. I surveyed the ground. By my calculation we had lost perhaps a hundred men but I estimated the Danish losses at five times that. As was normal, we slew the wounded and started to collect our booty in terms of weapons, armour, coins, hack-silver and gold and silver arm rings.

I sent ten of my scouts to collect their horses and then track the heathen army to see where they went. They had been gone less than an hour when Cei and the others came galloping back.

'They've re-organised and are coming back,' he yelled.

'Cei, over here. How far away are they and in what sort of strength?' I asked, running over to him.

'Under a mile away; it's difficult to estimate their strength, but I'd say around two thousand or so.'

Now it was our turn to panic. Ælfred, Pæga, Bishop Heahmund and I managed to restore some sort of order and gradually our army formed up on top of the ramparts to oppose the returning Danes. However, their leader, Halfdan, was too wily to make a direct approach and they appeared over the ramparts behind our position. King Æthelred, who had joined us in his little cart, was taken back to the baggage train by his gesith, despite his protests.

I cursed my folly in not sending Cei and the others back to track their approach but there was no point in regrets at this stage. We formed up facing the oncoming Vikings and formed a shield wall. However, we were at a distinct disadvantage, despite our greater numbers. Our youngest and least experienced warriors had been placed at the rear with our best fighters on top of the ramparts. Now boys of fourteen and fifteen and the fyrd of Dyfneintscir and Sūþrīgedcir were in the front rank.

✝✝✝

There was nothing that could be done immediately, but the other leaders and I pushed our way through the throng with the men from the top of the rampart so we could step into the breaches created when what was now the front rank fell. However, the latter were terrified and some of them started to push their way to the rear in any case.

There was utter confusion when the enemy hit us and they drove into us, slaying as they went. We must have lost hundreds of men in minutes before we managed to form a new shield wall with the ealdormen, thegns and more experienced warriors in the forefront. It took time but eventually we killed those Danes who had penetrated our ranks and held off the horde who were now filling the other side of the fort's interior.

They were hampered in their attack by the numbers of their own dead from the dawn attack and gradually we managed to force them back by virtue of our greater numbers.

It was then that Halfdan launched his master stroke. I had thought that there should be more Danes but assumed that some

196

had fled after the initial rout. I was wrong. Ubba led some eight hundred more Vikings over the rampart at our rear. Now we were hemmed in between two phalanxes of the enemy.

'Pæga, take men from the third rank back to hold the line against the Danes behind us,' Ælfred yelled.

The hereræswa waved to show that he had heard and he and Bishop Heahmund made their way through the press to take command of our rear. Both fought valiantly and managed to hold the line, but at terrible cost. Both were killed leading the fight back against Ubba.

I was exhausted by this stage and, although I didn't realise it at the time, I was bleeding quite profusely from a number of small cuts and nicks to my arms and legs. Then I saw Leofflæd fall out of the corner of my eye. I literally saw red. A red mist descended over my eyes and more adrenalin flowed through my body. I attacked the enemy in front of Leofflæd's body like a demon, my sword a blur despite my tired limbs.

Minutes later I had created a bubble around me as the Danes withdrew from my flashing blade. The men around me pushed into the tiny bridgehead I'd created and the enemy line buckled. I stood over Leofflæd as our warriors increased the gap in the Danish shield wall. More of our men poured into the gap as it widened. Now the Saxons at the front of the wedge were killing the less experienced Danes in the fifth and sixth rows of their shield wall.

Finally, the enemy broke and we chased them back up the ramparts over which they'd entered the fort. It seemed as if we'd won but Ubba was still fighting against our rear. As our men followed Halfdan's fleeing army out of the fort, Ubba was left in possession.

✝✝✝

As I fled I felt as if someone had knifed me in the guts. The thought that Leofflæd was dead made me wish that I'd been killed as well. What was worse, I'd been forced to abandon her body. Imagine my relief then when I reached the baggage train to find her alive and well. She had been knocked out by a glancing axe blow to her head. However, it could have been much more serious had she not been wearing a good quality helmet. Cei, Erik and two of our fyrd had fought their way clear, carrying her unconscious body to safety whilst I was doing my imitation of a berserker.

The blow to her head had made her sick and incredibly bad-tempered. I could only imagine how sore her head must be. She had vomited several times and that did little to improve her mood. When I threw my arms around her in relief I was roughly pushed away with a volley of curses. I didn't mind and stood their grinning like a loon.

I was full of gratitude and promised each of her rescuers a farmstead of their own if we survived the war and defeated the Danes. They were suitably grateful, but I sensed that they thought the likelihood of Wessex driving the heathen horde out of the kingdom was remote.

We formed up to defend the baggage train but the Danes gave up the pursuit before they reached us. I learned later that we had lost over three hundred men, but our estimate of enemy dead and seriously wounded was twice that number.

The death of both the hereræswa, Pæga, and Bishop Heahmund was a serious blow and it was with a heavy heart that we retraced our steps to the security of Wintanceaster after the monks had dealt with the wounded and loaded the more seriously injured into the wagons of the baggage train. One suggested that the Lady Leofflæd and I should travel in one of the wagons.

It was the first time I'd heard her referred to in that way but, of course, as the wife of an ealdorman he was perfectly correct. Needless to say we both refused: me politely, my wife indignantly.

We reached Wintanceaster at dusk that day, the twenty second of March. All I wanted to do was have a soak in a tub and then sleep for a year. The soak wasn't possible because of our wounds, many of which had required stitching and bandaging, so we had to be content with a wipe down by the king's servants. Just as we were about to go to sleep, a cheerful page arrived with a polite request that we attend the king in the main hall. I nearly threw something at the grinning boy, but then I realised that it was Ulfrid, the Lady Ealhswith's brother.

We hadn't seen much of Ælfred's wife since arriving in Wintanceaster two months ago. She had been heavily pregnant then and was now recovering from giving birth to a daughter, who the royal couple had named Æthelflæd. Little did I realise at the time what a pivotal role she was to play in the history of both Wessex and Mercia.

'Ah, Jørren, excellent. I'm sorry to drag you from a well-earned rest but the king has a vital task for your scouts,' Ælfred said as I entered the hall.

Æthelred looked pale and wan and he winced in pain as he gestured for his brother to continue. The sweet and sickly stench of rotting flesh hung in the air and I knew that the gangrene in his wounded thigh had got much worse. His wife, Wulfthryth, fussed over him and Bishop Asser knelt in prayer by the side of the chair in which the king sat. It would need a real miracle if he was to recover.

Then I noticed the king's two sons: Æthelhelm and Æthelwold, standing beside their distraught mother. The elder must have been eleven at the time and stared around him with a vacant look. I had heard that he was simple-minded and it looked as if the rumours were true. Æthelwold, who was two years younger than his brother, looked very much all there. He was staring venomously at his uncle and I was pretty sure that he would prove to be a problem for Ælfred when he was older.

If Ælfred was as ruthless as some kings I'd heard of, he would have disposed of both his nephews as potential challengers for the throne; either by imprisoning them well out of sight and mind, or by having them quietly killed. The fact that Ælfred treated them with compassion says much about how honourable he was.

'I want your scouts to track the Danes and let me know where they are headed to next, and in what numbers,' Ælfred was saying as my thoughts were dragged back to the present.

'Very good, lord.'

'One more thing; following the death of Pæga, Wessex is without a hereræswa.'

I'm afraid I immediately jumped to the conclusion that I was about to be offered the prestigious appointment, but I was brought down to earth with a bump by Ælfred's next words.

'Whilst I value your service and good advice, the ealdormen of Wessex don't really know you and they would never accept you in the role.'

He smiled to rob his words of any offence.

'However, the king and I would value your advice on who you would recommend for the appointment. We would, of course, like you to remain as chief of scouts and you will naturally have a powerful voice in the Witenaġemot as the Ealdorman of Berrocscir.'

I had the feeling that Ælfred knew exactly how my mind was working and was trying to let me down gently. I thought he was wrong. My military advice to date had been sound and I knew that I had distinguished myself in battle. None of the other ealdormen who had joined the army to date had impressed me. The only one who had, Ethelwulf, my predecessor as ealdorman, was dead.

I left feeling thoroughly disgruntled to give my scouts the bad news that they would be riding out again immediately. However hard I tried not to, I knew that I would resent whoever was chosen as Pæga's replacement. However, that didn't happen for some time.

The next day I went in search of the boy I'd captured at the Battle of Meretum. I asked Erik where he was and he said that the steward had taken him as a slave to work as a spit-boy. I was already feeling bad-tempered and I set off to find the steward and reclaim my property.

'Where is my captive?' I barked at him when I had run him to earth. 'The Danish boy I captured at Meretum. I am told you have taken him unlawfully and put him to work as a spit boy.'

'Oh him. He's useless for anything else; he doesn't speak any English and is a gormless fool.'

'He was not yours to employ, steward. And I'm an ealdorman, you will call me lord.'

'Yes, lord,' he replied putting just enough emphasis on the last word to make it sound like an insult.

I knew that I was being boorish and had probably just made a new enemy, but I didn't care. I went into the hall and found the boy, his flesh half scorched and dripping with sweat as he turned the spit on which a large boar was roasting.

'Boy, yes you. Stop that and come with me.'

He looked startled at being addressed in his own language, although I learned later that he was in fact from Sweoland and not Danmǫrk. Then he grinned and nodded, leaving the spit and coming towards me. One of the other spit boys, recovering at the side of the hall from his own stint, swore at him and rushed to continue the rotation of the boar before it started to burn on one side.

After he had washed the sweat and dirt away, I got one of the servants to find him a clean tunic and trousers before I interrogated him. His name was Bjarne and his father had been a hearth warrior sworn to serve Jarl Fionnbharr. He had been taken along as a ship's boy on the jarl's own longship until he turned thirteen, when he'd been accepted as a warrior under training by Fionnbharr, largely because of the losses the jarl had sustained in Wessex. The man who had used him as bait, and then been killed after I'd knocked Bjarne out, had been his father.

Getting information out of him was like extracting a tooth from a wolf. He was surly, defiant and swore at me a lot. Erik had joined me and he cuffed the boy around the head every time he cursed me and used far worse words back at him. Danish and Swedish were different languages but it seemed they shared similar foul language.

In fact, Bjarne spoke Danish quite well, as I found out later; you had to if you were part of the heathen army as the majority of its warriors were Danes. He said he knew nothing about the state of the enemy forces until I threatened to give him back to the steward as a spit boy. After that he became more cooperative.

He told me that Ívarr the Boneless had been killed fighting to keep a throne he'd usurped in Irlond. That was good news as we were always worried that he and his army would return and join his brother, Halfdan. He also told me that seven earls had been killed in the battles fought since the beginning of the year. The term earl was new to me but I learned that, whilst jarl meant chieftain and could mean both a leader of a warband or a major landholder, the latter were increasingly being called earls to differentiate them from minor landowners and captains of warbands.

Their army was disheartened over the severe losses they'd sustained in the past few months and many wanted to quit Wessex. A few had left already. This was music to my ears, if true. However, rumours that King Æthelred was on his deathbed had encouraged them to stay so that they could exploit the chaos they thought would follow his demise.

I went to see Ælfred and told him what Bjarne had said. However, he was sceptical and tended discount the testimony of a young Dane. Bishop Asser backed him up and maintained that heathens couldn't be trusted. I went away feeling even more frustrated than ever.

I was impressed by young Bjarne's spirit and decided to offer him a place with my trainee scouts if he would swear to be my man. Unlike Asser I knew that Vikings, like most Anglo-Saxons, would rather die than break an oath.

Bjarne surprised me but not swearing to be my man immediately when I offered him the choice of that or returning to be a spit boy. It showed how seriously he took giving his word. Erik explained that what bothered the lad was the fact that he's already given his oath. Erik said that his jarl was undoubtedly dead and therefore he was free to give his fealty to a new lord, but Bjarne stubbornly maintained that there was no proof of that.

'I'll give you two days to decide, either you give me your oath or you go back to the steward. Erik, take him away to join the other trainees.'

I had ten boys between the ages of eleven and fourteen training to join my warband. Some were the thralls we'd rescued and others were orphans from the streets of Wintanceaster who wanted to better themselves.

Bjarne asked to see me the following day. He'd been surprised how easily the other boys had accepted him and were even willing to teach him English. He had evidently overcome his scruples and he gave me his oath. In due course he proved to be one of my most courageous warriors. Erik was happy too. He'd been missing Ulf and Tove but now he had a fellow Viking to share experiences with. The two became fast friends, despite their age difference.

†††

It took a month for my wounds, and those of Leofflæd, to heal sufficiently for us to ride without fear of tearing the stiches and re-opening the various wounds we'd suffered. We found this extremely frustrating as both of us were eager to go and visit our vills at Silcestre and Basingestoches.

Of course, we received regular reports from the reeves. The inhabitants had returned and life was gradually getting back to normal. The land had been tilled and new crops had been sown. On the down side my scouts reported that the Vikings had returned to Readingum. Thankfully they seemed to have stopped raiding further into Wessex and their attention now turned to southern Mercia. No doubt the fact that King Burghred seemed loathe to oppose them made Mercia a more attractive prospect than Wessex, where they had suffered grievous casualties for little reward.

King Æthelred's health continued to decline and, despite the successful amputation of his gangrenous leg, everyone knew that he was not destined to live for much longer. We left in early April to visit my two vills in Hamtunscīr before travelling on to some of the various vills I now owned as Ealdorman of Berrocscir. The ealdorman's hall was at Readingum and many of my dozen vills in the shire were located between there and Eatun further to the east along the Temes. They were lost to me pro tem so I decided to base myself at Ferendone at the western end of my shire for the time being.

Ferendone proved to be a vill of a similar size to Silcestre. There was a hall, a small timber church and a dozen or so huts. It was surrounded by five farmsteads, all of which were now owned by me and each had a tenant. It was a pleasant place in the wide valley that runs from Oxenaforda in Mercia to Suindune in Wiltunscir. It had rich soil and was a prosperous settlement, as yet untouched by war. The reeve seemed honest enough, although the priest was uneducated and had a wife and a brood of small children. The latter didn't bother me, there were plenty of married priests, although the more devout held that clerics should be celibate. It was the fact that he couldn't read and barely knew anything of the Bible that concerned me. I would talk to Bishop Asser about him when there were less pressing matters to concern us.

The day after our arrival at Ferendone a messenger arrived to say that King Æthelred had died on the twenty third of April and that a witenagemot had been called at Winburne for the twenty-ninth of the month, the day after the funeral. I wondered why Æthelred was being buried at Winburne instead of at Wintanceaster, but apparently it was specified in his will. All ealdormen and king's thegns of Wessex, including the sub-kingdoms of Ēast Seaxna Rīce, Cent and Suth-Seaxe,   had been summoned, although it was unlikely that more than half would be able to attend in these troubled times.

I left Leofflæd to oversee certain improvements I wanted at Ferendone, especially the construction of a larger, stone built hall and a palisade, and set of for Winburne with an escort of eight men and boys. The rest of my warriors were split between the various vills I owned to train the fyrd and to select boys who would join my warband when they were ready.

I had foolishly assumed that the route between Ferendone and Winburne was safe. Nevertheless I had put out Erik and Bjarne as scouts. It would take at least two days to get there and so I decided to stay for the night at Basingestoches and then travel to Winburne via Wintanceaster the next day. We had just travelled through a large wooded area and were about to emerge into open country three miles short of Basingestoches when the two scouts came galloping back.

'There are Danes attacking your vill, lord,' Erik said breathlessly.

'How many?'

'Perhaps fifty, lord, but our warriors and the fyrd are making a fight of it.'

I had left five of my warriors at Basingestoches and the ceorls of fighting age numbered something over sixty. They slightly outnumbered the heathens but they might have been caught unawares and, despite their training recently, a farmer was no match for an experienced Viking warrior.

When we arrived my men were making a stand in the centre of the settlement whilst the women and children fled towards the woods. When they saw my eight men and me appear, they stopped and cheered. I gestured exasperatedly for them to continue to flee; there was no guarantee as to the outcome after all.

We dismounted at the outskirts and, leaving Bjarne to hold the horses, I signalled for my men to climb up onto the rooftops at the rear of where the fighting was occurring. I glanced around from my vantage point and saw several dead women, children and the odd male slave and villein in the streets around the central square. Men on both sides who had died in the fighting lay in groups where they'd fallen. I muttered curses at the Danes below us and we commenced sending arrow after arrow into the rear of their shield wall.

The result was utter confusion in their ranks and men started to fall with arrows in the necks, backs and legs. They had suffered ten casualties before the rear rank managed to turn around and use their shields to protect themselves. It was too dangerous to shoot over the rear rank because of the risk of hitting our own men. Instead we left our bows and climbed down to the ground.

I swung my shield, which was on my back, around and grabbed hold of a new weapon I'd devised recently. It was a mace; a short, thick wooden stock with a heavy ball of iron at the end. The blacksmith who had made it to my design had affixed thin, cone-shaped points to the ball. They were long enough to punch through the metal of a helmet and the leather arming cap underneath before driving into the victim's brain, killing him instantly. That was the theory at any rate and I'd been itching to try it out; now was my chance.

We formed a small shield wall with two men on each side of me and four behind. We banged shields with the warriors facing us and I swung my heavy mace overhand to crush the helmet of the man opposite me. I felt a jar as mace and head collided and he dropped from sight without a sound. I grunted in satisfaction and repeated the move with the man behind him.

My companions were still battling with the Danish shield wall but I had moved slightly ahead of them. Now the backs of those fighting the men of Basingestoches faced me. I swung my mace again and another Dane died. However, I had been foolish. I was protected to my front by my shield but my flanks were exposed. I felt an inexpertly wielded spear glance off the side of my byrnie and then an axeman on my left raised his weapon above his head to chop me down.

I thrust the point on the top of the mace into the eye of the spearman but I knew I was going to die at the hands of the axeman. Then one of my men appeared at my side. He thrust his dagger upwards under the axeman's byrnie and into his groin. The eyes under the rim of my attacker's helmet registered surprise, then agony. A second later I sideswiped my mace into his face, crushing his cheekbone and his jaw.

I stepped back and glanced to my right to nod my thanks to my saviour only to see that it was Bjarne, who I'd left with the horses. I was speechless with amazement. Rescuing the lad from life as a spit boy had saved my life.

The Danes had had enough. They had lost half their number, and for nothing. They ran and my victorious men ran after them. The ceorls of the fyrd weren't slowed down by the weight of chain mail and they were intent on vengeance. Six more Danes were killed by them and then my warriors and I - now mounted once more - overtook the remainder. Some turned to fight and that delayed us. By the time we'd disposed of them the remaining few had reached the trees and we let them go.

I gave the crushed helmets to the blacksmith to melt down and reuse the metal but we collected the byrnies, good helmets and the Danish weapons for the fyrd to make good use of. The dead Vikings, and there were none alive after the women had returned and cut the throats of the wounded with relish, yielded a small fortune in coins, hack silver, gold jewellery such as cloak broaches and arm rings. I kept my share, distributed half of the rest to my warband and gave the other half to the reeve to look after the widows and orphans.

Apart from the odd flesh wound my escort were unharmed. I took one of the Viking shields and the shortest of the swords and presented it to Bjarne together with a small silver arm ring. I was rewarded by an incredulous smile and then the boy's face grew serious.

'Thank you, lord. You do me great honour. I am your man now and always.'

My men could well have jeered as the boy's pompous little speech, but they didn't. They cheered and I noted Erik's look of pride at his protégé.

The next day I left the inhabitants to clear up the aftermath of the fight and we continued on our way once our few minor wounds had been attended to. When we arrived at Winburne we found the settlement full to overflowing. With so many dignitaries, both secular and clerical, present I was unable to obtain accommodation in the hall, or anywhere else with a roof, and so I had to camp in the open with my men.

It was no hardship of course, and I preferred their company to that of some of the nobles present, but I felt aggrieved that, once again, no one had thought to reserve appropriate lodging for me. Later I realised that the man in charge of allocating accommodation was the king's steward. No doubt he was exercising a petty revenge for robbing him of Bjarne's services as a slave.

†††

Before mass the next day I sought an audience with Ælfred but I was told that I would have to wait my turn by the sentry on guard outside the hall. He was in a meeting with the new Archbishop of Canterbury, Ælfric, Bishop Asser and the late King Æthelred's mother and her two sons.

'I have information that the Danes are on the move again and are not that far from Wintanceaster,' I hissed at him. 'Now, announce me or take the consequences.'

Wisely the man scuttled inside to have a quiet word with Ælfred. A second or two later he reappeared, leaving the door open for me to enter. I walked in and saw that there was another man near Ælfred who I didn't recognise. Everyone looked at me in annoyance because of my interruption but he positively glared at me.

'This better be important, Jørren,' Ælfred barked at me. 'What's this about the Danes? My latest information is that they are still ensconced at Readingum.'

'Yesterday I defeated a patrol fifty strong who were attacking Basingestoches, lord. That's all I know, but I suggest we should send out patrols to find out what exactly is going on. We are isolated down here in the south of the kingdom.'

'It's my job to advise the king on what action, if any we need to take,' the stranger snapped.

'The king is dead, in case you've forgotten, Lord Eadda' the Lady Wulfthryth, said with some venom, 'and the Witenaġemot has yet to meet and choose his replacement.'

Eadda was a name I'd dimly remembered hearing before. He was a king's thegn from Sūþrīgescir who I'd heard mention of as a fearsome fighter. Perhaps he was the new hereræswa? If so, he wasn't introduced to me. Perhaps Ælfred was too embarrassed to do so?

'Of course, lady,' Eadda said smoothly, but his tone implied that there was only one ætheling who was a candidate.

No one in his right mind was going to choose the twelve-year old Æthelhelm or his ten year old brother, Æthelwold. Both were too young to rule, especially at a time of crisis like this. However, Wulfthryth could be expected to promote her sons cause regardless.

Ælfred thought for a moment.

'What Ealdorman Jørren said makes sense. If the Danes are causing trouble again we need to know about it. Eadda, please send out scouts towards both Basingestoches and Readingum to see what they can find.'

'Yes, lord,' Eadda said with a curt nod and left the hall.

He would do as he was bid but it was evident that he thought it all a waste of time. I didn't understand his antipathy towards me at the time, although I later realised that he thought of me as a rival for his appointment and would do almost anything to discredit me.

I bowed to Ælfred and Wulfthryth and took my leave. However, I didn't return to my tent. Instead I went to find Cei and the rest of my warriors.

'I'm sorry to wake you but I have a task for you,' I told them when they had gathered outside their tents. 'We need to find out if the heathen army is still in Readingum. Eadda, who I believe may be the new hereræswa, has been told to send out his own scouts to see what the Danes are up to, but I have reason to believe that they won't try very hard. Make sure you avoid them as well as the Danes. Report back to me, and only to me.'

†††

It was three days before they returned. During that time King Æthelred had been buried with all due ceremony, the Witenaġemot had met and elected Ælfred to the throne, much to the disgust of Æthelwold in particular, and the new king had been crowned by Archbishop Æthelred. Most of the dignitaries who'd been in attendance had departed and Eadda's scouts had returned having found no sign of the Danes.

As they had only been away for just over a day, that was hardly surprising. There hadn't been time for them to cover the return journey of one hundred and fifty miles, make a cautious approach to Readingum and ascertain how many Danes were left there, let alone locate the main body of the enemy if they weren't there.

When my men came back they had not only found Readingum practically deserted, they had located the Danes encamped at Turkilestun, some fifty miles south-west of Readingum. I puzzled over this before going to see King Ælfred. Obviously Wintanceaster wasn't the target; they were too far to the west. The only thing I could think of was that they were heading for Wiltun, the previous capital of Wessex. Perhaps they thought that the treasury was still there?

I went to see the king and took Cei and Erik with me. This time I had no problem being admitted and found Ælfred talking to Eadda.

'Ah, Jørren; just the man,' the king said greeting me with a smile.

The warmth of his welcome contrasted sharply with Eadda's scowl.

'I was telling Eadda about the wall around your vill of Silcestre and the palisade that you are erecting around Ferendone. I'm convinced that it's the only way to defend Wessex against the Danes. Inside these burhs we can protect the people and prevent the enemy from controlling the immediate area.'

'They are a waste of effort and money, cyning,' Eadda said derisively. 'The Danes will either ignore them or pen our people inside until they starve to death.'

'I agree with the king,' I replied, shaking my head. 'The Danes don't have siege engines and they would lose many men trying to scale the walls. Halfdan and Ubba are already highly unpopular for the number of dead they have incurred so far. They won't risk losing significant numbers attacking a burh. As to starving the inhabitants, we must ensure that all available food and animals are housed in the burhs. That will also prevent the Danes from foraging.

'As to controlling the area, no burh should be more than twenty miles away from the next burh. We need to build a network of herepaths, based on the old Roman road system, to interconnect these burhs. This would mean that our people could reach safety quickly and our warriors will be able to congregate swiftly to fight the heathens wherever they appear. Lastly I suggest a system of beacons on the hilltops to give warning of any attack.'

Ælfred positively beamed at me whilst Eadda spluttered, trying to find fault with my suggestions. All he could come up with was the expense of doing as I had proposed.

'That's true,' I conceded. 'But can we afford not to. The Danes are losing men, but so are we. The harvest is disrupted and settlements and farmsteads are laid waste. Furthermore, the burhs could also be safe havens in which trade and manufacturing can carry on. Armouries, blacksmiths, royal mints and trading posts could all be sited within the burhs; and they could be used as supply depots for our army.'

'It's a fantasy. How long is all this going to take, and who is going to pay for it?' Eadda demanded.

'We all must. We have to rid Wessex of this scourge or we will all end up as thralls,' Ælfred declared in a tone that brooked no argument.

In response Eadda threw up his hands in despair. Cei coughed politely at my side, which brought me back to the reason I was here.

'Cyning, this isn't why I needed to see you. The heathen army has left Readingum, all but a small handful that is. My scouts found them at Turkilestun, fifty miles to the south-west. My guess is that they are making for Wiltun, a day's march from where they were yesterday.'

'Why did you send out your men; I'd already send out mine,' Eadda demanded loudly.

'It seems it's a good job I did. Yours didn't find the enemy, did they?' I retorted.

'Quiet!' Ælfred shouted. 'I won't tolerate this unseemly behaviour – from either of you. Why Wiltun?' he continued in a normal voice.

'It's where the treasury used to be, cyning,' I said quietly whilst Eedda continued to glower at me. 'Perhaps someone has told the Danes it's still there.'

'How many men do we have available?' he asked Eadda, seemingly having reached a decision.

'Just your gesith, cyning, and the local fyrd. Perhaps two hundred men in all.'

'We'll just have to hope messengers can catch up some of those who have just departed. We leave within the hour.'

Thankfully two of the other ealdormen and their households hadn't yet departed. They and their escorts made our total up to three hundred. I sent riders to Silcestre and Basingestoches to send every available man; my other vills were too far away. Ælfred's messengers managed to raise five hundred more so that, by the time that Wiltun hove into view we had around a thousand men. However, a significant number of them had little or no battle experience. It wasn't much of an army with which to tackle over two thousand Danes.

Chapter Fifteen

May 871

We camped three miles south of Wiltun and I sent my scouts forward to find out what was happening in the settlement. Eadda had protested loudly at the use of my men instead of his scouts, but the king had evidently lost faith in Eadda's men after he'd been misled by them. I had a feeling that the new hereræswa was treading on quite thin ice.

They returned with the news that the settlement had been pillaged and burnt. The Vikings were encamped a mile outside it on the north bank of the narrow river that ran to the south of Wiltun. I asked Erik for an estimate of numbers and he thought that there were no more than fifteen hundred. It was enough. King Ælfred had significantly fewer and the majority of them were local levies; farmers who were poorly equipped and trained.

'Our only chance is a night attack,' I told the king when he called a meeting of his senior nobles.

'Too dangerous,' Eadda responded immediately, 'men get lost in the dark or attack each other.'

'I'm not talking about the fyrd,' I replied, trying to keep my temper. 'I'll take fifty men, burn their tents and run off their horses. It'll unsettle them and reduce their morale. With any luck we'll kill a few as well.'

'Waste of time,' Edda muttered. 'Go ahead and get yourself killed. You'll not be missed.'

'That's enough!' Ælfred said sharply. 'Eadda, if you can't say anything constructive, don't say anything. Jørren, perhaps it's worth a try, but don't risk men's lives. We've few enough as it is.'

I nodded and left the king's tent to go and find Alric. I hadn't seen him since the meeting of the Witenaġemot but someone had told me that he and his men had joined the army yesterday.

'Perhaps we should use fire arrows,' my brother suggested, after we had embraced.

We had grown close again after his rescue but somehow we had gradually become more distant from each other. Perhaps it was because others had become close friends and the old intimacy wasn't there anymore? I was therefore surprised how much I had missed him when we both went our separate ways. Now we were reunited I realised how fond I was of him, but I'm not sure he felt the same way. Perhaps he was envious of the fact that I had children and he did not. My musings were interrupted when he spoke again.

'It'll cause confusion and do damage without risking our men's lives.'

It was a good idea. Undoubtedly the Danes would charge into the woods surrounding their camp, seeking revenge. My warband were adept at killing quietly at night and we could ambush small groups of Danes once they were isolated from the rest.

I gave Alric the task of killing the sentries at the horse lines and running off the animals whilst I took forty bowmen up wind of the enemy camp. Just before we parted Alric said something which I ignored at the time and bitterly regretted later.

'By the way, there were four men asking after you earlier today. They looked like experienced warriors, but they were more than that; I got the distinct impression that they were professional killers.'

'Perhaps my reputation had spread. Maybe they wanted to join me?'

'I don't think so. They didn't strike me as men who admired you; quite the opposite.'

I shrugged.

'We leave at midnight.'

†††

It was a balmy night for late May when we moved into position. It was dry with a moderate wind blowing towards the enemy camp from where we stood. More warriors stood concealed in the wood behind us.

Øwli and Cei had already checked that there were no sentries in the trees. The nearest ones, as far we could tell, were around the dying embers of the campfire nearest to us. We had built several fire pits at the edge of the trees where low fires burned just enough to enable us to set alight the oily scraps of cloth wrapped around the sharp end of our arrows.

When an owl hooted three times I knew that Alric had taken care of the sentries at the horse lines and I drew back my bowstring and sent my first flaming arrow speeding towards the nearest tent. Like us, the Danes oiled their leather tents to keep out the rain. Unfortunately this made them extremely flammable. The first tents hit went up with a whoosh and the fire spread so quickly that the men sleeping inside were either burnt to death or died of smoke inhalation.

Some reacted quickly enough to escape, but some of those were already on fire and ran around seeking a means to put out the flames. All they succeeded in doing was to spread the fires.

The four sentries had got to their feet when the fire arrows first hit home, only to be killed by more fire arrows. One fell into the remains of their campfire, scattering the smouldering firewood. The grass around the campfire was dry and caught light. Aided by the wind, the flames spread to the dry grass all around, adding to the confusion.

We sent four more volleys of fire arrows into the heart of the camp and then retreated into the woods. As expected, the furious Vikings charged after us. Some of the young boys training to be scouts collected our bows and quivers as we joined the others already waiting behind trees to ambush our pursuers.

I brought my breathing under control and waited silently, crouching behind a bush, for a Dane to appear. I was so intent on listening for their approach, coming from the direction of the camp, that I neglected my rear. I heard a soft footfall behind me and was in the process of turning to see who it was when I felt a sudden blinding pain in my head and I knew no more, slipping into oblivious unconsciousness.

When I awoke it was with a splitting headache. I was tied up, gagged and blindfolded, but could see through the material that it was morning. I was lying on a hard floor that moved and jolted, adding to my discomfort. Obviously, I was in a cart and being taken somewhere. I rapidly discounted my captors as Danes. They would have just killed me out of hand.

Besides, I could hear someone speaking English nearby; English with a Northumbrian accent. It was at that moment that I remembered what Alric had told me about four men asking about me. I knew then, without being told, who my captors worked for.

I'd quite forgotten about Ceadda the murdering rapist and his father, Cynemær. The man had sworn to kill me and I wondered why I was still alive. There could only be one reason: he wanted to kill me himself, probably slowly and painfully.

When they camped that night I was dragged from the cart and tied to a tree. Shortly afterwards my blindfold was removed and the smirking face of Hroðulf, Ceadda's accomplice, loomed into view. He unlaced his trousers and pissed all over me. His men laughed and came to do the same. I swore at that moment that they would die, although how I was going to achieve that, trussed up and stinking of urine, I had no idea.

✝✝✝

I wasn't given anything to eat or drink that evening and my stomach started to protest. My mouth was dry and my head throbbed from the blow that had knocked me out. I have to say I've had better nights.

I tried to free my hands but they'd tied me up so tightly that I worried that the circulation to my hands was so restricted that the tissue might die. All I did when I tried to loosen the rope was make it worse and rub my wrists raw. Eventually I fell into a fitful sleep.

The next morning I was allowed a sip of water and my hands were untied. I had no feeling in them at first and then the rush of blood into them actually hurt. They abandoned the cart and I was helped to mount a horse. However, they tied my feet together under its belly and one of them held a leading rein so that I couldn't ride off. It wasn't necessary. My steed was such a sorry nag that I doubt if I could have gone more than a few yards before they caught up with me.

I could tell by the position of the sun in the sky that we were heading northwards, but I didn't know exactly where we were. My captors avoided the main roads and stuck to small tracks. It soon became evident that they were lost. The man who was supposed to be guiding them had taken a wrong turn somewhere and an argument broke out. Hroðulf wanted to go back and find where they had gone wrong but two of the others insisted that would be foolhardy.

They might well be right. My warband were all expert trackers and, although it would have taken them until morning to find that I was missing, I hoped that they would be somewhere behind us. I felt the faint stirrings of hope, but then they faded. Ælfred would never give them permission to leave on the day of a battle. He had few enough men as it was without losing some of his best fighters.

In the end my captors decided to press on and hope they came to a settlement where they could ask for directions. However, the area seemed devoid of habitation. Rolling grassland was interspersed with woods but the only sign of life, apart from wild animals and birds, was the sheep that dotted the hillsides. I came to the conclusion that we were riding through the king's hunting forest to the north of Sarum.

It was after midday when we stopped again. Another argument broke out; this time two of my captors maintained that we needed to head north-east instead of north, but Hroðulf and the man who was supposed to know the area insisted that there was a danger that they might encounter Danes if they went too far to the east. It was true that only half the enemy army had been at Wiltun, but I was fairly certain that the rest would either be well to the east of us, or even back in Lundenwic.

'Any fool can follow the old Roman roads,' Hroðulf told the guide scornfully. 'Do you have any idea where we are?'

The man flushed with anger and his hand went to the hilt of his sword. In a flash the other three did the same and the guide forced himself to relax.

'We're in the royal hunting park north of Sarum,' he replied stiffly.

'And how big an area is that?' Hroðulf asked.

'I don't know; perhaps three hundred square miles,' he admitted reluctantly. 'But we are in the northern half of it.'

'Somewhere in an area of one hundred and fifty miles then?' another man said, spitting at the guide's feet. 'Great!'

The sip of water I was given did little to moisten my parched mouth and I nearly broke a tooth on the hard, stale chunk of bread that accompanied it. Despite my efforts to keep my spirits up, I was now wallowing in a pit of despair. No one knew where I was and I felt myself getting weaker on the bare subsistence diet I was given. If I didn't try and escape soon I'd be too feeble to do so; and it would probably take another week to ride to Bernicia, where Cynemær lived.

Later that day we emerged over a rise to see an old Roman road below us. My spirits rose. There was always traffic on such roads; in normal times at any rate. However, all I could see today was a farmer and a boy with a cart full of vegetables.

'Which road is this?' Hroðulf asked the wary farmer.

'Why, the one from Acemannesceastre to Silcestre, lord.'

Acemannesceastre meant *aching men's camp*, the place the Romans had called Aqua Sulis, though there was little there now except ruins and a monastery founded by Saint David two centuries before, or so legend had it. The mention of my vill at Silcestre warmed my heart. I was even more encouraged when I heard my captors discussing which direction to head in.

'Silcestre is where several old roads meet,' the guide said excitedly. 'There is one that goes from there due north into Mercia.'

'Very well, but I want to avoid the settlement itself,' Hroðulf said, to my intense disappointment.

'Why? We need more supplies, especially bread, cheese, lentils and barley, so we're going to have to stop somewhere and buy them,' one of the others pointed out.

'Very well, but one of us will have to stay outside the settlement with this piece of shit,' he said, indicating me. 'I don't want him to have the chance of shouting for help.'

If I was left with one man, there was a chance that I might be able to overpower him, but I suspected that they would tie me up before leaving. Unfortunately I was right.

The others had gone for perhaps half an hour, leaving me tied to a tree, when two girls aged about twelve or thirteen entered the clearing collecting wood. My guard immediately took an interest in them and started to talk to them instead of killing them, which is what he should have done if he wanted to survive. I vaguely recognised both of them; I seemed to remember that they were twin sisters, villeins' daughters from Silcestre. Both stared curiously at me whilst the man was trying to flirt with them and then recognition dawned in the eyes of one of them.

I shook my head furiously to tell her not to say anything. She tugged at the sleeve of her companion and whispered something to her. Both girls immediately ran back towards the settlement, leaving my guard staring after them looking perplexed. He should have been alarmed, but he was the dimmest of the four men and he merely shrugged, scowled at me and went to the stream to refill his waterskin.

I pleaded with him to let me have a drink and he came back with a cup full of water. I bent to drink from it but he threw it in my face with a derisory laugh. I swore to myself then that he would die of thirst if I ever managed to turn the tables.

It seemed an age before the other three men returned but it was probably less than an hour. My heart soared when I saw that they weren't alone. They had been disarmed and they were accompanied by Redwald, the two girls, Wealhmær and the other warriors I'd left to protect Silcestre.

My guard went for his sword, but his hand fell to his side when he saw several archers aim at his chest. I wept with relief when Redwald cut me free and we embraced. He quickly released me though, apologising and saying that I stank. I did, and so I went into the stream to try and get rid of the worst of the stench.

I promised the two girls a substantial reward after I learned that they had run back and told Redwald what they'd seen. He had already heard that there were strangers in the settlement and he put two and two together and made four. It took a little while for him and his men to locate the three strangers and then they came to rescue me.

My initial reaction was to think that he should have freed me first, but then I realised that he'd been sensible. If Redwald had done that he might have risked losing my other captors.

Whilst in the stream I had poured too much water down my parched throat and I was immediately sick. I soon recovered and ate and drank sparingly after that. Two days later I presided over the trial of Hroðulf and the others. I forgot about my desire to make the man who'd guarded me die of thirst; it wasn't in my nature to be so vindictive, however much he deserved it. All four were hanged from a large oak tree beside the main road outside the settlement. I had intended to leave them there as a warning to others, or perhaps send the heads back to Cynemær, but in the end I decided it was better if he was left wondering what had happened to them. Their bodies were therefore cut down and buried deep in a wood.

At some stage in the future I would have to kill him and his other sons to end the blood feud; otherwise he would only try again and the next time I might not be so fortunate.

Chapter Sixteen

Summer 871

Wealhmær and several warriors escorted me when I returned to Ferendone a few days later, just in case there were any Danes still around, but we saw none. Leofflæd was overjoyed to see me and embraced me so hard I thought she'd crack a rib or two. She had been told that I had fled abroad to avoid fighting the Danes at Wiltun. Of course, she never believed that I would do such a thing and threatened to kill anyone who repeated the scurrilous rumour.

She arranged a feast to celebrate my safe return and, tempted as I was to drink myself into oblivion to forget the whole miserable experience, I stayed sober enough to enjoy a proper reunion with Leofflæd in our bed that night.

It wasn't until the next day that I learned what had happened at Wiltun. Several of my warband who'd taken part were eager to enlighten me, but my wife had banned any talk of war during the celebrations of my safe return. However, as soon as I sat down in the hall to break my fast after morning mass the next day my warriors crowded around me.

'Sit down, for the love of Christ,' I reproved them with a smile. 'Cei, you are my oldest friend; tell me what happened.'

He gave me an appreciative look. He had always felt uncertain of our relationship. Although he'd been with me from the beginning, he had never forgotten his origins as a slave; and a runaway slave at that. I had a feeling that he resented the easy relations I had development with some of the other boys and young men who'd joined us as time went on. He had never really put his background behind him and, as a result, he tended to stay in the shadows. He certainly never showed his feelings openly. Now my words seemed to give him the confidence he'd lacked hitherto and he launched into the tale with gusto.

'As you know, the Danes numbered some fifteen hundred whilst the king's army was much smaller. Your brother Alric told us what happened at the war council the next morning. Eadda was all for withdrawing but King Ælfred wouldn't hear of it. He asked why you weren't present and sent one of the sentries to find you. The delay annoyed the hereræswa intensely, of course, but he couldn't conceal his delight when you couldn't be found.'

I wondered then if Eadda had anything to do with my disappearance. My abductors seemed to have found me remarkably easily.

'No one knew where you were but we were certain that there must be a good reason for your absence,' Cei continued. 'Of course, Eadda claimed that you'd run away like a coward and apparently your brother had to be restrained from hitting him. Anyway, against Eadda's advice, the king took up a position at the head of the re-entrant south of Brydancumb with the shield wall in the middle and archers along the hilltops on either flank.

'The Danes came charging into the re-entrant but those in the lead stopped and formed a shield wall as soon as they realised that they were walking into a trap. However, those behind milled about, uncertain what was happening. I was with our archers who were some distance away from the thousand or so Danes in the rear, but we were above them and we were able to rain arrows down on the rear ranks, despite the long range.

'Tens were killed or wounded and then tens became a hundred or more. This infuriated those Danes who were suffering casualties and they started to ascend the slopes towards us. They held their shields in front of them and this reduced the effectiveness of our volleys, but advancing like that slowed them down. The heathens were still suffering casualties but our archers were now in danger, so Ælfred ordered us to withdraw.

'Meanwhile, about five hundred Danes had advanced up the re-entrant to attack our shield wall. The two clashed and appeared to be evenly matched. Of course, our warriors held the higher ground and that gave us an advantage. I saw no more as we reformed to the rear and couldn't see what was happening.'

Others who had been in the Saxon shield wall continued the narration but there wasn't much more to tell. The enemy had suffered losses in the hundreds against about ninety on our side during bitter hand to hand fighting. Eventually the Danes withdrew to reform for another attack. We had evidently come off best during the clash between the two shield walls. However, the king's forces were still outnumbered by over two to one and he'd lost the element of surprise.

He therefore withdrew in good order leaving the Danes in control of the battlefield. Technically the day was theirs, but they couldn't afford many more victories like that.

The next day Halfdan and Ubba sent emissaries to Ælfred asking for a meeting. Both sides exchanged hostages and the heathen leaders met the king, Eadda and Bishop Asser in the middle of a ford over the River Nadder south of Wiltun.

None of my men knew the details, but apparently a three-year truce had been agreed whereby the heathen army agreed to leave Wessex in return for a payment of two tons of silver. They had been true to their word and had retreated to Lundenwic. It was only later that we learned that Northumbria had risen in revolt and the Danes would have been forced to withdraw soon in any case.

✝✝✝

My first priority was to seek an audience with the king to explain why I had disappeared. I had enough enemies: men like Eadda who were jealous of the fact that a Jute from Cent had been appointed as Ealdorman of Berrocscir   instead of a Saxon thegn. Even my name, Jørren, although a good Jutish name, sounded more Scandinavian than Saxon. I couldn't let the slur of cowardice go unanswered any longer than necessary. After that I needed to visit the shire's capital of Readingum and see what state it was in following the heathens' withdrawal.

I arrived at Wintanceaster only to find that the king wasn't there. He had called a meeting of the witenaġemot at Certesi in Sūþrīgescir to which all ealdormen, king's thegns and senior clerics had invited. At first I was annoyed that I seem to have been excluded but, as the king's steward explained, rather snidely, no one knew where I was.

It was fifty miles or more to Certesi and the witenaġemot was meeting the day after tomorrow. There was no time to waste. The Danes had left Hamtunscīr and Berrocscir so hopefully my small escort of Cei, Wealhmær, Erik, Bjarne and two boys called Acwel and Lyndon would suffice. The latter pair were both twelve and training to be scouts. Had I known when I first set out where the king was, I would have brought more men with me. The monastery at Certesi was a mere thirty miles from Ludenwic, where the Great Heathen Army was now based. My hope was that the Danes would be busy foraging in Mercia, stocking up with provisions for the coming winter, but no one could be certain of that.

I sent Erik and the two boys ahead to scout the route and set off at a fast pace. It was now midday and we would have to push our horses if I was to arrive at the monastery in time. I was fairly certain that the witenaġemot would meet immediately after mass and a hurried bite to eat. The road was clear, apart from the odd farm cart and a few other travellers, and we stopped for the night just after dark in a clearing by a small river a few miles short of Certesi. Of course, I wasn't expecting to camp and we had no tents, or even food, with us.

Acwel proved to have a useful skill and had tickled three medium sized trout when we'd stopped earlier in the day. It wasn't much of a meal for the seven of us, but it was better than nothing. It rained in the middle of the night and we awoke wet, cold and miserable. My cloak had kept out most of the water, but not all. Some of the others looked like drowned rats, especially Acwel and Lyndon. There was no time to dry out and just before dawn we were on the move again.

Thankfully the rain ceased as the sun rose in the east. When we arrived outside the gates of the monastery we found the area covered in tents large and small. They stretched along the west bank of the Temes and the south bank of a small tributary which joined the bigger river just beyond the monastery. The settlement itself lay to the west of the walled monastic enclosure. I could see why Ælfred had chosen it. It was convenient for the nobles of Cent, Sūþrīgescir and Suth-Seaxe, who had played little part in the war so far, whilst being easily defended in case of attack by the Danes. It wasn't quite so convenient for many of those from Wessex proper, of course.

We chose a spot away from the rest, on the north bank of another small river called the Bourne, which meant stream. Whilst the others got a fire going and took care of the horses, I sent Cei and Bjarne into the nearby settlement to see if they could buy some tents and provisions. I made myself look as presentable as I could in the circumstances and, taking Wealhmær with me as my banner bearer, I rode up to the monastery gates.

I arrived at the church during mass and entered to the disapproving looks of those nearest the door. I wasn't sure whether it was my unkempt appearance or the fact that I was late which upset them, but there was one face there that I recognised and who smiled when he saw me. I went and stood next to Alric, who nodded to Wealhmær before asking me the inevitable question.

'Thank the Lord that you're alive; we all wondered what had happened to you,' he whispered.

'I was abducted by Hroðulf and other thugs hired by Cynemær with, I suspect, the connivance of Eadda,' I whispered back.

'What happened to them?'

'Hanged by the neck until they choked to death. The fools made the mistake of stopping at Silcestre. Otherwise I'm sure that by now I'd be dead at the hands of Cynemær.'

'I'm glad that you're not, otherwise I'd have had to kill him to avenge you,' he replied with a grin.

'I'm going to have to kill him anyway, and his other sons, to end the blood feud,' I said grimly.

By now one or two others were looking at us; no doubt finding our sotto voce mutterings of more interest than the droning of Archbishop Æthelred's endless homily.

'You must tell me more later,' Alric said. 'By the way, Æscwin is here.'

That news gave me a jolt. Obviously he didn't mean my infant son but our eldest brother. I should have realised that he might be present as part of the contingent from Cent. It would be good to see him again, but I had no idea how he'd react to seeing me after I'd absconded with one of his slaves. I didn't have to wait long to find out.

✝✝✝

Officially there were ten shires and sub-kingdoms which made up Wessex at that time. However, Ēast Seaxna Rīce had been overrun by the Danes when they conquered the Kingdom of East Anglia and so there were only nine ealdormen present. Apart from the archbishop, there were another four bishops, including Asser of Wintanceaster, all of whom were also abbots of monasteries. There were four other abbots present, all of whose monasteries but one – Certesi – were in Berrocscir. I hadn't met the abbots of my shire before, but they hastened to speak to me after mass was over.

All were old men and I must have seemed a young pup in comparison. If they thought that, they were too well-mannered to let it show. We walked over to the refectory together to break our fast before the serious business of the day began and I resigned myself to having to sit with them and make polite conversation. However, Bishop Asser rescued me by saying that the king wished me to sit next to him.

I was conceited enough to think that I was being honoured. I should have realised that wasn't the case as I was the youngest, and therefore most junior, ealdorman present. Bishop Asser sat on my other side and Archbishop Æthelred sat at the king's right hand with an elderly man, who I later learned was Ealdorman Odda of Dyfneintscir, next to Æthelred.

Curious glances were directed my way and I noticed with a start that my brother Æscwin was staring hard at me, although I couldn't tell whether he was irate or merely incredulous. I smirked and then my expression changed completely when Ælfred turned to me.

'Why did you run away before Wiltun; it isn't something I would have ever expected of someone who I had trusted enough to make an ealdorman.'

'Cyning, I didn't desert you out of choice!' I replied, perhaps a little too forcefully.

'Have a care, Jørren,' the king shot back. 'Remember who you are addressing.'

'I apologise Cyning, but it is a false accusation put about by those who would harm me in your eyes. The truth is I was abducted and would have been killed had my captors not stumbled upon one of my vills.'

'Which vill?'

'Silcestre, lord.'

Ælfred appeared to be sceptical and so I pointed Wealhmær out to him. He was sitting with other household warriors near the door.

'He was there, cyning, and can verify what I say. He also witnessed the hanging of my abductors.'

'I believe you,' he said, albeit a trifle hesitantly.

I saw him glance at Eadda who was sitting with several ealdormen on one of the tables which abutted the high table at right angles. It came as no surprise to learn who had dripped poison into the king's ear about me. I pulled back the cuff of my undershirt to show my chafed wrist, which had been rubbed raw by the rope.

'I believe you Jørren,' the king said again, this time with more sincerity. 'I'm sorry I ever doubted your loyalty and your bravery. One thing puzzles me though. Why would anyone want to abduct you?'

I hesitated. I'd rather no one in Wessex knew what had happened at Eforwic. However, if the king was to trust me, I had to trust him.

'I killed a boy in Northumbria. He was under my command at the time but he'd murdered one of my warband, a good friend, and tried to rape the girl who is now my wife. I killed him to stop the rape.'

'Did you pay wergeld to the boy's family?'

'No, cyning. I couldn't afford to at the time and, in any case, the boy's father said he wanted my head, not my silver.'

'You need to settle this before the blood feud gets out of hand.'

'I know, lord. I fully intend to. May I have your permission to go north and settle matters?'

'What? No, of course not. I need you here. I meant that you should send the boy's father the wergeld he's owed.'

✝✝✝

My mind was so full of my conversation with Ælfred and concern about Eadda and Cynemær that I had forgotten about Æscwin. As we all walked back to the church for the start of the witenaġemot someone tapped me on the shoulder. I turned to find myself looking at my brother.

'I thought you were dead, and that runaway slave with you,' he began.

'I'm happy to see you too, Æscwin. I left to rescue Alric from the Danes, which I did. Perhaps you were about to congratulate me on my success?'

'You always were a snide boy,' he retorted.

'Yes, well. Now I'm a snide ealdorman. We can have this conversation at a more suitable time.'

I left him staring after me open mouthed. I regretted what I'd said almost immediately. I had hoped for a reconciliation between us but I feared that there was little chance of that now.

Benches had been arranged in the front of the nave for the ealdormen and the senior churchmen. The thegns and others invited to attend had to stand behind us. Three chairs had been placed in the chancel; the centre one for Ælfred, one for the archbishop and the last for the Abbot of Certesi who, as host, would be chairing the meeting. However, he didn't get far beyond his opening prayers and a few words of welcome before Ælfred took charge.

'You all know that Halfdan and Ubba have agreed to withdraw from Wessex for a period of three years. However, I have recently learned that a new Danish army under a jarl called Guthrum had landed at Beamfleote in Ēast Seaxna Rīce.'

It was not a place I had heard of before, but I later learned that it was virtually an island surrounded by streams that flowed into the Temes and the surrounding marshland. As a base it was virtually impregnable, the only approach being along secret paths through the wetlands or from the Temes estuary by ship.

'Reports about this new summer army vary from fifty to one hundred and fifty longships but, whatever the true number, the heathens have replaced the losses they suffered this year and they can probably now muster around four thousand warriors in total.'

There was an audible intake of breath at the thought of facing so many experienced Viking fighters. Wessex could probably field twice that number but most were members of the fyrd and, in any case, scattered throughout the south of England. Even if the king managed to assemble most of them together in one place, the Danes could attack elsewhere with impunity using their ships.

'We need to turn Wessex into a fortress,' Ælfred went on. 'East Anglia seems to be firmly under their control but Northumbria has risen in revolt against the puppet king placed over them and Mercia has only been subdued in parts. The heathens are therefore going to be busy elsewhere for the foreseeable future and we need to take advantage of that time to prepare ourselves for the next invasion.'

'How do we do that, cyning?' Odda, Ealdorman of Dyfneintscir asked. 'You have just said that the Danes can strike anywhere along

229

the coast or up the major rivers in strength whilst we can only move on land.'

'By fortifying settlements for use as well defended bases garrisoned by the fryd who are better trained and better equipped than hitherto. If we improve the existing Roman road network and build new cobbled roads where necessary, we link these bases or burhs together so that reinforcements can move speedily to where they are needed. By this means, we make Wessex a hard place for the Vikings to raid. The one thing we do know about them is that they hate to lose men. Kill enough of them and they will leave Wessex alone and concentrate on Mercia and Northumbria.'

'That's all very well, but who will pay for these burhs, roads and for the time ceorls spend training instead of farming their land Ælfred?' Wulfhere, Ealdorman of Wiltunscir, asked with a sneer.

'I will and you will, Wulfhere,' snapped the king. 'I'd rather pay to defend my kingdom than give the money to the Danes to leave us alone for a while. I'm sure that you would rather contribute what you can afford rather than have your lands laid waste, your settlements pillaged and burned and your womenfolk raped. One more thing, Ealdorman Wulfhere, I am your king and you will address me as such.'

'What? Oh yes. Apologies cyning.' Wulfhere muttered insincerely, stressing the last word.

Ælfred gave him a long hard stare before looking at the rest of us. He allowed his eyes to dwell on every corner of the nave before continuing. The muted conservations and mutterings as men digested what he'd said died away and we waited for his next pronouncement in absolute silence.

'I cannot claim that this strategy for defending our kingdom was mine alone. Credit for developing my initial idea came from the Ealdorman of Berrocscir and I am most grateful to Lord Jørren. Consequently he will assist me in coordinating the planning for the burhs and the new road system and thereafter tour the kingdom to assist you with its implementation, as well as reporting to me on progress.'

I groaned inwardly. I was already unpopular as an upstart and an interloper, now my new role as the king's enforcer would make me positively detested. I sensed Eadda's eyes boring into my back. No doubt he saw this as preferment for me at his expense. Normally he could have expected to have been put in charge of these defensive works as the hereræswa. If he wasn't already my sworn enemy, he certainly would be from now on.

Chapter Seventeen

Summer 873

For the next two years Wessex was left more or less at peace whilst the two Danish armies, one led by Halfdan and Ubba and the other by Guthrum, rampaged through Northumbria and Mercia. The year after they left Wessex the two armies put down the revolt in the north and over-wintered in Lindesege, the north-eastern corner of Mercia.

According to the reports I heard, this was a new settlement, not one which they had taken over. They called it Torksey and it wasn't just a camp for warriors. It was located on the River Trisantona to where their ships could bring their families as well as merchants and tradesmen. They came from Danmǫrk mainly, but also from Norweġ, Sweoland and Irlond. It was a strong indication that the Scandinavians were here to stay.

In March 873 the Viking horde left Torksey but the latter continued to operate as a trading post and a manufacturing centre for armour and weapons. For the rest of that spring and summer the two armies, called respectively the Great Heathen Army and the Great Summer Army, fought a number of engagements against the Mercians. They eventually conquered the north-east of Mercia. This became a Danish kingdom known as the Five Burghs which stretched from Torksay in the north-east to Ligeraceaster in the south-west.

The final battle of that year took place outside a place called Hreopandune, a settlement which had grown up around the important monastery dedicated to Saint Wystan. King Burgred had been heavily defeated and had withdrawn to the western half of Mercia. The heathen army had then spent the winter at Hreopandune.

But that lay in the future. In August of that year the building of palisades around those settlements in Wessex chosen to become burghs was well advanced, as was the construction or repair of roads linking them. Of course, I faced opposition and many a time I had to threaten the local ealdormen or thegn with the king's displeasure to get them to do what was necessary.

I had asked Eadda to take over the training of the fyrd to garrison the burhs and, although progress was slower than I would have liked, he attacked the task with gusto and it kept him out of my hair.

Ælfred expressed himself pleased with what had been accomplished and I took the opportunity to ask his permission for a month's absence. Work on the defences would slow in any case as those working on the burhs and the roads would be needed to get in the harvest ready for the winter. He reluctantly agreed but insisted that I returned by the middle of September at the latest.

I hadn't forgotten about Cynemær over the past year and I had sent Erik, Acwel and Lyndon north into western Mercia and on into Northumbria to find out where the thegn lived and who the male members of his family were. They had travelled disguised as uncle and nephews en route to Lindisfarne as pilgrims wanting to pray at the tombs of Saint Aidan and Saint Cuthbert. Avoiding Eforwic and the rest of Deira, where most of the fighting was taking place, they reached the monastery on the Holy Island of Lindisfarne without mishap.

It was when they started to ask about a supposed relative of theirs called Cynemær that they ran into trouble. It seems that Cynemær was not popular and so the three were seized and taken to the nearby fortress at Bebbanburg. This was the seat of Ricsige, who had succeeded his father, Ealdorman Edmund of Bernicia, after the disastrous battle of Eforwic seven years previously. Erik vaguely remembered seeing Ricsige with his father before the battle, but he doubted if he would recognise him now. Ricsige had been barely sixteen at the time. He was told that Ricsige now called himself Earl of Bernicia to distinguish him from the other ealdormen in his domain.

When they arrived at Bebbanburg Erik had been impressed with the stronghold on top of a windswept rocky outcrop at the edge of the North Sea. It looked impregnable. It stood on top of vertical cliffs and was surrounded by a high palisade. Two double sets of gates defended the steep approaches from the north and the south.

They were taken into the centre of the fortress and dismounted outside a large hall. All three were ushered inside where the Earl of Bernicia sat in conference with three other men. All three were in their thirties or forties but Erik said that Earl Risige looked to be no older than me.

'He was impatient at being interrupted,' Erik continued. 'It appears that the Witenaġemot of Deira had succeeded in ousting the puppet king imposed on them by Halfdan and had elected Ricsige as their king.'

I was taken aback. If he accepted he would become king not only of Deira but of all Northumbria. No wonder the Danes had been all too eager to leave Wessex. There was a very real possibility that they might be driven out of Northumbria. In the circumstances I expected them to march north in the spring, whether or not Ricsige accepted the crown.

'When the earl asked me what I was doing in Bernicia I decided that the time for subterfuge was past,' Erik continued. 'I admitted that I sought Thegn Cynemær whose men had abducted the Ealdorman of Berrocscir in Wessex. I explained that they were taking you back to Northumbria so that Cynemær could kill you personally. I confessed that my task was to locate this thegn and report back. I started to recite the background to the blood feud but Ricsige held up his hand.'

'I've heard enough,' he snapped. 'Cynemær has betrayed me and has joined the Danes in Eforwic with his men. I want his head just as much as this Ealdorman of Berrocscir, who I've never heard of.'

'I told him that he would know of you, lord,' Erik said with a smile. 'I told him that you were the leader of the group who had burned the Danish fleet before the Battle of Eforwic. He took more of an interest then and bade me tell you that he would deal with Cynemær in due course.'

'He released us the next day and gave us an escort as far as the border of Northumbria with Mercia in the west. We then made our way back here.'

I mulled over what Erik had discovered but I was not about to let others deal with my enemies. Perhaps I was being pig-headed but I had to be the one who killed Cynemær and his brood. Of course, Leofflæd tried to dissuade me, but my mind was made up. Now she changed tack and demanded that she be allowed to accompany me on 'my fool's errand,' as she termed it. I tried to talk her out of it, but to no avail.

✝✝✝

The knarr I'd hired glided the last few yards into the berth alongside the quay at Eforwic an hour before dusk. It had been a long, but thankfully uneventful, passage from Sandwic on the south coast of Cent, from where we had boarded, to the mouth of the Humbre and thence up the River Uisge. It was too late in the year for there to be many longships crossing the North Sea to join the heathen army at Lundewic and the only ships we saw were trading knarrs like ours. However our cargo was limited to a few dozen bundles of sheepskins and cow hides. That left room for a dozen of my warriors in addition to the normal ship's crew.

In addition to my wife, who was attired once more in tunic, trousers and byrnie, I had brought Erik, Cei, Ecgberht, Øwli, Uurad, Wealhmær, Wolnoth, Swiðhun, Redwald, Acwel and Lyndon along. It was just like old times, except that most of us were now in our twenties.

As soon as we had docked a tall middle-aged man wearing an expensively embroidered woollen tunic and accompanied by two bored looking youths wearing helmets and carrying spears came striding along the jetty.

'Who are you and what's your cargo?' he barked at the knarr's captain.

'Aldhelm out of Sandwic and we're carrying sheepskins and tanned leather hides for sale here. What business is it of yours?'

'I'm King Ricsige's port reeve,' the man said, evidently affronted at being challenged.

He seemed to notice us for the first time.

'Why have you got so many armed warriors on board?'

'Dangerous times, my friend,' I replied before the captain could do so. 'So Eforwic is back in Northumbrian hands? What happened to the Danes that Halfdan left here as a garrison?'

'We rose up and slaughtered them as soon as Ricsige and his Bernicians appeared before our walls,' he said proudly.

Then he peered suspiciously at me.

'Why are you so interested in the fate of a couple of hundred heathen Danes?'

'I just wanted to make sure that it was safe for me and my men to walk the streets of Eforwic,' I replied with what I hoped was a disarming smile. 'Tell me, what happened to turncoats like Cynemær who had sided with the heathens?'

The port reeve sniffed in distain.

'He fled south with his sons as soon as King Ricsige appeared two days ago; more's the pity. Why? What's your interest in him?'

'He and I have unfinished business,' I replied curtly.

The man appeared to be one of Ricsige's supporters but I had no doubt that there were several agents in the pay of the Danes still left in Eforwic and I wasn't taking any chances.

'Well, if you came here hoping to meet him you've had a wasted journey haven't you?' he said nastily. 'Now, let's have a look at these skins so I can levy the appropriate tax before you land them,' he said, turning back to the captain.

We took rooms in a tavern for the night as we would need to find and buy enough horses for our journey in pursuit of Cynemær. Of course, the presence of so many armed men arriving in Eforwic hadn't gone unnoticed and we were eating a meal in the taproom when a dozen armed men entered and demanded that I accompany them to the king's hall. I took Erik with me as doubtless Ricsige would remember him. My men growled in disapproval as the king's warriors disarmed us before carting us off like felons but I assured them that we were in no danger, and so it proved.

Ricsige did indeed remember Erik and he was pleased to meet someone who could give him an accurate picture of what was happening in the south. When I told him that it seemed likely that the Danes would head north in the spring to re-conquer his kingdom he grew concerned, but thanked me for the warning. Erik and I were guests on the high table and ate considerably better fare than my wife and the men were enjoying in the tavern. Afterwards our weapons were returned to us and Ricsige wished us good hunting on the morrow.

It took all morning to buy enough horses for us to journey south after Cynemær. I was eager to start before the trail got too cold, although I was fairly certain that he would be headed to Lundenwic and the main Danish army now that he was branded a traitor by his own people.

We left Eforwic just after noon. We were each mounted on a decent riding horse and we had bought a few pack horses to carry the tents and camping equipment we would need. We wouldn't be stopping at any more taverns or even at monasteries. I intended to ride at as fast a pace as I could without damaging our mounts, stopping to camp at sunset and leaving again at dawn. We were four days behind Cynemær and the others who had fled Eforwic and I estimated that, with no reason to rush like we were doing, it would take them about a week to reach Lundenwic. That gave us less than three days to catch him.

✝✝✝

Having questioned travellers heading north on the old Roman road, I was confident that my quarry was only one or two days ahead of us when we stopped for the night just north of Stanforde on the River Weolud.

Uurad and Wolnoth had been scouting ahead and came back to warn me that the bridge over the Weolud was guarded by a small fortified camp. We were now on the border between Mercia and the territory controlled by the Danes. Perhaps the men guarding the crossing were Mercians but I thought it more likely that they were Danes.

'Were you able to get any idea about numbers?' I asked the two scouts.

'Not really, but the fortress isn't big enough to hold more than about fifty,' Uurad replied.

'However large the garrison, it's too many for us to tackle,' I muttered in frustration.

'Why don't we pretend to be Danes?' Erik suggested.

'How?' I asked puzzled. 'The way we dress is different, as is our helmets. Alright a few of us speak Danish well enough, but we look like Saxons.'

'They'll send out patrols and forage parties,' he pointed out. 'We ambush one and take their clothes and helmets.'

I was about to point out that we didn't have time to wait for that to happen when Cei, who was on sentry duty just inside the wood, came running back to say that a party of Danes had just ridden into sight half a mile away.

We were a good two hundred yards off the Roman road in dense woodland and therefore hidden. Leaving our horses with Acwel and Lyndon, we grabbed our bows and other weapons and made our way to the edge of the trees. I sent Redwald and Ecgberht north to cut off any escape that way whilst Waelhmær and Uurad went to take up a position between the Danish patrol and their fortress. That left me with Leoflæd, Swiðhun, Erik, Cei and Øwli to spring the ambush. I prayed that there weren't too many Danes in the patrol.

Slowly they rode into view. They had no scouts out and were laughing and joking together as if they didn't have a care in the world. Their shields hung on their backs and their helmets from

238

the pommels of their saddles. Only two wore byrnies, the others making do with leather jerkins or padded gambesons. Behind the two in the lead rode a boy of perhaps eleven or twelve. He was dressed expensively but wore no armour and only had a dagger hanging from his belt. I guessed he was the son of a jarl, in which case one of the leaders was probably his father. I decided to use my first arrow to kill his horse and hope that he survived.

I gave a screech like a barn owl and six arrows flew towards the Danes. I saw with satisfaction that my arrow had pierced the heart of the boy's palfrey and it crashed to the ground. I had no time to see if the lad had survived. My second arrow struck one of the startled leaders in the throat and my third took a Dane who was trying to flee in the back.

The others had similar success. Only four got away. One galloping away to the north and three back towards their fortress. Hoping that my two cut-off groups would be able to deal with all four, we set about killing the wounded and gathering up the horses. The boy was trapped under his horse, which had fallen on his right leg. By the way that he was screaming insults at me, I assumed that he was unhurt but, when we lifted the dead horse off him I saw that his lower leg was broken.

'Shall I put him out of his misery, lord?' Øwli asked, drawing his dagger.

'No,' Leoflæd said before I could answer. 'He's only a young boy. He'll mend.'

'What's your name boy?' I asked him.

The boy glared at me and then tried to move his broken leg. He screamed as the pain hit him and he passed out. The other four rode in to say that none had escaped and we began to strip the patrol of their clothes and collected the helmets from their horses. In the meantime, Leoflæd and Erik set the boy's shinbone and splinted it. They sewed up the gash where one end of the break had cut thorough flesh and bandaged it. Once wrapped inside a tent, we tied him over one of the packhorses. Hopefully he would stay unconscious until we'd crossed the bridge.

The Danes scarcely looked at us as we rode past their fortress and over the bridge, calling out a few ribald remarks in Danish to the four warriors lounging at one end of the bridge. They replied in kind and then we were safely over and into the woods on the far side. Once we were out of sight we started to canter once again but had to slow down again because of the injured Danish boy, who had regained consciousness and was screaming in agony as he was bounced around.

We stopped and I poured enough mead down his throat from my flask to send him back into oblivion. We changed clothes back again and I told Acwel and Lyndon to follow us with the injured Dane at a gentler pace. Then the rest of us set off at a canter once more.

We caught up with the party of turncoat Northumbrian refugees thirty miles north of Lundunwic. We were now in territory which, although officially Mercian, was heavily patrolled by the Danes. I had scouts out ahead and to either side of us as we rode at a trot down the road. Cei was riding point and rode back to say that a party of fifty or more was two miles ahead of us on the road. Some were dressed in chainmail or leather jerkins and helmets but there were a dozen wagons laden with possessions in which women and children rode. There were also a few civilians, presumably tradesmen and merchants who had decided that Eforwic was an unsafe place in which to remain.

'How many men who will put up a fight?' I asked him.

He shrugged.

'There are about fifteen who look like fighters: a few nobles and their hearth warriors presumably.'

I nodded my thanks and decided to ride around them and block the road.

'I have no quarrel with most of you and you are free to go on your way,' I called out when the column came to a halt when we confronted them. I sat on my horse in the middle of the road flanked by Redwald, Ecgberht, Waelhmær, Cei and Uurad.

240

Leofflæd and the others remained hidden in the trees with their bows ready in case of trouble.

'Then what do you want with us?' one of the men wearing an expensive chainmail byrnie and thick woollen trousers tucked into calfskin boots called back.

'I seek a man named Cynemær and his brood; only them. There is a blood feud between us which I intend to settle here and now.'

'I am Cynemær, who the devil are you? I have no quarrel with you as far as I'm aware.'

'I've changed a lot since we last met, Cynemær. I'm Jørren, Ealdorman of Berrocscir. I killed Ceadda after he'd murdered one of my friends and tried to rape the girl who is now my wife. Remember me now? I'm sorry to tell you that Hroðulf and the rest of the thugs you sent to kidnap me failed. Their rotting corpses now lie buried in unhallowed ground near one of my vills.'

'You,' he hissed and rode towards me, drawing his sword as he did so. Five men, who were plainly his warriors, followed him together with a youth who looked to be about seventeen.

'You die now!' he shouted digging his spurs viciously into the flanks of his horse.

It leaped forward but I continued to stare at him, my sword still in its scabbard, as he pounded across the short distance between us. Suddenly the horse faltered and its forelegs gave way as two arrows struck its side. Cynemær just managed to leap clear as the horse rolled onto its side and died.

I calmly dismounted and drew my own sword. Cynemær's men, seeing their lord sprawled on the ground with me advancing towards him, charged towards me. They must have been stupid as they must have been aware that there were archers in the trees; but perhaps they thought that there was only one. At any event none reached me, three being killed outright and two badly wounded.

The rest of the column watched the drama unfolding in front of them in amazement. Wisely no one else tried to intervene. That is except one man, presumably Ceadda's other son who dismounted and ran forward to help his father to his feet. I held up my hand to indicate that no one was to interfere.

'You are another of Cynemær's sons?' I asked.

'Yes,' he hissed at me. 'Do you intend to kill me too?'

'Yes, regretfully,' I replied. 'Otherwise I will be forever plagued by your attempts at revenge.'

He stared at me open mouthed.

'But, b-but,' he stammered, 'I'm only seventeen.'

'So?' I replied. 'I've been fighting Danes since I was thirteen. I'll fight both of you at once and on my own. My men won't interfere. Is that fair?'

His eyes widened and I saw a speculative look in them. Obviously he thought that the two of them would make short work of me.

His father had recovered his sword in the meantime and once again he advanced on me. He headed towards my left and gestured for his son to attack my other side. I faced them, holding my own sword in my right hand and my seax in my left.

'Two against one isn't fair,' Cei cried to murmurs of agreement from my other men.

'This is my fight, not yours,' I snarled back, annoyed at having had my concentration broken. 'But thank you for your concern,' I added in a softer tone, just as Cynemær made his first move.

I swore at being taken off guard but just managed to parry his thrust. The way was open for his son to drive his sword into my side whilst I was distracted, but he was too slow. By the time he attacked I was ready and beat his sword aside with my seax. Instead of withdrawing to recover, the stupid boy tried to cut my leg from the same position. I swiftly chopped down inside his sword with my seax and cut deeply into the front of his right thigh. He screamed in pain and his own blade lost all power, bouncing off my chainmail covered chest.

At the same time I brought my sword up to deflect his father's attack and swung my seax around, spinning on my toes as I did so, to cut into Cynemær's side. His byrnie robbed the blow of some of its momentum, but several links parted and red gore started to seep out of the gap when I withdrew my sword. From the jar to my wrist I was certain that I had broken some of his ribs as well. He took several steps back and grimaced, trying to overcome the agony he was in. It was my chance to finish him off, but I'd forgotten about the son.

As I moved forward to attack Cynemær, his son gritted his teeth and limped forward and slashed at my left arm. My byrnie only protected me down to the elbow and his sword cut into my forearm before striking my radius. Luckily it didn't break, but pain shot up my arm and my hand opened involuntarily, letting go of my seax.

Thankfully the move had caused the youth intense discomfort and for a moment he wasn't able to follow up. A wave of nausea swept over me but I knew I had to overcome it or I was dead. I brought my sword up and thrust it with all the strength I could muster into the son's stomach. It wasn't a killing blow but it was sufficient to put him out of the fight.

I dimly heard Cynemær shriek 'no' as his son fell to the ground, clutching at his belly, then he ran at me, rage giving him the ability to overcome the pain he must have been in. I was feeling dizzy but I managed to move my head to the side to avoid the man's thrust at my left eye. The side of his blade scored a line across my helmet before he drew it back to thrust at me again. He never got the chance. I brought my sword up and shoved the point up under his chin, through his mouth and into the base of his brain.

I knew he was dead but his son was still alive. Nevertheless I let go of the hilt and blacked out. I knew no more.

✝✝✝

When I came to my arm hurt like fury. For a moment I wasn't aware of my surroundings but slowly my eyes focused and I saw Leofflæd's face as she gently bathed my forehead.

'Sometimes I think I married an idiot,' she said.

They weren't the words of loving care that I was expecting and I glared at her.

'You were lucky to survive fighting those two with no more than a nasty cut to your forearm. It chipped the bone but it didn't break. However, you did lose quite a bit of blood as a consequence.'

'Good to see you too, my love,' I managed to croak, my mouth dry.

She gave me some water and I greedily swallowed it, but immediately felt sick.

'Slowly, slowly,' she urged.

'Where am I?'

'In the infirmary of the monastery of Saint Alban. It was the nearest place to bring you after you collapsed. The monks say that Cei sewed you up well and the wound is healing nicely.'

'What of Cynemær's son?'

'Sons,' she corrected me. 'There was a younger boy in the cavalcade as well as his wife and two daughters. The one you fought died of his wounds and Erik is taking the rest of his family into Ludenwic to sell them as thralls to the Danes. That's an end to the blood feud.'

If only she had been right.

I was well enough to travel a few days later, although my arm was still quite painful. We travelled slowly, so as not to damage it further, through southern Mercia and thus back to Readingum, where Leofflæd and I were reunited with our two children. I was delighted to be back and looked forward to a less stressful time whilst my arm healed and I got to grips with all the myriad tasks that being an ealdorman entailed.

I had been away for more than the month that King Ælfred had allowed me and I sent him a message to explain. From his reply I gathered that he was less than pleased with me and bade me commence a tour of all the burhs under construction. He made it plain that he wanted them finished before winter set in.

I read his letter with annoyance and frustration. It was now late September and so what he asked was impossible. Construction had stopped at harvest time and, without me there to get the inhabitants back to work, little had been achieved recently. Although the harvest had been gathered in, threshing and winnowing still had to be done, and so had all the other preparations for the coming winter.

However, I couldn't flout the king's instructions and so, in the face of Leofflæd's opposition, I set off to make a tour of the burhs of Sūþrīgescir, Suth-Seaxe and Cent as being those nearest to Lundenwic and therefore, I assumed, those most in danger. I decided to start in the east and work my way back toward home.

My forearm still caused me considerably discomfort and riding a horse one handed was difficult, but I persevered. I took the same small warband with me as I had when I'd set off to seek Cynemær. I'd be in trouble if we encountered a large band of Danes, but I wanted to travel swiftly and taking more men, and supplies for them and the horses, would just slow me down.

I started at Cantwareburh; the Romans had left behind stout stone walls but alas they had fallen into disrepair. I was heartened to see that the repairs to the gaps with timber had almost been completed and I stayed the night with the archbishop. The next day dawned bright and clear but dark clouds gathered as we rode westwards and by the time that we neared Cilleham we were being bombarded by large hailstones. Our helmets and chainmail protected us from severe bruising but the horses became almost uncontrollable, both because they were being bombarded by chunks of ice and because of the accompanying thunder and lightning.

Unwilling as I was to do so, we needed to seek shelter and the nearest place was my brother's vill. We dismounted and led the horses into the first barn we came to where the villeins and slaves had stopped threshing to gape at the storm from the doorway. We pushed them to one side and entered the barn. Normally, it was the custom to ask the local lord's permission to shelter on his property but this storm was far from normal.

Although I hadn't spotted him, Æscwin was there supervising the work with his reeve. He came rushing over to confront the strangers who had flouted the normal rules for hospitality, but stopped when he saw me.

'You!' he said, startled.

'Yes, me, brother. Forgive the intrusion uninvited but it was that or be bludgeoned to death by giant hailstones.'

'I'm pleased to see you again. I fear that our last meeting didn't go as well as I'd hoped.'

I smiled. I had no wish to argue with him and his more conciliatory attitude this time came as a relief.

'No, and I'm sorry for my part in that,' I said, 'I hope you will forgive me now for taking Cei and setting off to rescue Alric.'

'Of course, although your sisters may not take such a charitable view. They worried themselves sick after you disappeared.'

'Yes, I must apologise to them. Are they here?'

'No, Godifu married the thegn of a neighbouring vill four years ago and Sibbe is now a nun at Cantwareburh.'

'I wish I'd known. I've just come from visiting the archbishop.'

'You move in grand circles now that you're an ealdorman,' he said with a touch of envy in his voice.

'There are times when I wish I was no more than a simple thegn,' I replied with a grimace. 'Responsibility for the defence works of Wessex is not a task for the fainthearted.'

'I gather you have two children now,' he said, changing the subject before I took him to task about the state of that part of the road between Cantwareburh and Hrofescæster that he was responsible for.

I did, but not after we had exchanged all the other news we had for each other, including an explanation of my injured arm. He grunted noncommittally when I mentioned the blood feud and I got the impression that he would not have avenged my death had things turned out differently.

He had three children of his own now, but they were all daughters. The lack of a son to succeed him as thegn obviously worried him, but I said that there was plenty of time yet. It was a trite thing to say and an uncomfortable silence followed.

I looked around me and became aware that Cei was staring intently at one of the slaves. The man kept his eyes downcast but glanced up now and then, a smile of pleasure lighting up his face. I realised with a start that it was Bedwyr's other son, Cei's elder brother.

'Do you mind if Cei greets his brother?' I asked Æscwin.

'No, provided he doesn't give him ideas. I've few enough slaves as it is,' he replied with a scowl.

The two greeted each other warily, one because he had run away leaving the other with more work to do and the other because he was overawed by the young warrior standing before him wearing fine woollen clothes, an expensive byrnie and a stout helmet with a nose guard. He wore a sword and a seax from his belt, weapons no slave was allowed.

Eventually they overcame their shyness and embraced each other. I caught snatches of their conversation, although I didn't mean to eavesdrop. I learned with sadness that both Bedwyr and his wife were dead and that Cei's brother, whose name I had forgotten, now had a wife and a daughter of his own. It was more than Cei had. Household warriors tended to marry late in life. Being the wife of one was not an attractive prospect. The husband tended to be away a lot and could be killed at any moment, leaving the wife and any children destitute.

By this time the hail had stopped and, after a fond farewell and promises to keep in touch, we set out again as the sky lightened and the odd patch of blue appeared. I was in an ebullient mood after the meeting with my brother but I was brought back to earth with a jolt when Lyndon came riding back to say that there was a Viking raiding party just ahead of us.

✝✝✝

'They are in a sorry state,' the boy reported with glee. 'There are perhaps fifty of them but only two are mounted. Quite a few have been injured by the hailstones, those without byrnies that is. Perhaps twenty are limping or have their arms in a sling.'

Even so, fifty was a sizable warband and I wasn't about to pit my dozen men against them, especially as I couldn't fight or use a bow. On the other hand, they were headed towards my brother's settlement and I had to do something to protect them.

'Cei, ride back and warn my brother that a large group of Danes are coming his way. Tell him to bring every man and boy capable of bearing arms and meet me at the black pool.'

The black pool was where we used to swim as children and was sited in a clearing in the woods not far from the road from Cantwareburh to Hrofescæster. It was where a stream fed a pond before splashing over some rocks and dropping a few feet, hardly a waterfall, before continuing on its way.

We reached there a good ten minutes before I expected our enemies to walk past on the road but there was no sign of Æscwin. I could only pray that he and his ceorls would reach us before we were overcome. I left Acwel and Lyndon there to guard our horses and to tell my brother were we'd gone.

We were just in time. The Viking raiders came around the bend just as we'd finished moving into position. Lyndon was correct; they were a sorry looking bunch, but still dangerous for all that. Only two men rode; both wore byrnies and helmets, as did about ten of their followers. The rest wore gambesons, leather jerkins or plain woollen tunics and cloaks. All had a sword or an axe, and a few carried spears. Only half had shields and they were all unharmed, having had the sense to shelter under them. Most of the rest had been injured to some extent during the storm.

They had neglected to put scouts out, a foolish oversight in enemy territory, and I surmised that they were poor Danish or Norse bondi who farmed for a living and had come to England in the hope of easy plunder.

Then I noticed the wounded in the rear of the column. My guess was that they had attacked Hrofescæster and had been repulsed with heavy losses.

We waited until the leaders and their immediate entourage had passed us and then I hooted like an owl. Three quick volleys sent a score of arrows to strike the column before they reacted. Consequently ten of their men had been wounded or killed by the time they managed to form a shield wall. To launch more arrows at them after that would be a waste so I gave the order to switch targets to those who hadn't been able to protect themselves, in essence the injured and the wounded. It wasn't something I enjoyed doing but I wanted to inflict as many casualties as possible to dissuade other jarls from leading their men into Wessex in the hope of plunder.

We had reduced the enemy numbers to around thirty by the time they organised themselves properly and advanced into the woods. I gave the order to withdraw but told Cei to fire one last arrow before we retreated. His target was the man who was evidently their jarl or hirsir. His aim was true and the man was struck in the chest. At such close range the arrow penetrating through his byrnie and other layers to lodge in his heart. His death caused the others to hesitate, but they came after us again after another man had harangued them, calling them cowards who would never reach Valhalla unless they avenged their jarl.

We arrived back at the Black Pool to find that my brother and his fyrd had just arrived. I nodded to thank Æscwin for bringing me over thirty reinforcements, but we didn't have time to say anything to each other.

'Form shield wall, my men in the front rank,' I yelled.

We had just formed up when the first of the yelling Vikings erupted from the trees. They came to a halt when faced with forty opponents. Although they had nearly as many men and they had the advantage of being more experienced fighters, they had lost so many already that day that they hesitated to lose more. After all, they had little to gain by fighting us, except revenge, and their new leader knew that.

After staring at us for several minutes the raiders vanished back into the trees and we all breathed a sigh of relief. A few hotheads were all for pursuing them, but I was confident that the survivors would slink back to Ludenwic. Cilleham was safe for now. Hopefully other Vikings would hear of their losses and be put off raiding south of the Temes.

It was my last skirmish that year, and indeed for some time to come, and a month later I returned to Leofflæd and my children at Readingum for the winter. Many of the new burhs were far from complete but, if the Great Heathen Army headed north to confront Ricsige, as expected, we would have the whole of next year, if not longer, to finish the project. King Ælfred would have to be content with that.

The story of Jørren's part in the battle for Wessex will continue in

The King of Athelney

To be released later in 2020

Printed in Great Britain
by Amazon

80201882R00144